THE RAT WHO KNEW

Novels by Beverly Hurwitz MD

The Tale of a Transplanted Heart
Who Has Your Back?
WAR in the OR
Is the Cat Lady Crazy?
Nobody Else's Business

Also By Beverly Hurwitz MD

Park City Hiking Guide
Park City Walking Guide

THE RAT WHO KNEW

Beverly Hurwitz MD

Surrogate Press®

Published in the United States by
Surrogate Press®
an imprint of Faceted Press®
Surrogate Press, LLC
Park City, Utah
SurrogatePress.com

ISBN: 978-1-964245-26-3
Library of Congress Control Number:

Book Cover design by: Beverly Hurwitz
Book Interior design by:
Katie Mullaly, Surrogate Press®

This book is dedicated to everyone
whose life has benefitted from
animal research.

PLEASE NOTE:

All of the people and places in this story are fictitious
with the exception of a few cultural icons.
Any resemblance to actual humans or entities is purely coincidental.
Of all of the rat breeds mentioned in this story,
only the Laudren rat is fictitious.

1

September 30 – Afternoon

"Tansy, wake up! Tansy! Can't you hear me? Wake up! Tansy, they took Freyja again. She was screaming. Didn't you hear her? Please, Tansy, wake up!"

"Huh? What? It's still light. It must be the middle of the day. Oh, Piper, what is the matter?"

"You must be deaf, Tansy. I've been shouting at the top of my lungs. They took Freyja. Didn't you hear her screaming?"

"No, please! Not again. Oh no, no! My poor baby. They keep taking her. My poor, precious baby. When? Who was it? Who took her?"

"Just a few seconds ago. Someone unrecognizable. I'm certain I've never seen him before. There are always these people around here who you just start to get used to and then you never see them again."

"Did they take anyone else, or just Freyja?"

"I only woke up when I heard her screaming, so I don't know if they took anyone before that. Hopefully, everyone else is still tucked in.

"Tansy, I really think you've gone deaf. I cannot believe you didn't hear the racket Freyja made. The poor little thing must be so terrified. I'm sorry I even woke you because there's nothing we can do, and now you're as upset as I am. I'm sorry, Tansy. I love Freyja too, and it broke my heart to hear her scream like that. She's so special."

"She's beyond anything I could ever imagine, Piper. Of all my children, there's never been one like Freyja. She could speak before any of the others could even babble, and she could barely speak when she started asking questions like 'why are we here?' How do you answer such a young one asking a question like that? It's as though she was born knowing. That must be what makes her so interesting to them."

"Freyja is truly unique, Tansy. I've been in this nursery twice as long as you, and I've never seen another baby with such abilities. They must see how extraordinary she is. Elsie knows, and my instincts tell me that Elsie will try to protect her."

"I believe that too, Piper. The problem is that Elsie hasn't been here so much of late. Do you know why? It's always so much better when she's here."

"I don't know, but it happens from time to time. She's gone for a while and then she comes back, same old Elsie, always patient and kind. But here's my question, Tansy. If it's Freyja's intelligence that interests them, why do they send her back anesthetized? It doesn't make any sense to knock her out if they want to see how smart she is."

"I don't get it either, Piper. She used to come back exhausted from all the stuff they made her do. But now, she comes back unconscious and when she wakes up, she can't tell me about anything that's happened.

"When she came back last week, she was irritable and anxious. She's had trouble sleeping and her appetite's down. So, for them to knock her out again so soon, I don't even want to imagine what it might do to her. I pray that's not what they're doing to her now.

"And then, Piper, I have to face the horror that they may never bring her back. I may never see that sweet baby face again. Oh, Piper, I honestly don't know if I can go on if I lose Freyja. Of all my children, she has given my life the most meaning. And she's so beautiful and loving. Even the thought of losing her makes my heart hurt.

"And I fear you're right about me going deaf. I'm starting to realize how hard it is for me to hear lots of things, especially the little voices of my youngest kids. It's making me feel inept and helpless, and without my children, I feel useless. I cannot face this life anymore if they take Freyja away."

"But Tansy, you must go on because of the children and for Freyja. Both you and she are resilient. You've both survived so much already. You will learn to compensate for your hearing loss, and both you and Freyja will go on to thrive. I believe in you, Tansy."

"I love you, Piper. Please be my ears and tell me if you hear anything about Freyja."

2

OCTOBER 1 – MIDDAY

Nurse Neil noted that Jenna Laudren arrived as soon as the patient was moved to his unit. Jenna's gray, well-tailored pantsuit and keenly cut short hair broadcast an all-business persona. She signed in as August Rincade's ex-wife. She greeted August by momentarily laying a hand on his shoulder. Then she wiped a tear from her eye before seating herself at the foot of the bed.

Along with Jenna, Elsie Rincade signed in as the patient's daughter. She kissed August on his cheek and sat at the side of the bed, stroking August's limp hand and silently crying.

It was hard to tell if this daughter was a girl or a young woman. She was short and slight, and she wore an oversized Mickey Mouse sweatshirt and a unique cap. It was fitted with some apparatus that positioned a speaker over her right ear and a microphone extending around to her mouth. On the other side of the cap was a multi-button control panel.

Long brown bangs draped over Elsie's high forehead. Thick lensed glasses seemed to balance precariously on her nub of a nose. Behind the lenses, her eyes appeared small and squinty. Neil watched her get visually close to his patient's monitors, and then she seemed to study the screens intently.

Neil found it hard not to stare. The bones of Elsie's right cheek and jaw appeared short and contoured, compared to the flatter cheek and longer jaw on the left, making her mouth look crooked. The asymmetry made the observer want to tilt their head to process what they were seeing.

About ten minutes after Jenna Laudren and Elsie Rincade signed in, another woman named Charlotte Swift-Rincade identified herself as the patient's wife. Obviously younger than Jenna, she wore skintight jeans and blue suede mules that showed off her long legs. A black cropped turtleneck revealed a bejeweled navel. Along with her long torso, a geyser of red curls on top of her head made her appear tall when seated.

Charlotte averted her gaze when the ex-wife Jenna nodded to her. Charlotte's half-smile to August's daughter Elsie went unreturned. Charlotte sat at the side of the bed and scowled at the sight of her unconscious husband.

Neil couldn't tell if August Rincade was aware of anything, let alone the presence of his family. His skull was wrapped in bandages and a bolt protruded from his head so that a device could measure the pressure on his brain. Another set of wires monitored his brain activity.

Hollywood handsome August looked old and pale, not that he ever got to spend much time in the sun. The right side of his face drooped downward. His chin glistened with drool seconds after Neil wiped it clean. His eyes remained closed. He showed no discernable response when either of the wives or his daughter spoke to him.

Although August was able to breathe without ventilator support, his condition was still critical. The doctors hoped that some familiar voices might stimulate his injured brain. This was the first time any-one in his family had seen him since the stroke and they each looked shell-shocked.

~ ~ ~ ~ ~

Sixteen hours earlier, August Rincade had been in the prime of his life, a well-funded scientist with a new wife who was helping him to hone in on a great discovery.

~ ~ ~ ~ ~

Fifteen hours earlier, August Rincade had suffered a massive stroke while in the company of a young woman who was not his wife or his ex-wife. The rapid drug screen performed in the E.R. was positive for cocaine and benzos.

~ ~ ~ ~ ~

The doctor came to talk to the family. He explained that it was much too soon to predict to what extent August might recover. It was unknown when the stroke had occurred. Some blood clots had to be extracted before the ruptured artery could be clipped. But August was seemingly a healthy, vigorous fifty-one-year-old, and the neurosurgeon wasn't ready to say that he had no future.

The family was also told that the young woman who had accompanied August to the E.R., had informed the triage nurse that August could get medical grade cocaine because he was "some kind of a scientist."

This escort had delivered August's car keys and wallet to the E.R. triage desk, about a half-hour after August had been taken to the operating room. The escort had also made a point of telling the triage nurse where August's car could be found in a downtown hotel garage. Then, this young woman did a skilled disappearing act.

August's cell phone never showed up, but from the I.D. in his wallet, the E.R. staff had been able to track down the family of the anonymous stroke victim undergoing emergency brain surgery.

~ ~ ~ ~ ~

Jenna Laudren had come to August's hospital bedside because she needed to know how to proceed if he was incapacitated. Together, they operated a neuroscience research laboratory that was funded by Jenna's family trust.

Jenna had wanted to break all ties with August when she divorced him the previous year; but the research coming out of the lab was too important to sacrifice the lead researcher. August, and his technical partner, Charlotte, were being invited to present their exciting discoveries at science meetings around the world. With his charm, good looks, and a beautiful assistant at his side, August was also expert at attracting the attention of journalists. The whole science world seemed to be holding its collective breath for August Rincade to come through with a cure for cocaine addiction.

Initially, Jenna had been thrilled with their reception by the larger research community, before she woke up to what was really going on. While she was working a hundred hours a week to keep the lab, the family, and the family trust functioning, August and Charlotte were spending their conference trips entertaining each other. And apparently, now that August was married to this marauder, he was cheating on her as well. Having to continue to work with both of them was eating at Jenna's heart and soul.

The issue of medical grade cocaine had Jenna so enraged that she felt homicidal. She couldn't fathom how August could be siphoning off their secured research supply. As far as Jenna knew, August had been committed to abstinence his entire adult life. He hadn't relapsed since going through rehab twice before his nineteenth birthday, more than three decades ago.

The controlled substances in their lab were kept in a vault that required three randomly selected staff members to be present to open and to verify the number of grams extracted, as well as the remaining weight of the supply, all while being recorded on video. All three people also had to witness and document how the cocaine was used. Jenna couldn't fathom how August could get around that. Theft of the cocaine could shut her lab down.

If it wouldn't hurt their research and her family's philanthropic foundation, Jenna would have called the police. But what a waste of resources to prosecute a criminal in a coma. And if she couldn't figure out how August could have stolen it, how could she prove that he did? Maybe it was the girlfriend's cocaine, and the girlfriend or escort or whoever she was, was just blaming it on August. Or maybe, August had relapsed since marrying wild woman Charlotte, who preferred to go by the name Charly.

Jenna was grateful that she had been able to salvage her self-esteem by identifying herself as a dedicated scientist instead of a jilted wife.

She had decided to wait to restructure ownership of the lab until after August published their final results.

Jenna had also been preoccupied with trying to find a researcher to replace August after he completed his current project. Now, she might have to do that much sooner than she'd anticipated. She had no intentions of funding her ex-husband's next project, even if he did recover and come up with something brilliant.

Jenna hadn't been impressed with any of the young scientists she had started to interview after she divorced August. The great inquisitive mind she would have wanted to take over her cherished lab was that of her son, but that was never going to happen as long as August was in the picture. Toby had zero use for his father and for the lab. It had become difficult for the two of them to even be in the same room.

When Jenna had called Toby to tell him of his father's stroke, his only response was, "gee, that's terrible for Elsie." Jenna wondered if Toby would even come to the funeral if August died. She also wondered if Toby would ever be able to expand his mind and come to appreciate the enormous contribution to human and animal welfare that's been made by research animals. Jenna was having difficulty coming to terms with the fact that even if August did die, it was highly improbable that Toby would ever be interested in taking over the lab or his father's research.

As Jenna sat observing Charly at the bedside of her comatose husband, she consoled herself that at least she wasn't facing the prospect of being married to a vegetable, if that's all that August had become. Now, he would be Charly's burden, and it was what the thieving homewrecker deserved.

~ ~ ~ ~ ~

Charly Swift-Rincade had come to August's bedside primarily because she wanted to kill him. Since receiving that call from the E.R. the previous evening, she'd been beating up on herself for being such a moron that she married a man who was unfaithful to his first wife.

Now, she was determined not to be a moron when it came to protecting her interest in their research. While her skills could get her a lab job anywhere, she had become totally invested in August's potential to produce a treatment that the whole world wanted.

Charly had spent a lot of mental energy trying to come up with a way for August to wrestle the science and the operation away from Jenna. Still, she hadn't hatched a feasible plan and now there was little hope that she could. She'd just have to team up with some other scientist if her genius cokehead husband wasn't going to get his marbles back. Their research was too important to let die along with him. And Charly thought that she knew a guy who had the credentials to maybe do it.

Besides, even if August fully recovered, knowing what she knew now, Charly wouldn't want to stay married to him or work with him anymore. August hadn't cheated on Jenna just because Jenna was too busy to be a wife. August cheated because he was just another cheating rat bastard.

~ ~ ~ ~ ~

Elsie Rincade, the unusual looking girl/woman, seemed detached from the other two women. She sometimes cocked her head as if hearing something that the rest of them didn't. But of the three visitors, Nurse Neil noted, Elsie appeared to be the most concerned about the condition of August Rincade.

3

October 1 – Afternoon

After leaving the hospital, August's wife Charly started ruminating about her future without her husband and partner. The first scientist she thought about who could maybe take August's place was her old mentor, Merle Nobakov. She didn't know if Merle would even talk to her, but she was pretty sure that he'd remember her. She'd probably poked a hole in his arrogant heart when she'd turned him down for a date, back when she was a college freshman and Merle was a graduate student and lab instructor.

Not many freshman girls elected to take Biology 101 that year because it was widely rumored that putting out for Merle was required to get a good grade. The gossip about Merle had just made Charly curious about him. She liked to learn from people who were good at manipulating others, having once endured abuse by a masterfully manipulative foster parent.

After attending two of his lectures, Charly quickly concluded that Merle Nobakov was probably as brilliant as he was creepy. Charly also managed to get an A in biology, despite having coldly rejected Merle's advances.

Though she never liked Merle Nobakov, Charly felt indebted to him for her career success. When she had first started college, she planned to be a clinical psychologist, probably because she wanted to understand why she'd always felt like a misfit.

Biology 101 provided Charly with a new sense of worth when lab supervisor Merle Nobakov noticed the speed and deftness with which she could artfully carve out a frog's heart. Merle convinced Charly that very few people had the ability to wield a tiny scalpel to within a millimeter of its edge, while peering through a microscope. Her degree of eye-hand coordination and steadiness was extraordinary and rarely encountered.

It was in an eighth-grade art class that Charly had started to appreciate that she was considerably more dexterous than most people, and she initially thought that would enable her to become an artist. But later on in that same art class, Charly came to realize that she lacked creative talent. She was only good at reproducing a likeness of what an artistic person had already created. She embraced this discovery and even started to dress herself that way. She'd look at online pictures of the funky clothes that talented people had created for their fashion dolls, and she'd imitate the outfits. There were oodles of options for a figure like hers.

Merle had advised Charly that she'd have a much better future as a surgical technician than as a psychologist. He claimed she'd be wasting her God-given talents if she spent her career listening to miserable people complain about their unhappy lives. Merle's arguments won out after Charly spent a week observing in a clinical psychology lab. She switched her major to biotechnology and acquired competence in genetic sequencing and chemical analysis of hormones and pharmaceuticals.

Now, the Laudren NeuroScience Foundation Laboratory was compensating Charly handsomely for her skills. There were few dissectionists in the world who could precisely excise the tiniest parts of tiny rodent brains more perfectly than could Charly Swift. Chances for research success were bolstered when August Rincade charmed Charly into becoming his assistant.

~ ~ ~ ~ ~

Throughout the past decade, Charly had noticed that Merle Nobakov's publications were showing up in elite neuropsychology journals. He'd become prominent in the field. Merle had become so successful, that numerous media outlets made a major scandal out of some erroneous data that had spilled out of his lab. It had recently been in the news that because of the errors, the infamous research scientist had been fired from his prestigious professorship at the renowned neuroscience institute where he'd spent his career.

Charly had concluded that the more respected scientists are, the harder they fall. Highly compensated baseball players got three chances to get a hit but underpaid scientists, not so many.

Charly also saw the situation as an opportunity. However, she worried that even if Merle responded to her communication, he would never accept a position in her obscure little laboratory. The Laudren lab's academic affiliations were so remote that they were almost fictitious. But who else was going to hire Professor Nobakov, now that he was damaged goods?

Perhaps, Merle Nobakov didn't even need to work anymore. His notoriety could sell books, especially if he exposed other erroneous studies. With his domineering personality, he could maybe make lucrative appearances on talk shows and podcasts. He could make a good living out of making science even more disrespected by all of those anti-intellectuals who owed almost every convenience in their lives to science.

After Merle's former department secretary connected Charly with Merle, Charly perceived that her old mentor had become mellower after a few decades, but she also sensed that he was still a master manipulator who she could learn from, so long as it wasn't lab data he was manipulating.

Still, the bigger question would be if Jenna Laudren would even consider hiring Merle Nobakov, assuming Merle would accept the offer and assuming it became certain that August was done for.

Charly kept telling herself she didn't really care if August was finished. She was one hundred percent through with the cheating bastard, even though she still cared about the projects they had worked together on for so long. If she could find some way to continue August's research, wouldn't that also be Jenna's goal?

There was no doubt that Jenna was totally invested in August's research. If the woman had been as dedicated to August as she was to the projects that her precious Laudren NeuroScience Foundation was sponsoring, maybe she and August would still be a couple. Jenna was so focused on the success of her holy family legacy, that she had no time for family.

Charly planned to get rid of her hyphenated Rincade name as soon as she could get divorced from her cheating husband. She certainly didn't want to be associated with his name anymore, especially if the cocaine-related death of a cocaine researcher became a big news story. Hopefully, if August did die in disgrace, they could keep the matter private, and she wouldn't be tainted by her partnership with him.

Charly kept struggling with the fact that if she could get Merle interested in working in their lab, it would be a hard sell to get Jenna to accept him in August's place; not just because he came with a tarnished reputation, but because his work on addiction wasn't that closely related to August's.

Merle had used Wistar rats for alcohol research and Zucker rats for his obesity studies. He had no experience with the Long-Evans rats that August was partial to, or the Laudren breed of rats that Jenna's lab had created.

Charly needed to delve more deeply into Merle's research to see if she could find some connection by which she could reel in both Jenna and Merle and make them both dependent on her skills.

4

October 2 – Morning

After seeing the state August was in, Jenna Laudren opted to shut down some of the lab activities for the week. She gave paid leave to those not caring for the animals. She wanted to take some potential new researchers on a tour of the facility without Charly present. But Elsie would be there, so she'd have to explain Elsie. These interviews had been scheduled before August had suffered a stroke.

Potential candidate Frank Murr's initial research had focused on the tendency of the Brattleboro rat to suffer kidney disease because it can't produce the hormone vasopressin to regulate kidney function. But coincidentally, it was discovered that vasopressin also influences social behaviors like addiction, or whether a partner of a monogynous species would stay faithful to its spouse. Perhaps infidelity was hormonally driven.

Frank claimed he had recently become more interested in addiction because his favorite nephew, who should have had a bright future as a software engineer, wound up addicted to cocaine, and every treatment that the family had tried had failed. To support his addiction, the kid had concocted a web-based used-car dealer scam. He got caught by a cybercop and he wound up in jail where he suffered a brain injury which left him incapacitated. The whole family was devastated, and Frank now had a vendetta against cocaine.

Jenna was thinking that maybe Frank could be a temporary fix for her lab if not August's replacement. She liked his ideas and his attitude, but a part of her wished she still had August's insight and help with such an enormous decision. Before he got captured by Charly, Jenna had always considered August to be a good judge of character. He could have been useful in selecting his own replacement had he not trashed his own brain.

Before she took Frank on a tour of the building, Jenna told him about how she had funded and developed the lab. She was the trustee for the wealth that her father had accumulated as an inventor and an investor.

Jenna's father, Jay Laudren, was a civil engineer who served as a utilities manager for a small city. He'd spent many a chilly night tromping around in snow and mud to address power outages and freezing pipes, while carrying around giant books of maps of the underground cables and water lines. As the city grew, the books became so bulky that they no longer fit in his subcompact car. He acquired an old used van, just so he'd have enough room in the back to open those books, the pages of which were getting old and frail. Then, Jay Laudren had a vision.

It was the dawn of the age of the computer chip. Tech-savvy Jay started to develop software that could read and reproduce the lines on the pages of giant utility maps. It took him three years to get the chip to market, but immediately, every utility company in the world wanted it. Then, just a few weeks before several competitors started putting out their utility-mapping chips, Jay sold his company and his patent to an investment firm for a fortune.

A week before selling the chip, Jay had reviewed utility proposals by a major developer who planned to build a suburban community where there had previously been a big farm. A few days after selling his chip, Jay noticed a for-sale sign on a five-acre parcel that would likely border a connector road between the new subdivision and the local highway. It was outrageously overpriced, but Jay immediately sunk a chunk of his fortune into it.

It took nearly a decade to fully develop that piece of land, but ultimately it became the essential suburban strip mall with all the necessary stores, eateries, and services, plus a twelve-thousand square-foot fitness gym, and an urgent care clinic. The rents paid by these tenants all went into the Laudren trust fund.

Behind the Laudren Retail Plaza, Jay built a laboratory for his scientist daughter Jenna. Concealed by a wall of mature evergreens, the ultra-modern Laudren NeuoScience Laboratory building was designed to be invisible to all of the traffic that delivered merchandise to the backs of the stores. Even many of the people who worked in those stores every day did not know that there was a research lab in their backyard.

"The Laudren NeuroScience Foundation provides as much revenue as our scientists need to do the research that we believe could be the most helpful to humanity," Jenna proudly told her potential recruit.

Frank Murr wondered who the "we" was in reviewing what expenditures were worthwhile. It probably wasn't a university-based board of scientists, economists, and ethics experts. Laudren was a small, independent player in the neuropsychology field, and Frank was surprised to learn that it had that kind of revenue. Jenna never spelled out the figures, but Frank figured it was in the range of tens of millions. A researcher could do great things with that kind of cash.

However, Frank didn't know about all the other Laudren dependents that the foundation also supported, though Jenna did give him a head's up about a family member who worked in the lab, her special needs daughter Elsie.

Jenna explained that her lab currently housed four units. In addition to August's addiction studies unit using Long Evans rats, researcher Celia Fromme and her team were currently using FSL (Flinters Sensitive Line) rats to study the treatment of depression. Along with a team of doctoral students, August and Charly co-managed the third unit which used the Wistar albino rat and the Laudren rat to study age-related hearing loss. The fourth unit was dedicated to breeding and training Laudren's own line of rats, which other researchers were starting to show interest in, particularly for the study of aging. The Laudren rat was also gaining notoriety for its exceptional trainability, so the Rincades were starting to get requests for these rats from some international researchers.

It took Jenna and August almost twenty years and dozens of generations, but the longevity of the Laudren rats had been developed to almost double the short lifespan of most other domestic rat breeds. It was only after creating the longer-living rats that their tendency to abuse cocaine was recognized.

Though now deeply invested in addiction research, Jenna and August were hoping that Laudren rats could also become models for deafness research. They had recently discovered that the majority of these rats retained remarkably acute hearing into their old age, while about ten percent of the breed appeared to prematurely lose their hearing. August was interested in finding out why. Rats were widely used for research into deafness caused by noise pollution, old age, and faulty genes. Laudren rats could point to a new genetic mutation.

Jenna was also currently researching the feasibility of breeding these smart, docile rats as pets, though that would require a much larger operation than her lab could accommodate. Rat lovers would be thrilled if their affectionate, clever little pets lasted more than two years. But without August to help, she wasn't sure she could undertake that enterprise, and she didn't think breeding and selling rats would be an attraction for Frank Murr, so she didn't bring it up.

"My daughter Elsie is the primary trainer in the breeding unit. We have two other trainers and a variable cast of students who intern for college credit in laboratory technology.

"I need to tell you about my daughter Elsie. She was born very prematurely with multiple congenital anomalies. The doctors had little hope for her survival, but she fooled everyone. She had a rough time of it though. She was almost six months old before we could take her home, and that's when things got really complicated."

"Yikes," Frank responded. "My second son was born six weeks prematurely and those weeks in the neonatal intensive care nursery were just brutal; the worst weeks of our lives. He's now twelve and he's doing okay, just some mild learning disabilities, but he's getting better. How premature was your daughter?"

Jenna revealed that she wasn't a very good incubator. Her firstborn, Toby, came three weeks early, but he only spent a few days on oxygen, and he was home in a week.

Toby was Jenna's pride and joy. He was now in his second year of veterinary school. He wanted to be a zoo doctor so that he could bring some comfort to those poor animals in captivity. But Jenna was confident that once Toby started to learn about how all those animal illnesses were treatable because of animal research, he'd have much greater appreciation for what his parents did.

"My second child decided to bail out of the womb when he was barely twenty-four weeks old, and the neonatologists couldn't save him. He would have turned twenty-two last week, if he'd survived."

"Before my kids were born, researchers were using rats to study preterm birth. Ten percent of U.S. babies are born prematurely, and the incidence of prematurity is increasing due to older maternal age. Rats can't remedy delayed human reproduction. The incidence of prematurity in humans also correlates directly with levels of air pollution and the rats also can't fix the bad air quality."

Jenna chewed her lower lip for a minute. This topic was obviously personal to her. Then she added, "I was fertile, but I had two more miscarriages, at which point I gave up. Toby was five years old, and we were resigned to his being an only child, when unexpectedly, I got pregnant again while using birth control…the one to two percent failure rate they warn you about.

"Like her lost siblings, Elsie decided to arrive thirteen weeks ahead of her due date, at the tender age of twenty-seven weeks, weighing twenty-seven ounces. She was smaller than the two-pound fryer that August had served us for dinner on the night she was born.

"As you'll soon see, Elsie has unusual facial features, underdeveloped vision and abnormal hearing. Up until she was three, we thought she was deaf. Then we came to understand that an odd-shaped cochlea on her left side can pick up frequencies that differ from what most humans can hear. With the use of a Vococorder, a tool that raises the pitch of low frequency sound, her right ear can hear if you speak clearly and slowly.

"Elsie also doesn't have much of a voice. Being intubated for the first three months of her life because her lungs were too undeveloped to breathe, caused vocal cord damage. She speaks with the use of a microphone."

"How inspiring, Jenna. It sounds like your daughter has overcome tremendous odds. Do you know the cause of her disabilities besides her premature birth?"

"Genetic analysis revealed that two of her forty-six chromosomes are missing a few pieces of DNA, and one of her other chromosomes shows an odd duplication of genetic material. Her chromosome profile has probably been screened by every major geneticist in the world, and nobody has ever seen another one like it. Elsie appears to be one-of-a-kind. You'll see when you meet her."

5

OCTOBER 2 - EVENING

Merle Nobakov and Charly Swift met in the upscale dining room of the West Willow Hotel. Charly wouldn't have recognized Merle had she not been looking for him. He was never particularly good looking, but he hadn't aged well. He was balder than a baby's butt, and he had a big belly to go with double chins. Even his fleshy lips seemed fatter. The pocket of his too tight jacket displayed a cigar that Charly could smell from across the table, along with his cigar breath.

Merle was only six years older than Charly, but he looked like he could be her father. His appearance might even disqualify him as a science celebrity on the talk show circuit, so maybe he actually did need a job. He was downright repulsive.

Merle would have recognized Charly anywhere. Her wild red hair, perfect features, and her Barbie-esque physique were still showstopping. Now she was also sporting an attention-grabbing tattoo of a rat in the middle of her chest, which she was showing off with a strappy little emerald green crop top under a vintage denim jacket. She was both the shabbiest-dressed and the sexiest person in the restaurant. Most of the diners couldn't take her eyes off of her. Neither could Merle Nobakov.

Even after two plus decades, Merle Nobakov was still infatuated with Charly Swift. Merle had also recently attended a science meeting where a video about Charly and August Rincade's most recent project had been shown, and Merle had been more than impressed with the high level of technology they had access to. Very few labs could afford such equipment. Merle had long envied August Rincade because Charly had partnered with him, but now Merle was also envious of their resources.

While they both perused the menu, Charly gulped down a gin and tonic before Merle had even picked up his glass. Then she flagged the waiter to ask for another, which she downed almost as quickly.

Merle chuckled to himself as he watched the ears of her rat tattoo turn red, as Charly's chest and face flushed, but he was also concerned. Was the object of his affection studying addiction because she was an addict? Could she only face her old mentor if she was schnockered?

By the time their meals arrived, Charly was chugging her third gin and tonic and she showed no interest in the food. As she watched Merle dig into his steak, she suddenly felt light-headed, and she found herself getting misty eyed. August would have enjoyed a steak the way Merle was doing just now.

The booze-infused moment turned out to be the first time since she had received that shocking phone call two nights ago, that Charly realized how much she missed August. Suddenly, her roaring rage at him had been replaced by a painful sense of loss. Yes, August was a cheating bastard, but she had loved the guy. The thought of working alongside of Merle in August's place, now seemed so revolting that she felt sick to her stomach.

Merle watched Charly's flushed face lose its color and he asked her if she was alright. She took the opportunity to excuse herself to the rest room. She entered a stall and purged herself of the alcohol. Then, for maybe three minutes, she just sat there and cried. Then she got angry at herself for being so emotional and for dragging Merle into this when it wasn't even yet clear if August could recover.

Maybe the best thing to do was to just keep Merle interested before some other independent lab came knocking on his door. She knew of some other researchers who could maybe be looking for a new lab, due to the devastating cuts in federal support for university research. She needed to check these people out in more detail before she made any commitments to Merle.

Then she wondered who she was kidding. She had no power to make commitments to anyone. Only Jenna did, and it was starting to look like Jenna was inclined to wait to see if August could recover. But Jenna was so protective of the lab that Charly was certain that Jenna was simultaneously looking over the same crop of researchers that Charly was thinking about. She composed herself and returned to the table.

Merle had already cleaned his plate, and he was gaping at Charly as she took her seat. He was also ogling her unfinished meal. His primary research interest in obesity was apparently personal for him.

There could be no doubt that Charly had been crying, but she gave Merle the biggest smile she could muster and gulped down a glass of water. "Apologies, Merle. Those drinks were stronger than I anticipated, and I'm afraid I've lost my appetite. Do you want to finish my halibut?"

"Well sure, if you don't want it?" As she passed him the plate, he asked her again if she was okay.

As she watched him dive into the food before she could even answer, Charly opted to just change the subject. She told Merle why she thought he might be able to help her lab with the addiction research. She had read about his intriguing research using deep brain stimulation for obesity.

Merle was one of several researchers who had demonstrated that the compulsion to consume excessive amounts of food could be reduced in fat rats by electrically stimulating certain areas of their brains. As with most lab animals who are bred specifically to study certain human problems, this breed of chubby rodents had been created specifically because their forebearers had been observed to be obese gluttons.

Different researchers had tried different electrical waveforms in different areas of the brain before it was tried on humans. A fifty-year-old man with life-long, morbid obesity was the first to have electrodes implanted in his brain. For six months after surgery, nothing happened. Then, the researchers changed the current, and the patient stopped craving food and lost weight. However, he went on to develop severe insomnia and he started to eat at night and gain weight. Additional adjustments of the electrical signaling caused other problems that ended the experiment.

Since the early 2000s, researchers had repeatedly tried to use variations of deep brain stimulation (DBS) with few successes. Most of the obese humans who were desperate enough to be lab rats for this brain surgery, either didn't lose much weight or suffered intolerable side effects.

But Merle Nobakov was convinced that electrical brain stimulation would eventually get refined enough to provide a safe treatment option for obesity, should the weight loss drugs ultimately lose their effectiveness or prove toxic.

He was now experimenting with transcranial brain stimulation instead of implanting electrodes inside the skull. Transcranial was better for the rats and for the researchers.

Charly said she hoped to bring Merle's experience with electrical brain stimulation to the addiction lab. August had a theory that electric stim in combination with a particular hormonal therapy could extinguish cocaine cravings. She'd get back to Merle if they could get something worked out.

Charly patted Merle's hand and then she got up and left. As she rushed home to freshen up, Charly hoped she was sober enough to go see her husband in the hospital.

Merle Nobakov wasn't at all surprised that his former student was still a prickly cactus, yet he still yearned to be with Charly Swift.

6

October 3 - Morning

Nurse Neil was discouraged about August Rincade's lack of progress in spite of the twice daily physical therapy to keep his limbs from stiffening, and the favorite music they were playing for him. August had remained unresponsive since his hemorrhagic stroke, two and a half days previously.

It there was no improvement in the next few days, his wife was considering having a feeding tube implanted in his stomach and transferring him to a chronic care facility. She wasn't holding out much hope that he was going to recover, although it now seemed less likely that he was going to die.

Neil was perplexed by the family relationships. The ex-wife and the daughter had visited three times each day. According to the registry, the current wife had not returned since that first day after emergency surgery and had only been in contact by phone.

Jenna and Elsie had both tried to talk to August throughout their visits. Elsie would bring her microphone right up to August's ear and say things that Neil couldn't quite hear without being intrusive.

For one moment the previous afternoon, when Elsie was speaking to her father, Neil thought he saw August's eyelids flutter. The rest of the time, August was so not-there that Neil decided that maybe he had imagined the eye movement. But he was invested enough in his patient's recovery that he mentioned it to the night nurse when he arrived for the shift change this morning.

"Well, that's interesting," Lorrie responded. "About an hour ago, someone in housekeeping scrubs came in here to dump the garbage. While I was over at the sink, I observed this person walk right up to August's bed and take a look at him before bending to pick up some little thing from the floor, and I also thought that August might have reacted to that person's presence. I thought he might have even been trying to open his eyes.

"I didn't really look at the housekeeper. He or she was wearing a mask and a surgical cap, and they were in and out of here in maybe twenty seconds. If you hadn't brought your observation up, I probably would have thought that August had just exhibited some kind of involuntary reflex."

"Does housekeeping typically come in here at that hour to empty garbage?" Neil asked. "I usually see them take the night's garbage about an hour into my morning shift."

"No, actually, now that you mention it. Unless there's been a spill, I've never seen housekeeping in here at that hour except this morning. And now that I'm thinking about it, the whole thing was weird, and I just have this feeling that August was somehow aware of that person's brief intrusion."

"Well let's keep looking for some hope here, Lorrie. If August is responding to anything, that's good news. I've read a little about him. He's a renowned scientist and I'd hate to see him in a vegetative state for the rest of his life. Please let me know if you see any other signs of responsiveness, because this poor guy is scheduled for gastric tube placement if he doesn't wake up soon."

~ ~ ~ ~ ~

Nurse Neil and his patient August spent an uneventful morning together. August didn't respond to being bathed, shaved, exercised or spoken to, not by Neil, and not by Jenna or Elsie. It appeared that Elsie was straining most of the muscles in her neck as she whispered in her father's ear, and for a brief second, Neil again thought he saw August try to open his eyes, but he remained essentially unresponsive. Elsie and Jenna had left with their heads hanging down.

When Neil came back from his lunch break, the relief nurse told him that she had just spiffed August up because another visitor was signing in. Neil was putting his password into the computer when a handsome young man wearing a backpack walked into the room. He introduced himself to Neil as August's son Toby, though he needn't have. The resemblance was uncanny. Neil had no idea that August had a son.

The young man put his backpack down and stood at the foot of the bed, just staring at August for a few minutes. Then he sat down on the chair by the side of the bed and said, "hey, Dad, it's me Toby."

Now, Neil had no doubt that he was seeing a response in his patient. The left side of August's lower lip was quivering, and it appeared he was trying to open his eyes, but without success.

"Mom told me they're going to move you to the Luciden Center where Grandma is a patient, and I just wanted you to know I'm rooting for you, Dad. I'm really sorry things haven't been better between us."

Neil almost jumped out of his chair as it appeared that August was trying to move his mouth, while his eyelids seemed to flutter. The monitors were showing big blips on the brain wave tracings.

"Keep talking to him, Toby, please! Amazingly, your father is showing more response than what we've seen since his stroke. Please! Keep talking to him."

Toby told his father about the courses he was taking. It was beyond demanding to learn the comparative anatomy and the pathology of so many different mammals. Toby tried to think of things that might be of interest to his father.

"Tigers are prone to kidney disease. Giraffes suffer from high blood pressure. Elephants have weak immune systems, but they rarely get cancer. Tuberculosis is common in monkeys. Zebras are prone to diabetes and heart disease. Rodents are vulnerable to tumors and cancers. The superior immune system of bats has researchers optimistic that a cure for viral disease is on the horizon. Bats can also teach humans about resistance to cancer and diabetes."

Next semester, Toby's curriculum would include another course on mammals and also a course that focused on birds, reptiles, amphibians and cartilaginous fishes. It was when Toby told his father that he was starting to understand the need for animal research that August briefly opened his eyes, not even long enough to look around, but it was a sign of hope for which Neil had been anxiously awaiting.

August then closed his eyes, and his brain monitor suggested he had gone back to a comatose state, but the lines on the monitor showed a little more amperage than before his son had spoken to him. Eye opening didn't always correlate with awakening in comatose patients, but Neil made sure it was documented in August's record.

Neil and Toby decided to let August rest at that point. Neil went back to inputting the computer and Toby continued to sit at his father's bedside, looking glum. After a few minutes, Neil sheepishly asked Toby if he could ask him a question about his sister.

"Of course! Everyone in healthcare should hear Elsie's story. Maybe the whole world should hear it. My amazing sister Elsie, as handicapped as she is, has a beautiful soul and a remarkably insightful mind."

Toby went on to explain that Elsie was a very premature baby who came home from her long neonatal hospitalization on the day of his seventh birthday. That weekend, family and friends came to the house for a big celebration, though they all stayed far away from Elsie. They sang Happy Birthday to Toby, but it was Elsie's survival they were commemorating.

Even as he opened the coveted toys he was gifted that day, Toby could sense that this precious new baby was going to change everything in his family's lives. He could feel the anxiety in the adults. Even their old, laid-back golden retriever seemed nervous.

"Elsie didn't have enough vocal power to cry to alert her caretakers of her needs, so she had to be continuously monitored. My Grandpa Jay was wealthy, and he built a whole wing onto our house to accommodate the private duty nurses that took care of Elsie around the clock. We didn't know then that Elsie wasn't going to need so much help as she matured out of infancy.

"Grandpa Jay was still sharp then. However, when Elsie was about seven and I was thirteen, he developed lung cancer which metastasized to his brain. He was successfully treated but some of his cognitive skills became compromised and that's when he turned management of his entire estate over to Mom.

"My mother was overwhelmed. She not only had to manage the finances, but she had to manage the Laudren Retail Plaza that provides the income that supports the trust and the neuroscience lab. She had to be present for building inspections, parking lot repairs, fire drills, police investigations of vandalism and emergency services for patrons who got injured on the grounds.

"Mom was constantly on the phone with landscapers or snowplow operators, or she was arranging for construction alterations as tenants came and went, or she was getting estimates for someone to replace damaged roof tiles or cracked pavement. She had to act as a rent collector and she often had to do battle with insurance companies, lawyers for the tenants' association, environmental inspectors, and tax assessors who overvalued the undeveloped portion of the land.

"It was a full-time job, and my mother already had three fulltime jobs, researcher, lab administrator, and parent. She was also constantly running to doctor appointments for Elsie, as well as regularly visiting Grandpa who could still function well enough for independent living, but who could no longer advise Mom about the business issues. My mom had to take over his finances to be sure his bills got paid.

"My grandmother Sara used to help my mother when Elsie was young, but eventually my mother wound up having to help Sara. My grandmother developed dementia to the extent that Grandpa Jay couldn't take care of her anymore, even before he had his own problems. Grandma Sara has been in a facility for about ten years, and she's been in an Alzheimer's unit for the past five years. She no longer recognizes her husband or my mother.

"My father tried forever to get Mom to hire an administrator for the trust or for the lab, but she couldn't let go of either. She still can't. She's so obsessed that she's actually possessed. She was a very good mother to me before all of this stuff landed on her plate, but it was mostly my father who raised Elsie to be the remarkable person that she is."

Toby went on to explain that Elsie became a hyperactive toddler who investigated everything in her reach, but she did not speak. She didn't respond to verbal commands, and she covered her ears when others spoke. She would also cover her ears for no apparent reason, but she wasn't showing any of the other typical behaviors that are commonly seen in autistic children.

"Though it's hard to judge the response of a baby outfitted with headphones, a pediatric audiologist surmised that Elsie couldn't hear much of anything in her left ear and she could not hear low frequency sounds on the right. They tried all kinds of hearing aids for her, but she wouldn't tolerate them.

"She did tolerate eyeglasses when she got fitted for some at twenty months. It's pretty hard to diagnose visual impairment in a baby, but a great ophthalmologist made a good guess, because after we figured out how to keep the glasses on her funny little face, we were able to start using sign language with her. She became fluent in sign a lot faster than the rest of us, but you had to be right up close for her to be able to see your hands and expressions. She still can't read signs from across the room.

"When Elsie was three, my parents learned of a special program in the city for children with visual and hearing impairment. It was an hour back and forth to get her there, but my father drove her every day for a few weeks until the teacher told him that the program wasn't right for Elsie. She was much more cognitively advanced than the other children. She seemed bored and she was spending almost all of her time with her left ear pressed up against the rear wall of the classroom.

"That intrigued my dad. He investigated behind that wall and found an alley with poorly maintained dumpsters and bountiful evidence of rats. Rats are nocturnal scavengers who shouldn't have been too active during the day when school was in session, but some rats will show up when humans throw out the trash. That's when August started to wonder if Elsie could hear the ultrasonic squeaks of rats."

Neil was intrigued by Toby's story about Elsie, and he had read a little about August's rat research. "So is your sister some kind of rat whisperer?"

"My poor sister's damaged vocal cords will never be able to squeak like a rodent, but she can hear more of the sounds they make than we can with our normal hearing. Elsie can hear a dog whistle. Her hearing is apparently superhuman.

"Hey, there's much more to Elsie's story, but I've got to go. I'm only home for a brief visit and I can't miss too many of my classes. I'll try to come back tomorrow if it'll help my dad."

Toby put his hand on his father's limp arm as he said goodbye. Neil again witnessed a flicker of August's eyelids and a tiny spike of his brain waves.

~ ~ ~ ~ ~

On the way out of the hospital, Toby stopped at the coffee bar across from the main elevator. He had just brought the cup to his lips when he saw her coming down the hallway. He quickly turned his back, pulled his collar up around his face and walked in the opposite direction.

Toby hadn't seen Charly since the day before he left for vet school when she had seduced him, and he did not want to see her now.

7

October 3 - Afternoon

Jenna had thought Frank Murr might be a good fit for her lab, but at the conclusion of the interview, he didn't seem too enthusiastic about signing on.

Jenna wasn't sure if that was a ploy to bump up the salary offer, or Frank just wasn't that interested. Her compensation package was generous by research-world standards, but he'd given no feedback to indicate that he'd accept an offer.

Carmen Abara was Jenna's next interviewee. Doctor Abara was a physician who had worked in inner city addiction clinics for almost a decade before leaving clinical practice to become an addiction researcher. She had partaken in studies that had demonstrated how adversity in early childhood predisposes individuals to substance abuse disorders later in life, by causing permanent changes in brain development.

If given unlimited access to a drug that induces a state of euphoria, rats deprived of maternal contact or exposed to chaotic parenting when they were pups, are much more likely to show behaviors like binging, intoxication and addiction, than are rat pups who've had good mothering. Carmen had spent years trying to come up with a formula that could reverse those early brain changes, but she hadn't yet succeeded. If there was a substitute for motherly love, it remained unknown. Like August, Carmen's primary interest was in the use of hormones to reprogram the addicted brain. Like Jenna, Carmen had also lost a sibling to a fatal drug overdose.

~ ~ ~ ~ ~

Elsie was in the breeding lab when Jenna gave Carmen the tour. Jenna had given Carmen a head's up about Elsie, but Elsie wasn't aware of their schedule, and she was playing with one of the rat pups when they walked in. There were always some animals that Elsie formed strong bonds with, but she had finally learned to stop rescuing them all as she came to understand the nature of her parents' research.

"That's a young one you've got there," Jenna commented.

Elsie shook her head and held up her index finger in a "but wait" gesture. She put on her cap with the microphone and said, "six and a half weeks, but watch what this baby can do."

Elsie put the baby rat in a box with two chambers separated by a see-through wall. The rat was contained in her chamber, but she could see Elsie put a treat down on the other side of the wall. She had to push a lever for the treat to be given to her. If she saw Elsie put two treats down, she had to push the lever twice to get her reward. Three treats required pushing the lever three times, and so forth. She wouldn't have been given treats if she pushed the lever an incorrect number of times, but she didn't make any mistakes.

Both Jenna's and Carmen's jaws dropped when the little rat was apparently able to count all the treats and push the lever seven times. Then, Elsie stopped the demonstration because she didn't want the pup's belly to get too full. She said she thought this baby could probably count higher.

"Can all of these rats that you're breeding here do that?" Carmen asked. "There's a widely held belief that the average domesticated rat's I.Q. is about 105, a tad better than the average human I.Q. of 100, but I'll bet that little pup is a lot smarter."

"I've never seen anything like that here ever, especially in such a young one," Jenna replied as she turned to Elsie. "How high can the mother count?"

Elsie said the mother rat had been able to count to five but not consistently. Most of the young rats could only be trained to push the bar three to four times and then they'd lose count after that, even when it seemed that they understood the task, though some got better with more training and maturation.

"What are you calling this little genius?" Jenna asked her daughter.

"Freyja," Elsie said and then said it again. She wanted to be sure her mother heard it correctly because she had big plans for this baby.

"Elsie gives names to the breeders and the pups she becomes attached to," Jenna explained to Carmen as she checked the baby's ear tag. The one she's calling Freyja we call C6/E4-F2/5/6, which means the mother is from the sixth generation from our C line, the father is from the fourth generation from the E line, and this pup is the second born female of five pups in this couple's sixth litter.

"We started our lines with three types of domestic rats and one wild rat. We think the wild one may have contributed some exceptionally smart genes to the mix. For months, this wild rat had been raiding the dumpsters behind the retail plaza that my family owns. She could get into them no matter how heavy a rock the tenants put on the lids. She was so smart that we were unable to trap her. On a security camera, we saw her using branches and rocks as tools to get the bait and escape, time after time. But my husband came up with an ingenious trap that finally caught the poor girl. Since Freyja is a C, she's that wild rat's great, great, great, great, granddaughter."

Jenna turned back to Elsie. "Are any of the other pups in this litter showing this level of trainability?"

"They're just starting to be ready to train. Freyja is an outlier by far," Elsie said, as she gently put the baby back with its family. The mother rat immediately started to vigorously groom her little one as if Freyja had been contaminated. Then she groomed herself and her other four babies as the three women looked on at screens that projected images from cameras inside the rats' quarters.

Elsie's crooked mouth broke into a sort of a smile. "Tansy is an absolutely wonderful mother. She gets better with every litter."

Jenna turned to her potential recruit, Carmen, "And Elsie gets better at training these pups with every litter. That actually makes it difficult for us to judge if the litters are getting smarter or if Elsie is. We're using another trainer with the next litters to see if we can tell if Elsie's talents are accelerating our rats' development. She's like a great professor stimulating young minds. She just has a way with them."

8

October 3 – Late Afternoon

Toby hadn't let his family know he was coming home. After he visited his father, he picked his friend Brigham up at the airport. He almost scared Maya to death when he and his buddy came in through the back door. Then, Maya almost hugged Toby to death.

Toby and Brigham had become close friends, and Brigham had come to visit with Toby at home because he wanted to see what an animal research lab was actually like; even though Toby had assured Brigham that the Laudren lab undoubtedly treated the animals better than most research facilities. In his second year of veterinary school, Brigham still wasn't sure if he wanted to take care of animals or do research.

Since he had invited his friend to stay at the house, Toby had told Brigham about Maya, the Laudren-Rincades' live-in housekeeper for more than a decade. Although she had her own apartment in the suite that had been built for the nurses who took care of preemie Elsie, for all practical purposes, Maya was a member of the family. She had actually been more of a mother to Elsie than Jenna had, and Toby also felt a special bond with this woman.

"My mother met Maya during an incident that occurred in the parking lot of our family-owned retail plaza. My mother was walking towards her car on a windy day with groceries in one arm and holding the hand of my disabled, six-year-old sister Elsie with the other. Then, a runaway shopping cart came at them from behind and knocked my mother off her feet, and my frightened sister went running wildly into the path of a backing-up pickup truck.

"Maya was a grocery store bagger who was helping another customer load up her car when she sprinted to rescue Elsie without a second to spare. She consoled my terrified sister, helped my mother up and gathered up the dropped groceries. When my mother offered her cash in thanks for saving Elsie. Maya refused the reward.

"My parents had just lost a housekeeper then, and my mother wondered if this quick-thinking, kind-hearted person, who had related so well to Elsie, might be interested in such work. She found out from the store manager who the bagger was and when the woman's shift ended, she intercepted Maya as she left the store.

"My mother talked this scared refugee into letting her take her to dinner. Then she brought her home after dinner and Maya never left. At that time, this poor woman didn't even have belongings to collect or a home. All she owned was a barely running old car and the clothes on her back."

Toby explained what little he knew about Maya's background. She had grown up in the Dominican Republic, very poor but provided for by a loving mother. She was fifteen when her mother died and a relative who came to rescue her, sold her to a human trafficker who sold her to a brothel in Texas. When she was eighteen, a client helped her escape, and she found refuge in a migrant camp. She survived for the next twelve years as a fruit picker and lost a husband along the way. He got food poisoning and without medical care, he died from dehydration. She gave birth to their son shortly after her husband's death.

Maya's son José ultimately transitioned from working in the migrant camp to working in Jenna's lab. Jenna was also paying for José to train in laboratory technology at the college. She also paid for his room and board on campus.

Maya had never been willing to tell her employers how she had earned enough money to buy her citizenship identity from a black-market broker, but she did finally obtain papers that enabled her to get a drivers' license and a job as a grocery store bagger. She had been sending part of her wages to two younger siblings back in the Dominican Republic and she was still doing so.

After Toby showed Brigham to the guest room, Brigham excused himself to make some phone calls. Toby took the opportunity to ask

Maya how his mother was doing. In recent weeks, his mother had been running to doctors for some mysterious pain in her chest and belly. Toby called Jenna regularly, but she would just tell him that she was fine while he suspected that she wasn't.

"I'm worried about your mother, Toby. She goes to work every day, but she spends her evenings sitting with a heating pad on her belly, and she's losing weight. I know she's been to multiple doctors and had all kinds of tests, but so far, there's no explanation for her symptoms and no relief with any of the medicines she's been treated with, which is more than a few. At least, that's my impression. Last weekend, she wouldn't even eat my yuca fritters and that's probably, of all my Dominican cooking, the food she loves best."

"Uh-oh, this is starting to sound serious. I appreciate you're leveling with me about Mom, Maya. I know you hate getting between us. Thanks for being candid. And Maya, I'd be ecstatic to eat those fritters. I also told Brigham that your sancocho stew is to die for, if you feel like whipping some up. Brigham's a meat-eater."

"I can do that, Toby. But get after your mother about taking better care of herself. I'm really worried about her. She always runs herself ragged, but especially now with her medical problems, your father in the hospital and chauffeuring Elsie around, she doesn't even have time to eat.

"I hope you're here to visit your father, Toby. He could die. Both you and August need to get past your differences."

9

October 3 – Late Evening

Nurse Neil had taken on a double shift to help out a colleague, and now he was excited that he might get to see his patient show some additional signs of waking up. Since August's son Toby had visited, the brain wave monitor had recorded occasional bursts of activity, even without a stimulus like the pinch of a toe. But then, August's brain waves had gone back to a slower state and stayed that way, until the moment when Charly Rincade walked into the room and gave her husband a peck on the cheek. Then August's brain responded robustly. So did Neil's.

Visitors to this unit were usually prohibited in the late evening, but apparently, Charly had managed to get past the registration desk. Wearing sparkly silver sneakers and a shocking purple bodysuit, she probably could have walked into the treasury at Fort Knox. The ears of her rat tattoo had apparently been dusted with silver glitter where it peaked out from her cleavage. Her mood was much less dark than when she had first come to visit.

"Wow, Mrs. Rincade. Give him another kiss. I'd love to see his brain waves spike like that again. That's the most awake he's been since he arrived."

Charly obliged by kissing August on his droopy, open mouth and he opened his eyes wide. Neil expected smoke to start coming out of the brain wave monitor, but August's eyes closed again, and the brain waves slowed. The effect had been potent but temporary.

"So, how's he doing? And please call me Charly. It's short for Charlotte."

Neil pursed his lips. "Had you come this morning, I would have told you that there's been no progress, but as of today, I'm starting to have hope. Your husband's level of consciousness appears to have improved in your presence and also when his son was here."

Now, it was Charly's eyes that widened. "Toby was here? Today? By himself? When?"

"Maybe ten minutes ago. I wouldn't say your husband responded as dramatically to his son as he just did to you, but there's no question in my mind that August is sensing that his people are here."

Charly heaved her shoulders, and her rat tattoo wiggled its ears. It was a truly unique tat. "I can't believe that Toby showed up. He and August have been estranged from each other for years. Their relationship is pathetic. August is an animal researcher, and Toby is an animal rights activist."

"Hmm; oil and water. But I was here throughout the visit, and I overheard Toby tell his father that he had come to understand the necessity of animal research. That was actually when your husband became responsive."

"Well, hallelujah! If the two of them can resolve that issue, then maybe they can resolve some of their other issues and learn to get…." Charly suddenly realized that she was talking about pre-stroke August. He wasn't going to be hard to get along with in his present state.

Charly couldn't decide if Toby had eaten humble pie because he truly felt guilty about his battle with his father, or because it pleased his mother and sister. Maybe he just wanted to be the good guy for Elsie's sake. It certainly didn't take courage to say such things to August when he was in a coma. Toby probably wouldn't have had the balls to say it if August was aware. She wondered if he could be aware but "locked in."

Charly asked Neil if Jenna and Elsie had visited, and Neil told her how often they had stopped in. Charly rationalized that Jenna was probably there only because Elsie wanted to be. Elsie was unable to drive, and her father thought she was too vulnerable to Uber or take cabs by herself. August used to drive Elsie everywhere. Now Jenna was going to have to take that on or Elsie would have to become an Uber girl.

As Nurse Neil continued to observe Charly observing her comatose husband, he couldn't resist an impulse to ask her about that rat on her chest. It was so provocative that it was in direct competition with all of Charly's other attention-grabbing features. "Your tattoo is so unique; it must be quite the topic of conversation. Where did you get it?" was all he could think to say.

Charly put a hand to her chest and proudly said, "Isn't she adorable? My Riki. I had her done when I was attending a conference in Japan last year. Rats symbolize good luck in Japan where the animal is revered for its intelligence and industry. In China, the rat represents wisdom and wealth. Some cultures believe that rats can predict the future.

"And in the world of medical science, rats and mice have taught us almost everything we know about health, disease and healing; ninety-five percent of what we know to be precise. Riki serves to remind me that humans owe their lives to lab rats."

Neil wasn't expecting such a profound explanation for a crazy tattoo, but Charly's little spiel did awaken his curiosity. "Well, that puts a whole new spin on a creature I always just thought of as a filthy, dirty rat."

"Dirty?" Charly's voice got louder, and she tapped her fingers against her tattoo as she informed Neil that rats are amongst the cleanest animals on Earth.

"Healthy, well-fed rats spend fifty percent of their waking hours grooming themselves. They use their tongues and their little hands to rub and brush their fur, systematically from nose to tail, six or more times a day. They'll clean themselves after any experience. They take extra care with the fur on their face and ears. Rats regularly gnaw and grind their teeth to maintain good dental health.

"Rats will also groom their friends and family members, and some pet rats groom their human parents. Pet rats can also be trained to use a litterbox. Rats are more far more fastidious than most human beings when it comes to personal hygiene."

Now, Charly had Neil mesmerized. She was as bright and feisty as she was attractive, but it was her dedication to rats that most intrigued him. He hoped she might be as dedicated to his patient.

"Well, that sure dispels a common myth.

"Say, Charly. Can you please tell me more about August? I'm going to be spending more time with him than anyone, especially if he starts to wake up. If I knew more about him, I could talk to him about things that would be more relevant than just the idle conversation I've been trying to make. I try to talk to him as much as possible without becoming annoying."

"Well, you can start with rats. Anything about rats would be of interest to August. He especially loves rat jokes. You know, what's a rat's favorite dessert? Mice cream. He's spent his entire career studying rodents' human-like behavior in his search for a cure for cocaine addiction. It's the absolute hardest addiction to recover from and August almost lost his life to cocaine addiction when he was a teenager."

Charly went on to tell Neil about August's history. His mother, June, like his grandfather, had exceptional mathematical ability, and she'd earned a scholarship to a special residential school for gifted kids. In the spring of her junior year, to the shock of everyone who hadn't realized she was pregnant, she delivered August in her dormitory bedroom and then brought him home to live with her parents.

"DNA identification wasn't available in the 1970s, and June refused to name August's father. Her parents suspected it was one of her teachers, though it could as easily have been one of the other students. I'd bet it was a scientist, but whoever it was, June was determined to protect him.

"June left school to take care of August, but when August was almost five, June went out on a date with a new boyfriend and never came home. A few days later, her body was found in an abandoned apartment. The coroner's report indicated that her blood showed a toxic level of cocaine, and that she had probably died from a cardiac arrhythmia.

"August's grandparents adopted him and provided well for him. His grandfather was a successful importer of Old-World textiles. He brought prized materials to clothing and furniture manufacturers all over North America, and he could speedily calculate in his head exactly how much yardage was needed for their projects.

"August's grandmother had been a librarian before becoming August's primary caretaker. She had a soft spot for her abandoned grandson, and while her husband traveled around with his suitcase full of fabric samples, she overindulged the little boy who kept asking when his mommy was coming home.

"August was a super smart kid, but he also had a rebellious streak. He was exceptionally good at outsmarting anyone who tried to reel in his adventurous nature. When he was going into sixth grade, he and two other kids got caught egging the house of a fifth-grade teacher they didn't like, and August's grandparents were outraged. They grounded him for the final days of summer.

"Home alone, depressed and angry while hearing his friends play outside, August discovered that he felt a lot better after taking some sips from his grandfather's bottle of whiskey. Neither of his grandparents drank much, but they kept some liquor around to entertain guests.

"August's grandfather was on the road that week and his grandmother was busy preparing for a big Labor Day event her library was sponsoring, so August wasn't getting much supervision during his home confinement. He quickly figured out that he could replace gin with water without his grandparents noticing, so he put the whiskey bottle back and emptied and refilled some bottles of gin, tequila and vodka.

"Some loose wire in his brain had turned him into an alcoholic in less than two weeks. Maybe his unidentified father had bequeathed him some addiction genes. Fortunately, he got caught by his teacher who smelled alcohol on his breath on the first day of sixth grade. August wound up spending the rest of that school year in a residential rehab facility for juveniles, where he recovered.

"The self-control wire came loose again when August was sixteen and madly in love with the high school beauty queen, who introduced him to cocaine. He spent the next three years in and out of rehab and miraculously, he recovered without ever relapsing again, until now." Charly's eyes grew angry as she looked at her stroked-out husband.

"That's a remarkable story, Charly. August's ex-wife told us what music he likes. Tell me some other things that interest your husband besides his career. Does he play any sports or follow professional teams? What are his hobbies? Does he have favorite movies or places he likes to travel to? Who are his heroes?"

Charly looked pensive. "Actually, August is so addicted to his research that he has little time for much else. He's either in the lab, or chauffeuring Elsie somewhere, or attending meetings or studying. He reads constantly and sometimes, I can't even distract him by sitting naked in his lap.

"He has very little interest in professional sports other than a headline boxing match now and then, but I think that's because boxing is an activity practiced by male rats. Rats box the same way that humans do, only they throw their punches faster, they can jump over their opponent's head, and they don't hurt each other once they've figured out who's going to be the champ. They also wrestle when playing or asserting dominance, but they still don't hurt each other."

"So, what does August do for fun?"

"He's sort of an episodic adrenaline junkie. On the rare occasion that he'll take a vacation, he'll go skiing or scuba diving or hiking to Machu Picchu. He has an old friend from college who also practices sobriety, and occasionally, they'll meet up somewhere and go surfing or rock climbing or something else they barely know how to do and are getting too old to do."

"What about favorite TV shows?"

"August rarely watches TV, but he does like to watch the inspiring people who compete in ninja warrior competitions. The fantastical obstacles that the human ninjas have to overcome sometimes inspire the obstacle courses we design for training our rats. Actually, the ninjas could learn a lot from rats about climbing walls.

"August tries to avoid political news unless it impacts research. He does follow science, medical and environmental news, but he mostly reads research journals. Because there's so much to read, we rarely entertain. August tends to socialize mostly with research colleagues so he can talk science, but maybe that's because scientists are boring to other people. August and I were research partners for seven years before we married. Our skills complement each other."

Charly seemed to get sadder as she painted this portrait of her husband. Neil also sensed she was getting ready to leave.

"Thanks for sharing all of this with me, Charly. Clearly, I'm going to have to learn more about rats to find a portal into August's consciousness, but you've inspired me to learn more about them anyway. Just please kiss him again before you go."

August didn't seem to respond much to Charly's kiss this time. Neil postulated that his neural circuitry was still recovering from the recent big discharge. He hoped Charly would visit again, but he wasn't sure if it would be more for August's benefit or for his own.

10

October 4 - Morning

After Toby and Brigham changed from their street clothes into lab scrubs, masks, bonnets and booties, Toby gave his friend the customary tour. Charly was analyzing blood samples when Toby and Brigham walked into her lab. Decked out in her leopard-print lab coat and surgical cap, gloves, mask and safety goggles, Brigham didn't get to see the hottie that Toby had primed him for, and he was disappointed. So was Toby.

Charly didn't even turn towards them as she said, "Hey, Toby. I heard you went to see your father. Congratulations! Now, you can have some peace if he kicks the bucket. You should also go spend some time with your sister. Her eyes have been red rimmed every day since your father was hospitalized.

"I have to run the sequencing on these specimens right now. Bye-bye." Charly pointed to the door.

Toby had hoped that having Brigham along for company would serve as a buffer for an encounter with Charly, but instead, it was a highspeed highway to humiliation. He hadn't known what kind of reception he'd get from the woman who stole his heart and then married his father, but he should have anticipated that it would be cold. Charly could definitely qualify as an ice queen, but today she was also hurling ice picks.

Toby wasn't even sure why he had ever loved her, but he still did. It had been that way since he was seventeen, shortly after she became his father's research assistant. Only because he wanted to be around her, he'd hang out in the lab when he wasn't in school. She taught him a great deal about the technology side of research. She also taught him about sex.

Toby hustled Brigham out of Charly's lab. They went to the employee lounge to grab some coffee before visiting Elsie in the breeding unit. Since it wasn't included in their veterinary curriculum, Toby gave Brigham a crash course on rat reproduction.

"Most rat breeds reach sexual maturity at two to three months of age. The female becomes fertile for several hours every five days. A couple may copulate repeatedly during that time period. Six to twelve pups are born about three weeks later and need maternal care for another three to four weeks.

"Females might stay with their mothers and share a nest. In nature, rats live in social groups often led by a dominant male, and females will travel far to avoid mating with their relatives. Six litters annually are typical though theoretically, one rat couple can produce more than a thousand offspring in a year, and the math gets mind-boggling after that.

"Reproduction slows down in cold weather, so global warming is proving to be a bonus for rats, which is why big cities are now hiring rat czars. Rats choose to live wherever humans live, and they thrive in big cities. They like the buildings, sewer systems, and our abundant food waste. City rats especially like pizza, Chinese food and pastries; options country rats don't usually have.

"In our lab, we limit our breeders to four litters a year though eight is possible. My parents created a new breed of lab rat with longevity advantages that also has a strong affinity for cocaine, so other researchers are becoming interested in them, which could increase our small-scale breeding operation."

"Is breeding profitable?" Brigham asked.

Toby laughed heartily. "Nothing my parents do is profitable. All they generate is debt. Everything gets paid for by my mother's trust fund, including the nice salaries that go to her cheating ex-husband and the woman who stole him. I think it's killing my mother that she can't just bounce both of them out of her precious lab, but for my mother, the neuroscience foundation that she and her father created with his wealth is the most important thing in the world.

"The real question is: can the lab fulfill its mission without the brilliance of my father?"

"So, what will happen if your father doesn't make it, Toby?"

"I wish I knew, Brigham. About eight months ago, my mother posted a notice in a widely read research journal, calling for proposals to develop a cure for cocaine addiction along the lines of my dad's research. She received dozens of interesting as well as idiotic ideas from around the world. I think she's still sorting through them.

"It can take hours to review the literature behind any one proposal. My mother has her doctoral degree in research methodology, so she not only evaluates the validity of a research idea, but also the methods of investigation. She's determined not to waste her precious resources on hopeless hypotheses that have no chance of producing a cure.

"Weeks before my dad had a stroke, Mom interviewed several researchers whose ideas she likes, but for various reasons, none of them quite fit her criteria or they weren't interested in her offer. I think the biggest issue is that the projects that my father designed require someone with highly specialized skills, and none of the other researchers had their own Charly to bring along. For the kind of research my father does, Charly's skills are both critical and hard to come by."

"So how did this Charly person come to be this vixen you had your little fling with?"

"Charly's is a sad story, Brigham. My dad told us her history shortly after she came to work in the lab. She grew up in Seattle in the golden age of grunge. She was in and out of foster care whenever her heroin-addicted prostitute mother got sent to jail, which was apparently quite often. She suffered some perverse abuse in one of those foster homes that she doesn't talk about.

"When Charly was thirteen, her mother died from a heroin/cocaine 'speedball.' Shortly afterwards, Charly was fostered by a good family whose hearts she won over. Those people adopted her and from there, she got to go to college where she discovered that she had exceptional talent as a dissectionist. She's also trained in numerous other high-tech lab modalities. It could take two people to replace her.

"Like my mother, Charly's also a rat lover. In one of the foster homes she lived in, she befriended a rat that lived under the house's back stoop, after her foster father killed the mother and wiped out the rest of the nest. Charly fed the surviving baby, and that rat would look for her every time she came out of the house. It never ceases to amaze me that Charly can both revere these animals and dissect them."

"But when you think about it, Toby, isn't that what vets do? We restrain or anesthetize frightened animals, stick needles in them, carve out their genitals, sometimes chop off their ears and tails, pull out their teeth, cut out their tumors, and perform other horrific procedures in order to conquer suffering and disease and save lives.

"How different is what vets do from what researchers do in their quest to relieve suffering, cure disease and save lives? We'll do these things to individual animals as veterinarians. Your parents do it to a population. Neither my dog nor your father's rats can give consent. So really, what is the difference?

"And how did your mother become a rat fancier? You never told me about that."

"The difference, Brigham, is that I am not going to intentionally sacrifice the animals I'm trying to save. The difference is that I respect the animal's life."

"I don't see it that way, Toby. To me the difference is numbers. You're trying to save one life; they're trying to save many. You have the same reverence for life but seek to save it in different quantities by different means. And don't forget that most vets also practice euthanasia.

"But I want to hear about your mother. How did she get to be a rat lover? I find this rat stuff too bizarre. Explain it, please."

"You better get used to it, Brigham. Dumb gerbils and hamsters are yesterday's pets, and smart rats are the next big thing. Just go check out all of the YouTube videos of adorable domestic rats shooting hoops and driving little custom cars. Pet rats also come dressed in designer coats featuring an array of colors and patterns to satisfy all of those vanity/novelty pet owners.

"Utterly social, rats form strong bonds with their adoptive humans like dogs. They know their names and they'll obey verbal commands and hand signals. They can identify human speech phrases. They're affectionate, playful, and they can be trained to do anything a dog can do and more, because their brains are more human-like, and they have hands.

"Rats are also easy to feed; they are such opportunistic feeders that they'll eat almost anything once they've systematically and carefully checked that it's not harmful, by gradually increasing their exposure. Rat feeding behavior illustrates why your toddler doesn't even want to taste new foods. Distrust of unfamiliar food is a built-in survival system. The caveman who would eat anything that looked interesting, probably didn't live to pass on his genes.

"The downside of rats is that they usually only live two years, which can be advantageous for the rat parent who's bored with having to take care of a pet, but traumatic for the human who's lost their best friend.

"The most tragic thing about domesticated rats is that some owners think they're disposable. Also, people who don't have a lot of time to spend with their pet will need more than one or their rat will die of loneliness. Actually, having just one is never recommended."

"Whoa, Toby. I didn't know that you're also a rat worshiper. I can see where you get it from, but I still want to know where your mother got it from."

"My mother grew up with pet rats. Her younger sister Shelby was allergic to cats, dogs, birds and seemingly, everyone in the family, but my mother's parents wanted their kids to have the experience of pets, so 'Snowflake' and 'Shasta' became my mother's best friends. Then it was 'Pansy' and 'Petunia,' then 'Thelma' and 'Louise,' and I don't know how many others before my mother started to breed the Laudren rat that she hoped could live longer.

"Remind me to show you a photo album in our house with pictures of all of the pet rats that my mother grew up with and you can even see in the pictures how much personality these critters have. Compared to the pictures of my mother's sourpuss sister Shelby, I'd much rather have hung out with the rats. I guess they also help humans to learn to live with loss and bereavement since they don't last very long."

"I can relate, Toby. I'm still grieving over the death of our family's beloved dachshund. She got to be sixteen and she was my best friend for most of my life. I can't imagine losing a pet you love so much every two years. Maybe it's familiarity and comfort with death that enables someone like Charly to do what they do. This is really enlightening for me, Toby."

As Toby guided Brigham towards the breeder unit, he reminded him to speak slowly and clearly for Elsie's sake. However, neither Toby nor his friend were prepared for what they saw when they entered Elsie's lab. Elsie was holding a squeaking rat pup up to her left ear and shaking her head as if she was following a conversation.

11

OCTOBER 4 - MORNING

Watching Elsie looking like she was speaking with a baby rat turned Toby's face tomato red. He was certain Brigham would think his entire family was insane. "Elsie, what are you doing with that pup?"

Elsie looked excited. "I have to show you this, Toby. This baby is some kind of an Einstein. Hi, Brigham. I'm so glad you came. I love to show off our wonderful Laudren rats.

"This is Freyja. She's not even seven weeks old and she's learning so fast she's like an adult, plus she can already figure out things that most rats will never be able to do. She's also more vocal than most rats, or maybe she just has a deeper or louder voice, so I just hear her better. Does Brigham know about my hearing?"

Toby hadn't yet informed his friend about this. He had only told Brigham that Elsie had vision, vocal and hearing issues.

"So, Brigham, if audiology is in our curriculum somewhere, we'll learn about hertz, the unit of measure for how many times an energy wave wiggles its way between two points in one second. The more frequently a wave vibrates, the higher is its hertz level and the higher pitched it sounds.

"Humans hear sound from energy waves that vibrate between 250 and 20,000 hertz. Dogs can hear energy waves that cycle as frequently as 35,000 hertz, so they can hear a high-pitched whistle that humans can't, except in the case of my sister. She can hear things that humans consider ultrasonic.

"Elsie's left inner ear structure is different than the right side and it allows her to hear some higher frequency sounds that even dogs can't hear. But neither of her ears hear sounds in the low frequency range of human speech, so she struggles with deep voices."

"I can't hear most of what rats can hear," Elsie added. "It's suspected that they can hear and squeak at frequencies all the way up to 115,000 hertz. I'm sure I don't hear a great deal of the sounds they make communicating with each other, but I hear enough squeaking to believe that they vocally communicate. I can tell when they're crying or laughing and I'm also learning to recognize their voices."

"Laughing?" Brigham asked.

"Yes, they definitely laugh when they're being tickled and when they are playing. But right now, I'm working with this incredible rat pup who I honestly believe is trying to tell me something. I think she's trying to teach me her word for 'more.' She says it whenever I give her a treat. Although I can't reproduce her words, it's as though she's trying to train me.

"Toby, you know how we test our rats' ability to count. I want you to watch what Freyja does."

Toby explained the counting test to Brigham while Elsie set up the box. Freyja got all of the counts right, even though Elsie didn't present them in numeric order. Then, Elsie showed the baby rat five treats but only gave her four, although Freyja had correctly pressed the lever five times.

There could be no doubt that this baby knew that Elsie had miscounted. First, she waited patiently while looking at Elsie's hand. Then, she waited impatiently, wiggling her ears and flicking her tail. Then she started to flail her arms, jump up and down and squeak like a toddler throwing a tantrum. She settled immediately when Elsie gave her the fifth treat and told the rat, "You're welcome."

Elsie turned to Toby and Brigham and said, "you normal people can't hear it, but Freyja emits a sound after she gets the last of the treats that she's counted that I strongly suspect means thank you."

Both Toby and Brigham were looking at her in disbelief, so Elsie said, "let me put Freyja back with her mom and I'll show you what we do here besides communicate with rats."

"As you can see from the cameras, our breeders are housed in multi-room condos that allow socialization, but also privacy. The females have family units with nurseries, and the males have bachelor pads. Male rats do not parent their offspring. In nature, alpha males will kick their sons out of the nest."

Especially if their sons are also alphas, Toby refrained from saying aloud.

"Nesting materials and a variety of toys and places to hide are provided for all of our rats, unless we're doing deprivation studies. My parents don't like to do those and neither do I. We change the toys frequently to stimulate learning.

"Temperature and light are strictly controlled because the chemistry of all plant and animal life is dependent on the diurnal cycle of light and darkness. We feed our rats nutritious food except when we're looking at the effects of junk food.

"Sugar, of all substances, has been shown to have the most negative impact on the health of humans and rats, but in spite of its many adverse effects, both species will continue to consume it. Animals have been given the ability to taste sweetness for nutritional reasons, but it is the pleasure of sweetness that makes it so addictive. It's now known that early introduction of sugar into babies' diets primes their brains for addiction. Sugar should be considered a gateway drug.

"In our lab, we've used treats sweetened with saccharin to train our rats for some experiments, but it appears that the experience of sweetness promotes the development of brain circuitry that continues to crave sweetness. It's why you can't eat just one jellybean. Perhaps it's our ability to experience both sweetness and bitterness that prepares us for life.

"Our primary research investigates the influence of hormones and brain chemicals on addiction behavior, and the light/darkness cycle of earth controls the release of those hormones, so regulation of light in our lab is crucial to our projects. At night, the caretakers use only infrared light that the rats can't see. A lot of the testing is done at night because that's when rats are normally active.

"For our current line of Laudren rats, we have two males that each mate with three females, so we have six pedigrees. One male shows addiction behavior and the other doesn't. None of the females show addiction behavior. We'll soon test all of Freyja's siblings for their addiction tendency, though I'm not so sure I'm going to do that to Freyja.

"If we're testing the effectiveness of a chemical that reduces drug seeking behavior in rats who have unlimited access to cocaine by pushing a lever, then we can see how it works if we give the treatment drug in the morning to one group, versus giving it at night to a second group, versus a third group that's not being treated."

"So where does your little Freyja fit into all this?" Brigham asked.

Elsie smiled again. "You saw it first, you animal doctors. My little Freyja may become the mother of a whole new breed of genius rats, never utilized for addiction studies, as long as I can keep Charly from dissecting her."

"I heard that," Charly said as she slunk into the room wearing snakeskin print scrubs with a low neckline. "And just who is it that I'm not dissecting?"

Both Brigham and Toby turned to face her and were transfixed by her rat tattoo. Charly was wearing a necklace that made it look like there was a little snakeskin collar around the cartoonish rat's neck.

"That's new," Toby blurted out, pointing to his own chest.

"You ought to see the other tattoo I've got," Charly said, looking down.

Before Toby could respond, Charly dangled his father's car keys in front of his face. There was no mistaking August's keychain with its Chinese Zodiac rat image.

"With your friend here to drive your car, please go pick up your father's rat-mobile at the downtown West Willow Hotel. The hospital staff was told by his lady friend that it was parked on the lower floor of the garage in the last row. Drop it off at my house and leave the keys in the flowerpot next to the front door. I won't be home."

As Charly sauntered out of the room, leaving Toby and Brigham with slack jaws, Elsie grabbed Toby's arm. "I want to go with you. I was in Dad's car just a few hours before this all happened. It smelled of coffee and French fries, and Dad announced that the odometer turned to 50,000 miles, just as he and I came back from lunch. He complained that the manufacturer's warrantee was now up, and the car was undoubtedly going to start to act up.

"And give me a moment to get a travel cage for Freyja. Mom and Dad are going to kill me, but I'm adopting her. I want her to have more experience and stimulation. And I'm just going to show the mother rat that Freyja is with me and she's okay. The mother gets frantic if anyone else takes this baby from her nest.

"Dad anesthetized Freyja once when she was three weeks old to get some brain imaging because she seemed so precocious. Then Charly had her knocked out again because this rat is so unique, and they wanted to focus on some other parts of her brain. Anyway, her brain looked normal, and I do not want to upset Tansy, her very protective and loving mother."

12

October 5 - Midday

After dropping August's car off at Charly and August's townhouse, Toby dropped Elsie off at the hospital to visit their father. Toby planned to visit his father later. At the moment, he wanted to take Brigham for a late lunch at the local vegan restaurant.

There were no good vegan options near the campus of their vet school, probably because very few veterinarians were vegetarians. Even if their diets didn't include cats, dogs and horses, the menus of the local restaurants clearly catered to diners who enjoyed eating cows, pigs, baby sheep and chickens.

Toby had also learned that Brigham's family incorporated deer, elk, goose and duck into their diets, though Brigham had grown up opposed to the hunting traditions of his father, uncles and grandparents. However, he did like to eat the trout that his father liked to catch, while Toby was bothered by new research suggesting that even fish are capable of basic math.

The last place Toby and Brigham had gone to dinner together was at a popular chain restaurant that featured wine bottle stands made from upside-down taxidermal armadillos. It so upset Toby that he swore he'd never return to the place. He was thinking about asking his mother if she would sponsor a vegan chef training program at the college of his vet school, even though Jenna didn't share Toby's vegan fervor.

~ ~ ~ ~ ~

Elsie got to August's hospital room before Jenna arrived to meet up with her and bring her back to the lab. She had Freyja's cage concealed in a shopping bag in which she had poked some holes that enabled the rat to look around.

In the car, Elsie had positioned the cage so that the baby rat could see the world go by. Freyja's eyes, ears and nose appeared to be working overtime to take it all in. Her little nostrils were so busy that Elsie worried that the baby's olfactory lobe might blow up. The only scents she had previously smelled were those of her food, the other rats, the humans who handled her, and the antiseptics used to keep the lab clean.

Elsie was aware of how keen a rat's sense of smell is. Along with their curiosity and the ability to get into tight spaces, the trainability of rats had led to their being used in search and rescue missions for humans trapped in collapsed buildings. With teeny GPS packs on their backs, they could signal to rescuers where a trapped human had been found. Also, due to their trainability and great sense of smell, rats were being used for the detection of hidden land mines.

Elsie wished she could know how the contrast from the limited lab environment was impacting the brain of this precocious baby. She relaxed when it became apparent that no one suspected she was carrying a rat in her shopping bag when she walked through the hospital hallways.

Nurse Neil was excited to tell Elsie that her father's brain wave patterns were showing more frequent bursts of activity, suggesting he had a chance to come out of the coma. There was even a blip on the monitor when Elsie greeted him.

Elsie turned up her microphone and told Neil that she had a new concern about her father's cocaine overdose. She asked Neil to come close to her father's ear so he would be able to hear what she was about to say.

Elsie and August had gone to lunch together on the day of his stroke, and he had been very excited about some new technology he wanted to bring into the lab. It was expensive, but certainly within Jenna's means.

August had explained to Elsie that eye doctors have been using an imaging technique called OCT, optical coherence tomography, to scan the retina for problems like macular degeneration and glaucoma.

OCT bounces light waves off of the retina to create three-dimensional images.

August had recently learned that ear doctors were now starting to use OCT to look down ear canals to see the inner structures of the ear. If OCT could allow them to see a rat's teeny, tiny cochlea, both the rats and Charly could be spared from her having to do difficult dissections. August had been offered an appointment with someone who could show him the OCT setup at the college animal lab, and he was supposed to go there after work.

Elsie had wanted to go with her dad to see the equipment, and he had welcomed her, but the timing conflicted with the scheduled training for the rat pups who would be waking up from their daytime slumber. It was important to keep them on their training schedule. All of August's behavioral research depended on all of these rats learning how to push a lever in order to receive a reward. They also were trained to push a lever to avoid something adverse, like being spritzed in the face with fox urine.

So, Elsie stayed behind for the training, and August went to this lab appointment by himself. Then, when Elsie, Toby and Brigham went to pick August's car up in the West Willow Hotel garage, Elsie made some unexpected observations.

For starters, Toby had to move the driver's seat back and raise the steering wheel just to be able to get into the car. Whoever had last driven the car could not have been the size of her father. The front passenger seat where Elsie usually sat had also been moved. It was much further back than usual.

Elsie also smelled cigarette smoke. Nobody who normally rode in that car was a smoker.

When Toby arrived at the garage exit turnstile, he couldn't produce a ticket that would have indicated when the car entered the garage. He had to pay for the month plus a penalty.

These observations verified Elsie's suspicions about what might have happened to her father. She just couldn't believe that August would undo a lifetime of abstinence on a whim. While Elsie understood how August could have been unfaithful to her mother, she couldn't see that he would do the same to Charly. He seemed happier when he finally made the break from Jenna. Although she missed him at home, Elsie had been happy for him.

The whole story of how August had landed in the hospital because of a cocaine induced stroke wasn't making sense, and her observations in his car had now saddled Elsie with an eerie sense of foul play.

"Neil, I learned some things today that have me worried that my father didn't voluntarily use cocaine. How can we get him tested for a knock-out drug like flunitrazepam."

"You mean Rohypnol, the date-rape drug?"

"That and any others you check for in rape victims. I don't think he was sexually assaulted, but I worry he could have been profession-ally assaulted. I just do not believe that my father could have done this to himself. He's fought his whole adult life to stay abstinent and there's simply no explanation as to why he would have relapsed now. Things were going well for him. This is going to sound weird, but I smell a rat."

Neil was jolted by Elsie's theory. "I'll get the attending physician to order a panel of those drugs as soon as she does rounds. I see here in the lab guidelines that a big dose of Rohypnol can show up in the urine for five days after its ingested, and we can probably get the test results back in a day. Some of these knock-out drugs can also show up in hair much later than that.

"Do you have any idea why someone would want to hurt your father?"

"My father's a good guy. People like him. Outside of our family, everyone thinks he's great. The only thing I can figure is that someone is so jealous of his research accomplishments and funding, that they want to knock him down, or scoop his projects, or discredit him because his findings conflict with their research.

"Competition for funding in the research world can be intense, but because of my mother's philanthropy, my father hasn't had to compete.

His situation is enviable. Now, there are scores of researchers out of work because their funding has been cut off by an anti-science administration. Some of these renowned scientists have been offered lab positions in Europe and Asia, so that our most brilliant minds might be siphoned off by governments that appreciate the contributions of science to humanity.

"However, some of these displaced researchers could be desperate to find a way to continue a project that they've committed their life's work to, by taking over someone else's lab. Professional jealousy is a powerful poison. I'm afraid my father could be a victim of his own success.

"Or maybe, whoever is flooding our country with cocaine wants to get rid of anyone who could get in the way of inducing cocaine addiction, a very profitable business.

"In the last few decades, the U.S. government has taken down some of the scandalous pharmaceutical manufacturers who legally disseminated addictive substances to large numbers of people, but it hasn't had much success suppressing criminal suppliers.

"There are thousands of hidden drug labs in neighborhoods everywhere in this country. Closing off the foreign flow of fentanyl and other drugs of abuse will just create thousands more domestic labs.

"To save us from the extremely high cost of addiction, we need to find and fund preventive and curative treatment. Curing just one person saves tens of thousands of dollars in crime victimization, law enforcement, incarceration, and medical and social services for the addict and family members that have been compromised by this illness.

"Addiction is a widespread, debilitating disease that costs society more than even a disease like diabetes, yet right now, addiction research is being defunded. Without philanthropic people like my mother, there may be no more research for this human ailment.

"Neil, please don't mention any of this to my mother or brother or August's wife Charly until the results of the drug test come back. There's so much conflict in my family already that I don't want to stir anything up unless my theory has merit. Will you keep this confidential until the tests come back?"

"Certainly, Elsie. What's the best way to reach you?"

"Thanks. My number's in the registry. When you get back the test results, just send me a text saying positive or negative."

13

October 5 - Afternoon

Toby dropped Brigham off at the house before heading to the hospital. Brigham wanted to call his girlfriend and his parents to tell them how enthused he was about his experience in Toby's family's lab. His encounter with Elsie and her genius rat pup had inspired him. He had an entirely new perspective about these reviled creatures, and about the prospect of becoming a researcher.

Brigham was starting to fantasize about being the heir to the Laudren NeuroScience Foundation. If he had unlimited resources and totally free reign to study anything about the brain or about neuro degenerative diseases, he didn't know what it would be. His favorite uncle, a dynamic, athletic attorney, had become crippled by Parkinson's Disease. Brigham had a childhood friend who now suffered from rapidly progressive multiple sclerosis. The kid started to have balance problems at age sixteen and by age eighteen, he was in a wheelchair.

Brigham was also interested in the issue of food addiction. His mother had struggled with obesity for decades. Now she also suffered from diabetes, even though a weight loss drug had enabled her to drop forty pounds. But the drug had also caused her to suffer vision loss. She had to discontinue it, she gained back her weight, and she was now also suffering from depression.

Brigham could think of numerous other research questions that had gnawed at him over the years. Why can't we remember our early life? Why are some very smart people unable to read? Is it the brain that hurts when you have a headache? Why does a virus like rabies go straight for the nervous system? Why, when most old dogs sleep most of the time, did my sweet little dog suffer from insomnia?

Brigham's list of questions was starting to make his head spin when he also started to question why his friend Toby was not thrilled to be heir to this diamond mine of discovery. Toby was one of Brigham's classmates whose interest in the science of veterinary medicine exceeded the emotional magnet of interspecies relationships. Plus, Toby had grown up in this science-drenched environment. He had advanced biology knowledge that probably even surpassed that of some of their professors.

Brigham had grown up on his family's ranch, herding cattle and being an on-call obstetrician during the busy calving season. With a herd of more than a hundred Black Angus, his father, brother, uncles and he all took turns being awake at all hours of the day and night to make sure that every cow and calf came out alive. Brigham had managed his first breech delivery when he was fifteen. Like most ranchers, Brigham's father had veterinary medicine knowledge from experience, but he did not know the science.

Brigham became interested in neuroscience when one of their cows was stricken with mad cow disease, (bovine spongiform encephalopathy or BSE.), extremely rare in North America. Brigham had been distressed to see this poor old cow become uncoordinated, anxious and ultimately violent.

Representatives from the U.S. Department of Agriculture, (U.S.D.A.), the Food and Drug Administration, (F.D.A.), and the Center for Disease Control, (C.D.C.) all came to investigate and make sure this cow was safely disposed of. If the prion that causes mad cow disease gets into the food supply, it can cause fatal human disease, (Creutzfeldt-Jakob Disease or CJD). Brigham wondered if research into mad cow disease was still being funded.

Brigham had appreciated how reverently Toby had spoken about both his mother's and his father's science careers. Toby had also boasted about the skills of his father's research partner, besides being smitten by her. Brigham couldn't fathom why Toby wasn't planning to follow in his family's footsteps.

~ ~ ~ ~ ~

Toby was anxious about returning to his father's bedside. He scanned the visitor parking garage for Charly's car before heading into the building. He couldn't face her again today, especially here in front of his father. He tiptoed into August's room and was relieved to find that he was the only one there besides Neil, who gave him a welcoming nod.

"Any progress?" Toby asked.

"Yes, indeed. I'm certain your father was trying to respond when your sister was here a little while ago. His eyelids were twitching more frequently. I think I saw some activation of muscles around his mouth. I also think we're at the point that we all have to be extra careful about what we say. I have a strong feeling that August can hear and comprehend far more than he can respond to.

"Your mother also came when your sister was here. She only stayed briefly but she talked to your father. It clearly moved the needle on the brain wave monitor when she told him that she didn't think there was a scientist in the world who could replace him, and that he better wake up and get back to work. His projects were waiting for him."

Toby looked stunned for a moment. Then he squeezed his father's limp hand and said, "Dad, did you hear that? Even Mom wants you back."

Neil watched as Toby's face scrunched up as he leaned in towards August's ear. "Dad, I want you back too. I'm sorry for everything. Please, Dad, come back to us. At least come back for Elsie."

Neil witnessed sadness every day in his neuro nursing career, but the snuffling tears that Toby suddenly lost control of put a lump in Neil's throat. He handed Toby a box of tissues and patted him on the back. Then, he looked at August and did a double take. A tear was trickling down the cheek of his unconscious patient. He pointed to it and Toby reached forward and gently brushed the tear from August's cheek. Another one trickled down, more freely.

"I think he hears you, Toby. Crying activates the nervous system. It causes the release of feel-good chemicals like oxytocin and endorphins. Humans are the only animal known to shed emotional tears and unconscious people do sometimes cry. I think maybe both you and your father need to let those tears flow."

14

OCTOBER 5 - AFTERNOON

After a few minutes of crying, Toby composed himself and asked Neil how he came to be a nurse. It was a career he had never considered. Toby was impressed by Neil's dedication to the noble role of giving total care to a totally disabled person.

"It's the typical story for people who go into healthcare. Many of us seem to want to fix what went wrong for someone we loved. My father had a stroke when I was eleven and he didn't get the care he needed. It helps me to be able to give good care to your father. Even if I can just spare him from bedsores, I feel like I've righted a wrong.

"The medical treatment of stroke victims doesn't differ too much from one doctor to another. The nursing care or lack thereof, may be the bigger determinant of recovery in these patients."

"Do you have a family, Neil?"

"I do. My wife of eighteen years is a pharmacy technician right here in the hospital. I have a sixteen-year-old son who wants to go to medical school and a fourteen-year-old daughter who wants to be a marijuana farmer. She thinks weed is a much better mood smoother than all of those pharmaceuticals her mother dispenses.

"I'm thinking my wife's and my kids' career choices will probably all be replaced by artificial intelligence, but I don't think AI will be able to empty bedpans and replace nurses. Who knows what it and robots will ultimately take over?

"My family's not quite as heady as your family, Toby. I was amazed by your sister in here yesterday. With her vision and hearing difficulties, how did she become so educated, so sophisticated? It's not just that she has the knowledge of an old professor, but she also has the wisdom."

"It is extraordinary, isn't it? Her interest in my parents' lab at age eight exceeded mine at any age, though I did start to appreciate the science around age twelve.

"Up until she was five, Elsie relied on sign language to communicate, but she had started to teach herself to read at age four. She had a bunch of bedtime story books, but there was one particular book that she'd want me to 'read' to her most nights or at least flip through the pages with her. One night, her brain connected the big letters to the big animal pictures on that book's pages and immediately, Elsie became absorbed in any print that she could see alongside of a picture.

"At age four and a half, an audiologist figured out a hearing correction for her right ear and she started to understand spoken language. I spent a lot of time saying the words she was reading. We found videos with subtitles and with the right magnification of the screen and amplification of the soundtrack, she quickly learned how to speak.

"The local school systems had no suitable classroom for her. She could not see a teacher using manual signs well enough to be in a deaf class, and the blind classroom teacher spoke with a soft voice that Elsie couldn't hear. My mother hired a tutor for her and my parents took her to kiddie events for socialization, but it started to become too painful. Other kids would run away from her because of her apparatus and her facial features.

"Plastic surgeons didn't want to try to remodel her until she stopped growing and when she did, she decided that she didn't want to be a lab rat for a procedure that's rarely ever done. She's seemingly become resigned to a life of hiding away in a lab and finding cures for humanity's afflictions. Like both my parents, her prime loves in life are science and learning.

"When Elsie was thirteen, the tutors said they had nothing more to offer beyond what Elsie was learning from surfing the web. Like my father's long gone mother June, math comes easy to her. Algebra equations and sudoku are her idea of fun. She also has a tremendous appetite for biology.

"With magnification on a big desktop, she reads voraciously. She's been reading about neuroscience since she's about ten. I cannot even fathom how advanced her understanding has become in the almost six years that I've been off at school."

"So, could Elsie take over your father's research if your father can't recover?"

Toby sighed deeply. "Intellectually, my sister could absolutely continue my father's research or maybe even advance it, but I don't believe my mother would allow her to become the leader of the Laudren NeuroScience Foundation.

"In an environment where new research gets published every day, brilliant research can easily go unnoticed. Without good marketing, the very best products or research studies can just sit on shelves while great marketing popularizes the worst products and information.

"My father was a good scientist and with his debonaire persona and the resources to rent vendor booths at conferences, he was also a good marketer. His booth showed captivating split-screen videos of treated and untreated rats behaving differently when given unlimited access to cocaine, and conference attendees would line up to get a chance to speak with him.

"Dad would get to talk to and charm a lot of scientists and addiction specialists to whom he also gave copies of his work. That's how he got eyeballs on his studies. That's how his research got enough attention for others to try to disprove or duplicate it. Only when other scientists conduct the same experiment and get the same results do researchers become respected.

"Elsie could be the right person to take the science further, but she doesn't have the experience or the ability to do the marketing or the comingling that supports the creative currents of research. Her disabilities leave her isolated. My parents and our housekeeper Maya and some people in the lab have been her only social contacts since I left for college.

"Her social intelligence comes from watching television. She especially likes crime shows and medical dramas. When Elsie was younger, she came to view the world through soap operas, but I suppose most people get their perspectives from TV.

"Meanwhile, my mom is now looking into having artificial intelligence continue my father's research. And if my father is finished, I suspect my mother will hire a known-name researcher to bolster the reputation of the lab."

"What's your sister's relationship with your father's wife? Your sister is spending much more time here with your father than Charly is."

"Elsie and Charly got along okay before the affair ended my parents' marriage. I suspect that Charly would never have chosen to share my father with his disabled daughter who has to be chauffeured everywhere.

"I also think that Elsie would rather not be sharing my father with Charly, and for my father to not be living at home anymore is terrible for Elsie. So, she resents Charly for stealing her father in addition to breaking up the marriage. Who she really should blame is my father. My father was everything to her."

Toby took another big breath and put his head in his hands. Neil watched tears roll down August's cheek. Then August opened his eyes. Neil grabbed a penlight from his pocket and watched his patient's pupils show some constriction when he shined the light into his eyes.

Previously, August's pupils had been dilated and unresponsive. However, August didn't seem to see Neil's fingers waving in front of his face and he again closed his eyes. Still, the pupillary response was a hopeful sign.

15

OCTOBER 5 - EVENING

Elsie thought she'd know what to do if her father's drug screen was positive for a knockout drug, until it happened. She suddenly felt more helpless than she could remember feeling since early childhood. She knew she couldn't handle this alone, but she didn't know who to turn to.

In the darkest place in her mind, she was considering whether either her mother or her brother could be capable of trying to get rid of her father. She also realized that if she called the police, they'd both become suspects.

Her mother had been cheated on and cruelly abandoned by her husband of twenty-eight years. Jenna had ample reason to feel angry and hateful towards August, and she'd spent most of the past year interviewing candidates to take his place as the lead investigator in her lab.

Jenna also had the resources to hire some drug addicted escort to seduce and poison her ex-husband. Maybe he was supposed to have died, and the stroke was an accidental outcome.

Elsie didn't want to believe that her mother was capable of harming her father, but she was concerned about how bitter Jenna was becoming. It almost seemed that her mom was self-destructing. Every week she went for another medical test and tried another treatment, but nothing worked. None of the many doctors she had consulted had been able to find a cause for her pain and weight loss, while Elsie could see that her mother was trying to do battle with unadmitted anxiety and depression.

Elsie also wondered if someone who had sent her mother a research proposal that Jenna had rejected could have targeted August. She knew where her mother had filed those proposals, and she wondered how long it would take to investigate the people who had been interested in gaining access to the lab. Simultaneously, she realized she had no way to investigate those people beyond their internet presence. She wasn't a detective who could go knocking on doors to interview the associates of a potential suspect. Between her vocal and hearing impairments, even using the phone was a challenge.

As for her brother, it was widely known by anyone associated with either Toby or August, that father and son had been at war since Toby was a teen. Even before Charly's arrival, Toby had been resistant to helping out in the lab on the rare occasion that either of his parents asked him to give a hand. He thought what they did to lab rats was cruel. He also felt like he did enough to help out because he spent so much time assisting Elsie.

Toby also felt like his childhood had been stolen because parental attention focused on his disabled sister. When Elsie's issues took over the Rincade household, Toby saw his status go from number one to caretaker. Although he loved Elsie and liked being her teacher, he also resented his whole family because while he helped take care of Elsie, he felt neglected.

Toby became especially resistant to helping his mother out when his father and Charly went off to meetings. Then, when he started hanging out in the lab because he so obviously had become infatuated with Charly, he also became increasingly hostile to the entire idea of animal research.

Elsie recalled that the war escalated when as a high school senior, Toby submitted a letter to the editor of the local newspaper regarding animal rights, and the editor published it. Both August and Jenna were furious with him for broadcasting his objections to their practice of inducing addiction in lab animals who had no choice in the matter, while humans did.

Things got even worse when Toby started to suspect that his father and Charly were having an affair. Jenna was still in denial at the time, but Toby was aware of what was happening, and he became outraged that his father was cheating on his mother and cheating with the subject of his desire. He resorted to being obnoxious to try to drive a wedge between them, and August became increasingly disgusted with Toby's behavior.

Elsie has witnessed these goings-on both at home and in the lab until Toby went off to college. Father and son tried to avoid each other thereafter, and when circumstances threw them together, the hostility between them almost made the air crackle.

To Elsie's way of thinking, Charly had just toyed with Toby because she could, and because she wanted to make August jealous. She had been trying to steal August from Jenna for several years and doting on Toby was just one of the many arrows in her quiver.

Elsie had figured out early on that Charly was totally empowered by her ability to entice and manipulate men, and Toby had been much too starry-eyed to see that he was being used. When Charly started paying too much attention to Toby, August decided it was time to leave Jenna and seal his relationship with Charly.

Still, there was no way Charly was ever going to switch her affection from August to Toby, even if the son did get rid of the father. Toby had to know that by now. Couldn't he finally see that she was just an opportunist? Elsie couldn't fathom that Toby would have arranged to have August eliminated, but to a police investigator, Toby might look like the perfect suspect.

Elsie even wondered about Charly. Could her father have done something that so enraged Charly that she took the ultimate revenge? Elsie suspected that a furious Charly might be capable of anything. Elsie had always admired Charly for her fearlessness and her independence, but she also thought she was too brazen.

Elsie was also starting to wonder if Charly wasn't just a sport fisherwoman who liked to throw the fish back after reeling them in. Or perhaps, August had been a fun play toy for her when the two of them went off to conferences, but maybe he wasn't so much fun to be with the rest of the time when he spent most of his days and nights engrossed in his research.

Elsie also worried about how a police detective might react to Charly if she used her sex appeal to try to frame Jenna for her own crime. Elsie was pretty sure that both Jenna and Charly would like to get rid of each other.

If something happened to their mother, Toby would become the manager of the Laudren family trust, since Jenna had cut August out as soon as she filed for divorce. When asked to be the trustee at that time, Toby had promised Jenna that he would carry on the family's philanthropic commitment to neuroscience. But being the primary heir to the trust could also put Toby on a suspect list.

Then, Elsie wondered if she herself could be considered a suspect. Would some detective think that she was so angry at her father for breaking up the family and abandoning her that she wanted to kill him? Then, she wondered if that could be true, but she quickly dismissed the idea. She was very angry with her father, but he was also the person she most loved and needed. Losing him would be the worst thing that could happen in her life.

Maya was the one other person that Elsie considered asking for help, but then she worried that Maya was also angry with August for leaving the family. Maya and Jenna had become very close, and Maya was one hundred percent on Jenna's side in the matter of the divorce. Maya had also made it known that she disrespected August for abandoning Elsie.

However, Elsie didn't believe that Maya, who had risked her own life to save six-year-old Elsie from being hit by a truck, was capable of anything so diabolic. Maya probably had a purer soul than anyone in her family.

However, she couldn't tell Maya about her theory before telling her mother. Without August, both Jenna and Maya were her only allies, and she always had to carefully tiptoe around that triangle because her mother was jealous of Elsie's relationship with Maya.

Elsie opted to think about it more instead of calling the police. She also wanted to wait before telling anyone else in the family. She first wanted to see if Nurse Neil could help her get some more information. He seemed genuinely interested in her father's case.

16

OCTOBER 6 - MORNING

Coincidentally, Charly and Jenna arrived at August's bedside at the same time. It was Neil's day off and a nurse named Lorrie was on duty. Lorrie had seen Jenna and her daughter Elsie before, but this was the first time she was present when Charly was visiting. The contrast between the wife and the ex-wife could not have been more striking.

Jenna wore a navy blue, man-tailored business suit. A light blue scarf at her collar was precisely knotted, but it only served to accentuate her paleness. Her short hair was too perfectly not gray and styled to show off small diamond stud earrings. Her manicured nails were unpainted. She was too thin, and she radiated grief.

Charly, the younger woman, had an explosion of red curls tied up on the top of her head that bounced or cascaded with her every movement. The rat tattoo above the top of her black leather camisole appeared to be adorned with glittery green eye shadow, matching the eyeshadow and the color of Charly's eyes, as well as her lacy leggings. Red nail polish, black combat boots and a white faux fur cropped jacket completed the outfit. The whole look was arresting, but it was the rat tattoo that Lorrie couldn't take her eyes off.

Lorrie had heard from Neil about the rat connections of August and his family, but this enchantingly whimsical character inked onto Charly's chest had suddenly turned her into a fan of these lowly creatures.

~ ~ ~ ~ ~

One of the most difficult aspects of the divorce for Jenna and August had been untangling the powers of attorney that they had entrusted each other with. Reluctantly, Jenna had turned power of attorney for herself over to Toby, only because she felt she had no other options, except for Elsie who would be the backup if something happened to Toby.

Jenna didn't know if August had turned his power of attorney over to Charly or Elsie, but neither of them had brought the issue up when August's doctor recommended placing a permanent feeding tube into his abdomen. The temporary feeding tube that went through his nose was too small for efficient feeding, and after so many days, it starts to irritate the nose, throat, esophagus and stomach.

Also, if August could start moving his extremities, he might try to pull the nasogastric tube out, which could be traumatic. Without any discussion, all of August's people appeared to approve of this measure for keeping him alive.

Lorrie was holding a tablet with the consent forms for the gastric tube surgery, but she didn't know which of the two women to hand it to. Jenna perceived the nurse's confusion and motioned for her to give the tablet to Charly who responded with a nod to Jenna. She quickly signed the forms, gave August a kiss on the forehead and left.

Jenna sat down at the head of the bed and told August about the feeding tube procedure. She told him that she knew that his brain was too good to not recover and that he needed his nutrition so he would have the strength to heal. She told him that he had to wake up so he could continue to see Elsie's amazing development.

Lorrie saw increased brain wave activity on August's monitor as his ex-wife offered him words of encouragement. It was the most activity she had seen since his hospitalization six days ago. She made a note in his chart while Jenna continued to sit in silence alongside of August and stroke his hand. Then she stopped stroking, and she felt August's fingers flex a little as she started to pull her hand away.

Jenna was startled at first. She looked at his face and thought she saw his eyelids flutter. She started stroking his hand again and again when she stopped, she felt him try to move his fingers. Then she repeated the sequence to show Lorrie what she had just observed, but this time August didn't respond.

Lorrie wondered if Jenna had just experienced an involuntary reflex. She desperately wanted to see this patient beat the odds, but she did not want to give the family false hope. She told Jenna that this could be a good sign, but she wouldn't postpone the placement of the feeding tube because of it.

~ ~ ~ ~ ~

Lorrie found herself perplexed by the dynamics of this family. The difference in how her patient's wife and ex-wife behaved during this morning's visit was remarkable. Lorrie was most curious about this ex-wife who visited so much more frequently and was so much more attentive than the current wife.

"Neil told me that you and your ex operate a neuroscience lab that's searching for cures for addiction. My father was an alcoholic, so it's a topic that resonates with me. May I ask how you and August came together to do this kind of work?"

The question whipped up Jenna's inner turmoil. Though she had done everything in her power to emotionally divorce herself from August, she was now feeling more emotionally connected to him than ever. She hoped he could hear her tell this empathetic nurse about their simple love story.

Jenna was an undergraduate student and August was a doctoral candidate when they met at a neuroscience conference. They were both brainiacs with similar goals and it took them less than an evening to fall in love. For a year and a half, they only saw each other every other weekend which created a great deal of passion in their relationship. In the early years of their marriage, August had been a doting husband and father through all of Jenna's difficult reproductive struggles. He was also the most dedicated scientist she had ever known.

Jenna told nurse Lorrie of August's mother's death from cocaine and his battles with juvenile addiction. She told her of August's stellar academic credentials and early research notoriety. She emphasized how fanatically committed he was to finding a cure for cocaine addiction.

Jenna described herself as the middle child of Jay Laudren a successful inventor, and Sara Goldstein, a nurse until she started prematurely showing signs of dementia. Sara's cognitive decline was what prompted Jay Laudren to set up a foundation to support brain research.

Jenna spoke of her older brother Everet who had their father's engineering brain but suffered from severe dyslexia. When he turned eighteen, he dropped out of school and joined the navy, hoping to acquire a trade. Once during a home visit, he told Jenna that he was working in a naval ship's metal shop where making hash pipes was his primary activity. Later that year, he died from a multi-drug overdose.

Jenna also had a younger sister Shelby who always struggled socially. Shelby seemed to have an affinity for people who could do her absolutely no good, but even then, her friendships quickly disintegrated. She went off to college to study mechanical engineering and the next thing her family heard was that she was living in some kind of religious commune to which she had given all of her possessions, including her new car.

Jay and Sara were both horrified and mystified. Neither they nor any of their three children had ever shown much interest in religion. The religious sect Shelby became involved with spread globally, but it ultimately gained fame for child abuse and violating labor laws in multiple states.

Jay and Sara gave an inordinate sum of money to an infamous cult rescuer who tracked Shelby down, kidnapped her, and supposedly deprogrammed her. She returned home and made a great show of recovery, and Jay bought her another car and paid tuition for her to go back to school. She went right back to her religious cult, and when her desperate parents again offered her an escape ramp, she refused to come home. Jay then made the decision to cut her out of the family trust forever.

So, by default, Jenna turned out to be the sole recipient of her father's wealth, though the trust was paying for care for both of Jenna's parents as well as for her father's sister who needed home health aides around the clock. Jenna's aunt was cognitively intact but she was trapped in a broken-down body, and she refused to move to an assisted living facility. A portion of the trust was also set aside to cover the costs of Elsie's disabilities.

But most of the trust's revenue was committed to funding research to help victims of brain dysfunction, and Jay had left it up to his scientist daughter Jenna to figure out how to spend the money. When Jenna fell in love with August, his research goals became the mission of her family foundation.

"How great that you use your wealth to help others. I appreciate you sharing that with me," Lorrie said as she started to disconnect August's monitor leads. She told Jenna that August was scheduled for a bath and change of linens.

Before she got up to go, Jenna caressed August's hand one more time, and again, she felt his fingers try to move. Her instincts told her that he was trying to communicate and that lightened the heaviness in her heart.

17

OCTOBER 6 - AFTERNOON

Jenna dropped Elsie off at the hospital before she drove herself to the surgical center for another imaging study. Although Jenna had been certain that her heart had exploded when her pain first started, her heart was quite healthy according to EKGs, stress tests, lab tests, multiple imaging studies, data collected from a halter monitor that Jenna had to wear for thirty days, and three consulted cardiologists.

A GI doctor with scopes had found a healthy gut at both ends. Ultrasound ruled out gallstones. Pulmonary function tests were fine. An orthopedist identified an old vertebral fracture that didn't explain belly pain, although a chiropractor had pushed on her back shortly before Jenna's pain suddenly started. Coincidental they presumed.

Jenna was now on her way for an abdominal CT scan. The pain just wouldn't quit, she was getting skinny, and one persistent doctor didn't want to miss something.

~ ~ ~ ~ ~

Elsie was hoping she'd have time alone with her father's devoted nurse Neil, and that Charly wouldn't show up at the same time. Then, she walked into her father's room and found Charly sitting at August's bedside. Charly gave her an unexpected smile.

"He might be waking up. The nurses are seeing more and more eye opening. They think he knows when his people are here."

Elsie responded with a deluge of tears. "Dad, I know you can hear me. Wake up, Dad! You can do this! I know you can. We love you, Dad, and you can come back to us. Please, wake up!"

Neil wondered if Elsie was shedding tears of sorrow or tears of joy. A difference in the chemistry of different kinds of tears was a subject of interest for this nurse who too frequently got to witness grief.

During the week that he had been taking care of August and interacting with his patient's relatives, Neil had felt inspired by the scientific missions of this family. The poor outcomes of some of his previous patients had resulted from cocaine overdoses. Even Neil's young teenaged daughter had been devastated by the loss of a friend to a drug overdose. Two thirteen-year-olds from her middle school had died from taking a drug that they'd purchased online. They thought they were buying oxycodone, but the pills were laced with lethal doses of fentanyl.

Neil was reliving his daughter's distress when Elsie's sniffles prompted August to open his eyes. For almost maybe twenty seconds, August appeared to be looking around. Neil, Elsie and Charly all held their breath until August's eyes closed again. Then, they all exhaled simultaneously.

"That's the most purposeful eye movement I've seen," Neil said. "It's a very good sign that he may be coming out of the coma. With comas, some victims wake-up suddenly, some wake-up gradually. Some wake up in stages, some only come partially back, and some come back and then relapse back into a coma. We really don't know how to predict who will recover, fully or partially. There's still so much we don't know about altered states of consciousness.

"I hope you can all keep coming to visit August as often as possible. In my experience with comatose patients, there is no more powerful drug than the support given by those who care."

"Except for maybe cocaine. Isn't cocaine the most powerful drug, August?" Charly said with a sneer while glaring at her husband.

"And by the way, Elsie, I called the college animal lab regarding your father's appointment to look at the OCT set-up there, and they told me there was no such appointment. I don't know what you think you heard, but no one at the college animal lab had made any appointments with August."

Elsie's neck muscles strained as she told Charly that she had been sitting next to her father in the car when a woman called to confirm his appointment. She had heard about the timing of it and that August was supposed to meet the person at the coffee bar in the lobby of the science building, where she would be able to provide him with a visitor's badge. She also gave him specific directions about where to park his car. It was a brief conversation.

"So, he even set you up as a witness," Charly fumed. "Of course he had an appointment, but it wasn't with the lab personnel that he supposedly went to see. The administrator at that lab said that she'd have known if any of the technicians were demonstrating any of their equipment, especially the OCT. She'd also have known if anyone had procured a security clearance to bring an outsider into the lab."

Elsie's face started to redden. She turned her microphone up to max and said, "Charly, listen to me! I think it was Dad who was set up. Someone did this to him. I asked that he be checked for evidence of a knockout drug, and the test just came back positive. I also asked Neil if he could find out more about the person who turned dad's belongings over to the triage nurse."

Charly's jaw dropped and she seemed stunned into silence. The widened eyes of both women turned to Neil.

"It just so happens that the triage nurse who admitted your father did the midnight shift last night and I was able to check in with her before her shift ended and mine began this morning. Her name is Marcy. I was told by another nurse that I know that Marcy has done E.R. triage for almost a decade and she's a topnotch judge of character as well as medical urgency.

"Marcy remembered the person who showed up at her triage station with August's belongings, maybe about an hour after he was dropped off by the ambulance. Marcy said she remembered this woman because she was pretty, petite and dressed like a professional, but she also appeared to be stoned. When she dropped August's stuff on the triage counter, she loudly announced that he had medical grade cocaine because he was a scientist. She also loudly announced where his car was parked, and then, she abruptly disappeared. Marcy also mentioned that this woman had a slight foreign accent, but not one of the more common ones she's used to hearing in these parts.

"I went to the security office and asked to see the tapes of the E.R. entrance around that time period. I froze a few frames that show someone that could maybe fit Marcy's description of the woman who brought in August's belongings, but only the back of that person. On her next shift, Marcy said she'd check out those images to see if she can identify the person she remembers. I told her how important August's research is.

"In turn, Marcy told me she appreciates what August does. She revealed that she has one son who's a physician, and another son who's a homeless drug addict. She doesn't even know if he's dead or alive since he recently stopped calling to beg for money. Marcy was very sympathetic to my concern about August. I also want to know if he's a victim."

Charly looked like she'd been punched in the gut. She blinked a lot and shook her head, but initially she said nothing. Then, she looked at Neil and then at Elsie with daggers in her eyes, and finally said, "and you knew this when?"

Neil responded. "Just today when the test results came back. Elsie's the one who asked for the tests to be done, thankfully. The E.R. doctor was totally preoccupied with getting August into neurosurgery for a brain bleed, and the results of the urine test showing cocaine and a benzo didn't come back until after August was in surgery.

"Seeing a positive benzo result on the routine drug screen that's done in the E.R. for unconscious persons, wouldn't have gotten the doctors' attention. Cocaine addicts commonly use benzos to calm the anxiety caused by their cravings. Addicts get terribly anxious when they can't maintain their supply and then they wind up addicted to Xanax or Valium or some other benzo. When August showed up with a brain bleed and a stoned-out escort, the doctors didn't have reason to suspect a drug like Rohypnol.

"If August had been knocked out with Rohypnol, it would have been easy for someone to blow a boatload of cocaine up his nose. And by the way, he doesn't show any of the nasal damage we see in chronic cocaine abuse."

Elsie came close to August's ear. "Dad, I know you can hear us. Now we know, someone did this to you. You have to wake up. You have to tell us what happened."

Then Jenna walked into the room. Elsie swung around and said, "he's waking up, Mom. And we just learned that Dad had a knockout drug in his system in addition to the cocaine, so he may be a victim here. He didn't do this to himself. He has to wake up and tell us."

Jenna just gaped at Elsie, put her hand over her mouth and shook her head, while Charly glared in her direction.

Just then, August opened his eyes.

18

October 7 - Morning

Toby planned to stop in to say goodbye to his father after dropping Brigham off at the airport, but Brigham wanted to see the lab one more time before returning to school. Toby suspected it was really Charly that his friend wanted to see, but so did he. He hated her for that, for having a fishhook so deep into his heart. He also hated himself for not being able to pull the damned hook out.

His mother had persuaded him to stay home one more day and he had become concerned about her. Her CT scan showed that the main artery to her digestive organs, the celiac artery, could be compromised. Now, she needed an arteriogram to further pin down this rare diagnosis.

No wonder it had become painful for her to eat. Her stomach and all of her digestive organs were being deprived of their blood supply whenever she ingested food. In ten weeks, she'd lost sixteen pounds. No wonder she couldn't figure out what it was that hurt. It was most everything in her torso.

Toby was worried. If he lost his mother, he would have to take over the trust. It was a bitter pill that he would also be responsible for maintaining the lab. Initially he figured that if his mother didn't survive; he could hire his father to run the lab. Oops! His father was in no condition to run anything.

Elsie could do it, but she'd need someone like Charly to do the technical part. Elsie's vision was too limited to do any of that. Of course, he could hire Charly, but then he might have to watch her seduce the next researcher that they hired. The thought of being Charly's boss brought Toby just a fleeting moment of pleasure before reality rifled through his fantasies. Even if Charly was his employee, she would still be there to tantalize and torment him. He was no match for her manipulative ways. He had to let her go.

Toby also didn't feel ready to take over the trust. It was a responsibility he didn't know if he could handle, and he wished he had never agreed to do it. He had other plans for his life. His mother simply had to get past her illness. He couldn't back out now when she was having all of these traumas. He couldn't live with himself if he did. Besides, he needed the financial support in order to finish school. He had to give his mother more support.

~ ~ ~ ~ ~

Toby's thoughts turned back to giving Brigham the insider tour. He was relieved to find Charly wasn't there. He took Brigham to see Celia Fromme's depression lab instead.

"How do you know if a rat is depressed?" Brigham asked.

Toby explained. "They behave the same way that depressed humans do. They become less active, they lose weight, they sleep more, and they have trouble learning new things. The FSL (Flinter's Sensitive Line) rats that Celia uses have been bred specifically because their depressed behaviors are exaggerated and therefore easier to observe, and also because these behaviors improve with certain antidepressant drugs."

"So, is the whole breed of these rats depressed?"

"Actually, one of the things they do to see which ones are really depressed is what's called the swim test. Rats are excellent swimmers and climbers, and they are also masters at getting out of tight spots. However, if put in a water tank with no possible route of escape, they eventually stop trying to get out and they go into a floatation survival mode, barely moving.

"The rats that give up swimming and climbing the fastest are considered to be the most depressed, though personally, I think those rats might just be the smartest. These human assumptions are one of the things that I don't like about animal research."

"Can you induce depression in a rat?"

"Absolutely. Just isolate it. Rats are extremely social and if isolated, they die of loneliness, even if all of their other needs are met.

"Celia is now using transcranial magnetic stimulation (TMS) to treat depressed rats, and that modality is already being used in humans. Picking the right brain regions, the right electrical input, and the right patients for it is a current research challenge. Its role in the treatment of addiction also needs further investigation and my father has been considering that for his next project."

As they headed from Celia's unit to Elsie's breeder lab, Brigham was starting to grasp how versed in this science Toby was. He asked Toby why his father had been studying the relationship between hormones and addiction.

"It's super complex. It's based on the fact that when cocaine-exposed mother rats have a choice between taking care of their newborns or hanging out in the cocaine room, they initially choose to take care of the babies. Once their little rats start acting like adolescents, some of the rat moms go back to the cocaine room.

"Maternal behavior is driven by an array of hormones that are activated during pregnancy and birth. After birth, the distinct smell of newborn babies also activates hormones and feel-good brain chemicals like dopamine, which drive parental attachment. It's the chemistry of love. It may be this chemistry that fails to happen in women who suffer from post-partum depression. It can also be the chemistry that's missing when premature infants like my sister and the rest of our family didn't get to spend Elsie's newborn life together.

"So, the question becomes, what combination of hormones can reduce the cravings for cocaine, as it does for the addicted mothers of newborn rats? My father is, was, very close to that answer.

"Our lab has also been carefully monitoring the rats whose addiction has been successfully treated with hormonal formulas, because rats are especially prone to mammary tumors. No one wants to develop a treatment that causes cancer later in life, so his study spans the lifetimes of the rats."

~ ~ ~ ~ ~

Toby and Brigham found Elsie in the breeder unit playing an electric xylophone. Her rat pup was in the lever/reward box.

"Hey you guys! Watch this! Freyja can remember a twelve note sequence no matter how many variations I try to confuse her with. When I first play it for her and give her a reward, she tilts her little head from side to side and wiggles her ears as though she's maybe singing it to herself. Once she's heard the sequence twice, she won't push the bar for any other notes I play. She doesn't get a reward if she pushes the lever for any other sequence. She's so far retained the sequence for two days and I can't wait to see how long she holds onto this. Rats have superior memories for the routes they travel. Maybe they can also learn songs."

Once again, Elsie's enthusiasm for this baby rat's intellect had left Toby and Brigham awestruck. As her brother stood there just staring at her, Elsie said, "you need to go see Dad, Toby. He might be waking up. And before you go back to school, we need to have a family meeting about some new lab test results. You should meet with Mom and me at home, after you go see Dad."

~ ~ ~ ~ ~

As they left the Laudren NeuroScience Laboratory, Brigham thanked Toby for what he considered a great experience. He also told his friend that he couldn't understand why he wouldn't want to embrace a golden opportunity and carry on his family legacy, especially since it seemed he was already immersed in the science of it. He could contribute so much more than just being another clinician.

Meeting Elsie had been a life-changing experience for Brigham. His academic curiosity had become supercharged. Finding preventions and cures for devastating illnesses now seemed like a more important way to apply science than did just taking care of the afflicted.

Maybe Brigham could even find a cure for a dreadful prion infection like mad cow disease, if he could ultimately develop more of a relationship with Toby's philanthropic mother Jenna.

19

OCTOBER 7 - AFTERNOON

A big bang came at the end of Neil's shift. He was signing care of August over to the evening shift nurse Marshall, when Charly Rincade made a surprise appearance. She had never previously visited in the late afternoon. Neil introduced her to Marshall. She nodded dismissively as she went to August's bedside, gave him a kiss on his cheek, grabbed his limp hand, and told him she was going to find the bastard who did this to him.

"August, you have to wake up and tell me what happened. I'm so sorry I blamed you. But I'm going to get whoever did this to you, to us, so help me." She abruptly turned in the direction of the two nurses.

"I just dropped my power of attorney documents off in the hospital lawyer's office. From now on, you will only discuss August's medical status with me, not his kids, ex-wife, friends, associates, employees, admirers, outside consultants, or anyone else I haven't authorized. Is that clear?"

Marshall was astonished. Even beyond what Neil had described, August's wife Charly was an absolute spectacle. In thigh high red suede boots, a cherry red halter top, ultrashort, ripped denim shorts, and a yellow fishnet cardigan down to her knees, she made you look. But once you noticed the tattooed rat with a gold crescent necklace adorning its chest, as well as Charly's ample chest, you were compelled to stare.

"But of course, Mrs. Rincade," Marshall said, trying not to look like he had been thrown off his horse. Then he opened his mouth as if to say something else, but nothing came out.

Neil stepped in. "Are the others still allowed to visit? I think it's critical to August's recovery. He certainly responds to his kids. His daughter comes two to three times a day."

"With her mother, Jenna?"

"Sometimes with her mother and sometimes with a lady named Maya and sometimes with a lady named Renée, who I understand works in the lab. Maya and Renée just say hello to August and then they leave Elsie here for a while. I feel very strongly that August knows when his kids visit. His brain responds even though the rest of him can't."

Charly hesitated. She looked back and forth at August and Neil a few times. Finally, she said, "you're a good nurse, aren't you, Neil? Okay, I'll let them visit for now, but August's medical status and test results are to remain strictly confidential. For all I know, it could be one of his family members that did this to my husband. They all hate him because he married me.

"Also, I want the incriminating labs repeated. I'm going to calculate the dose he was given by the decrease in the metabolites in his urine between the first and second tests. Pharmacologic kinetics should give us confirmation."

Marshall suddenly had an eerie new sense of who he was dealing with. "As you wish, Mrs. Rincade. I'll ask the attending physician to order that test as soon as they come by on rounds."

"You will *tell* the attending physician to order that test, and the sooner the better. And make sure the times as to when the specimens were collected are clearly and accurately documented."

Charly turned back to an unresponsive August. "I'll get whoever did this, August. I swear I will. You have got to wake up. You have to help me find out who did this to you."

Neil watched his patient's brain wave monitor as Charly continued to rant. His brain was showing increased activity, but August wasn't physically responding as he had with some other family interactions. His eyes remained closed.

Neil mouthed "good luck" to Marshall as he signed out of the computer and left. As he was walking down the hall, he could feel the anger in Charly's boot steps as she left August's room behind him. He detoured to a men's room rather than have to share an elevator ride with this woman. It was always difficult to not gawk at her and her new vibe had left him puzzled and annoyed.

However, Neil had to really ponder her accusation that there was so much rage in this family that one of his relatives had caused August to suffer this catastrophic brain hemorrhage. He especially wondered about August's son Toby.

~ ~ ~ ~ ~

After dropping Brigham off at the airport, Toby drove to the hospital. He drove around the visitor parking lot twice to be sure he didn't see Charly's car. Then he drove around it again to make sure his father's car wasn't there. Charly could be using his father's car just to keep it running, though she didn't like his car because he occasionally transported rats in it. She also didn't like having rats in her car. Although Charly worked with rats all the time, she wasn't the one who cleaned up after them.

The Laudren lab employed other people to maintain the rats' housing. One of those people, Pearson, a wiry little man with limited abilities had lived in a tiny apartment in the facility since it was built. He was so devoted to taking care of his "ratties," that he wouldn't take a day off or even take a paid vacation. Jenna arranged to have prepared food delivered to him, and she made sure he got medical and dental care.

Toby wondered how they'd ever find as dedicated a worker as Pearson if they lost this man. His mother was smart to make sure the guy stayed healthy and well-nourished. Toby also appreciated Pearson because, unlike most men, he was totally impervious to Charly's charms. He'd just say, "Good morning, Mizz Ratty Lady," when she'd first arrive in the morning, and then he'd ignore her for the rest of the day.

Toby procrastinated some more in the hospital cafeteria. Vegan choices were sorely lacking from the menu. He did buy a cup of coffee because it smelled really good, and his father was a coffee fiend. August drank coffee all day long. It was the stimulant that took the edge off of cocaine cravings. Toby wondered if the smell of coffee could be a wakeup signal to his brain. When he finally got to his father's room, he introduced himself to Marshall and asked how August was doing.

Marshall swallowed hard and rubbed his chin. "As you can see is all I can say."

"Umm…my sister Elsie said there's been a new development with his labs, something important."

Marshall bit his lip. Then he said, "I'm sorry, Toby. A little while ago, Mrs. Rincade revoked our permission to share information about your father's medical status without her authorization."

Toby looked shocked. "And that includes his children?"

"I'm afraid so. But she hasn't limited your visiting privileges, so please, spend some time with your father and talk to him. We believe visits from family are helping."

Toby shook his head in disbelief and cursed Charly under his breath. "Did you hear that, Dad? Charly doesn't want us to know how you're doing. But I know you're waking up. You have to come back for Elsie's sake. You have to, Dad. Please, come back to us." Then he waved the cup of still steaming coffee under his father's nose.

~ ~ ~ ~ ~

Nurse Marshall Humphreys documented that at 5:35 pm, August Rincade wriggled his nose to the smell of coffee, opened his eyes, looked around the room, and tried to move his mouth. He also tried to make a sound. It was more of a deep rattle in his chest than a spoken word. Then, August made a sound that vaguely resembled a scream.

"You're okay, Man. You're safe." Marshall told August. "You've been in a coma, and you just woke up. You're in a hospital intensive care unit. I'm your nurse. I'm Marshall. I'm here to help you, August. You're going to be okay. You've had a hell of a week but you're going to be okay. Welcome back, Man. You're going to make it."

"If you can understand what I'm saying, blink your eyes once."

Toby watched in awe as August deliberately blinked his eyes. Still, he looked disoriented and frightened. His eyes were darting around, and half of his lower lip quivered.

Marshall turned to Toby. "Fear and agitation are not uncommon when someone awakens from a coma. As you can see is all I'm allowed to say."

20

October 7 - Evening

"He's awake," Toby shouted as he came into the kitchen where Maya and Elsie were eating. "He woke up while I was there, just a little while ago"

"Thank God," Elsie said. "I knew he'd come back. Did he know you were there? Can he talk?"

"I can't really say. He became very agitated, and the nurse had to give him a quick-acting sedative. The nurse said some coma victims become seriously terrified when they wake up. They have no idea where they are or how they got there or why none of their body parts work. It can take hours to days before they grasp their situation.

"The nurse was concerned that August was so disoriented that he might have dislodged his monitors or pulled his feeding tube out, so he had to physically and chemically restrain him. Dad was actually trying to move his left hand or maybe his fingers.

"I was relieved that this nurse knew how to handle the situation. It was scary for a few minutes. Whether Dad recognized me, I have no idea. I just let Nurse Marshall take over. He thought Dad might be much more amenable to interacting after he starts to show some semblance of a sleep-wake schedule. Sometimes, that takes a few days. Then he might be more coherent.

"Where's Mom?"

Maya explained that Jenna was on the phone trying to get an opinion from a doctor friend of hers. She offered Toby some pasta salad and he ate hungrily while Elsie explained what was going on with their mother.

"They think she might have something called MALS, short for Median Arcuate Ligament Syndrome. The MAL is a big ligament that wraps around the aorta and anchors the diaphragm to the spine. This ligament is actually part of the diaphragm, so it goes up and down when we breathe.

"Sometimes, this ligament falls into a position where it pinches the celiac artery and the celiac plexus, the big nerve bundle that sits on top of that big artery that supplies blood to all of our digestive organs. So, every time a person with MALS takes a breath, the artery and the nerves get pinched.

"The doctor Mom consulted today said he thinks the chiropractic adjustment repositioned the vertebrae that this ligament is attached to, and now it's crimping her artery and nerves which upsets the whole nervous system. Maybe that's why she seems so anxious and can't sleep. She didn't used to be like that."

"This sounds horrible. So, what's the solution?"

"If they can confirm the diagnosis, then it requires a major surgery to cut that ligament. It's like carpal tunnel surgery when they cut the wrist ligament to free up a compressed nerve to the hand. The MAL is a much bigger ligament and it's much harder to get to, so recovery could take months. However, finding a doctor who knows how to do this surgery is proving difficult.

"MALS is just a suspicion right now, so they'll do an arteriogram to confirm it. Nobody wants to perform a big bad surgery if it's not going to help. But I do think this diagnosis perfectly explains Mom's symptoms, while apparently, not a lot of doctors have ever even heard of MALS. Most of the patients whose online stories I read were considered cuckoo before their MALS was finally recognized and successfully treated.

"And to be honest, I was starting to wonder if Mom's pain wasn't just the emergence of repressed rage. She's furious that Dad left our family and abandoned me. Then she went ballistic for those initial days that she thought he was stealing the lab's cocaine. Now she's angry that someone has tried to maim or kill her lead researcher."

Just then, Jenna came into the kitchen and sat down where Maya had fixed her a dinner plate. She scrunched up her face and pushed the food away. Her failed attempt to smile at her kids indicated the pain was intense at the moment. Though she always tried hard to be stoic, sometimes, she couldn't hide how awful she felt.

"Dad woke up, Mom. Tell her, Toby."

Toby recounted his experience at August's bedside and managed to bring a smile to his mother's distressed face. Then he told Jenna and Elsie about Charly cutting them out of the information loop, provoking their mutual outrage.

"How can she even have the right to do that? He's our father. And what did that new lab test show, Elsie? You didn't tell me, and the nurses wouldn't tell me because of Charly's gag order."

"It showed traces of flunitrazepam, otherwise known as Rohypnol, the infamous, illegal date rape drug. I asked Dad's team to order that lab test and check him for knockout drugs because I just couldn't believe that he would have voluntarily overdosed on a drug he's spent his whole life trying to conquer.

"Even though most of the flunitrazepam was probably out of his system by the time they sent off a specimen, the test still came back positive. They must have given him a big dose."

"Who's they?" Toby asked.

"That's what we have to find out. But how can we do that if we don't call the police?" Elsie responded.

"Well, we have to call the police before Charly does," Jenna said.

"Maybe she already has," said Toby. "The fact that she doesn't want any of us to even know what's going on with Dad makes me think that she thinks that it's one of us is who poisoned him."

"Uh oh!" Elsie said. "I suspect that she who calls the police first, gets to accuse the people who didn't, and I knew about this since early today when Neil sent me a text. So, aren't the police going to wonder why we didn't call right away when we figured out that we knew that Dad was poisoned?"

"I'm calling them right now," Jenna said.

"I'm going to my apartment," Maya said. "You guys better have your stories straight."

21

OCTOBER 7 - EVENING

The police person who took Jenna's call had told her that an Officer C.C. McAllister would call them back within the hour.

"So why did you go to a chiropractor?" Toby asked his mother while they waited. "I thought you didn't believe in chiropractic?"

"Well, I didn't, and I sure don't now. It was a monstrous mistake that I regret every day. I was desperate to get rid of some nagging back-pain, right between my shoulder blades. Everything else I've tried over the years hasn't helped. Anti-inflammatories give me gastritis, and the firmer mattress makes me feel stiff. Physical therapy made zero difference, and the pain just gets more nagging.

"The whole spinal manipulation approach seems to be gaining traction as people become increasingly disenchanted with pharmaceuticals. I sometimes wonder if the drugs cause as many problems as they solve. Renée at the lab is being treated with a blood pressure drug that's caused her to develop diabetes. Gary, the guy who edits the rat videos, has neuropathy in his feet because of an antibiotic. My attorney Stan now has kidney failure, likely caused by being on a heartburn drug for more than a decade.

"Recently, I read the story of a woman who took a prescription for osteoporosis and wound up with so much bone pain and fractures that now, she can't even walk. Becoming chronically sick or disabled because of a drug reaction is a very frightening risk. So, I thought maybe I should at least try spinal manipulation.

"The guy who manages the gym at the Laudren Retail Plaza raved about this chiropractor, a young woman who took over some old guy's practice in the strip mall by the highway. The new chiro was described as high tech but holistic. A lot of the gym rats thought she was terrific.

"It turned out that this woman was an exhibitionist hottie like you know who, so no wonder the men liked her; though I'll admit she was also warm and personable. She paid a lot of attention to my history. She did a bang-up job of putting me at ease, until she actually did a bang-up job of cracking my back. I still can't believe I submitted to what she did.

"I think something happened when she pushed on the middle of my back from the top, while dropping the table under me at the same time. It was shortly after that when I started to feel this burning sensation in the middle of my torso. And for the last three months, it's just continued to burn, sometimes much worse than others. I'm sorry, Toby. It's getting really hard to take."

"Geez, I'm so sorry, Mom. Is there anything I can do to help?"

"Toby, there is definitely something you could do that would give me great peace of mind. I may be headed for a risky surgery. If they do these other tests and confirm that I actually do have MALS, my only potential pain relief lies in submitting to that surgery. All of the organs of my abdomen will be retracted out of the way for the surgeon to get to the celiac artery. Assuming the surgery is successful, it can take many months to recuperate. There's also the risk that I may not survive.

"Even if your father wakes up and by some miracle, returns to his old self, and by some impossibility, even returns to our family, I could never again trust him with the lab or the foundation or anything else. But, Toby, I trust you. You have the smarts. You are driven by a sense of justice that I see maturing as your education advances.

"I want you to get your veterinary degree and the career that you want, but at the same time, our foundation is going to give some young scientist the opportunity of a lifetime to make a difference in people's lives, or maybe even in the lives of animals. Isn't that just a little bit tempting?

"It would be so helpful to me if I knew what you'd do if I turn the trust over to you, maybe even temporarily if I have to travel to some medical mecca to find a surgeon with MALS experience. There's only a few in the country."

"Mom, why not just turn the trust over to Elsie? She's more than capable. Certainly, she could manage it all for a few months if you're out due to surgery."

"Toby, I wish that Elsie was my best option. I think Elsie's potential is just starting to really bloom, and I can't wait to see where she's going to go, but here's the thing, Toby. For nineteen years I've been living with this bitter pill. Your father and I talked to maybe a dozen leading genetic experts when it became evident that Elsie could survive, and I'm terribly afraid that Elsie might have a limited lifespan.

"As you know, she has three minor defects in her chromosomes. Even though no one in the world seems to know what her genetic profile means, we have known since her infancy that one of those defects is associated with premature aging. My mother and I also have that same genetic error and we're wondering if that's what caused Grandma Sara's early dementia, which I hope won't also be my fate.

"Elsie's other genetic defect, a deletion, has been associated with the development of CLL, chronic leukocytic leukemia. The effect of her third chromosomal abnormality and the combination of these defects remain unknown. Also, it seems probable that Elsie will not pass her genes onto another generation, and I fear that Elsie may not live long enough to carry the trust to fulfill its mission. Even if Elsie were to find a partner, I doubt she'd take the risk of passing her chromosome anomalies to another generation, assuming that she even could.

"Toby, I'm optimistic that you will pass your father's and my genes on. You're a healthy person with healthy genes. You can have financial security for the rest of your life, but do you really know what it is you want to do with your life? And could you take over the trust if I need you to?"

Toby's posture slumped. "Does Elsie know that her lifespan may be limited?"

"What do you think, Toby? I've never told her, and I doubt her father ever has, but don't you think she's researched every detail of her chromosome profile? Nothing escapes your sister's curiosity, but she never has brought it up with me, so I've remained silent. If she knows, she lives with it gracefully as she does with her disabilities. I wish I could make her the primary trustee, but I fear the trust and the foundation cannot be sustained that way."

Just then, Elsie came into the room. Freyja was sitting on her shoulder.

"Watch this, Mom, Toby! Freyja, head!" Elsie pointed to the top of her head and the little rat climbed up Elsies cap and sat on top of her head.

"Freyja, left shoulder," Elsie pointed, and the rat obeyed.

"Freyja, right hand." Elsie didn't point but the rat ran across her back to her right shoulder and then down her right arm to her hand. Then without a gesture, it obeyed her verbal command to go to her left shoulder. She gave it a treat, and it gave her a little bow. Then it cleaned its face and ears and turned to study Toby and Jenna. It's nose and whiskers wiggled wildly as it surveyed the humans who were watching it.

"I know all about my genetic risk for an early demise, Mom. But it's okay, I don't live for the future. I live for today, like Freyja here. I've already outlived this little critter more than twenty times. Only right now, I'm living for tomorrow morning so I can go see Dad. Can you imagine if he really came back to us?"

Before Jenna could answer, her phone rang.

Officer C.C. McAllister from the county police department wanted to interview her on a Zoom computer interface.

22

October 7 - Evening

"I understand you believe your ex-husband was poisoned," a raspy voice said, as the pasty, jowly face of an older woman filled the screen on Jenna's desktop. Jenna shook her head yes as her eyes jumped around, looking for some verification that she really was talking to a police officer.

C.C. McAllister picked up on Jenna's skepticism and backed away from the camera. She tilted her computer and panned it around so that Jenna could see a cubicle within a sea of cubicles. Multiple voices droned in the background and grew softer as C.C. adjusted the volume.

"Our station starts to get very busy in the evening, so just try to ignore the background noise. Please give me the particulars about who your ex is, and who you are."

"My ex is August Rincade. He's a fifty-one-year-old research scientist who's in the Fifth Hill hospital in a coma right now, or maybe he's starting to come out of a coma. He's also my business partner. We share ownership of a research laboratory.

"I am Jenna Laudren, owner and principal of the Laudren NeuroScience Foundation and Laboratory, and the Laudren Retail Plaza. I was married to August Rincade for twenty-eight years until last year. He left our family to marry his research assistant.

"About a week ago, August was supposedly going to see a technician in a laboratory at the college who was going to demonstrate a costly device for examining the inner ear. A few hours after he left for that appointment, I received a call from August's current wife Charly. She said that August was in the hospital for a cocaine-induced hemorrhagic stroke and he was undergoing emergency brain surgery. They didn't know if he was going to make it."

"So how come the wife called the ex-wife?" C.C. McAllister asked.

"I employ both August and Charly, and I would have continued to do so until they could bring an important project to its conclusion. They are my lead researchers. However, if August dies, Charly is not only out a husband, but she'll also be out of a job, a very good job I might add. She has ample reason to stay in touch with me."

C.C. scratched her short gray hair. "So, what do you do in this laboratory? Did you say you own it?"

"My ex-husband and I have co-ownership of the lab, though it's funded by my family's philanthropy trust of which I'm the principal and administrator. Our foundation's research seeks to cure cocaine addiction. We're also exploring the possibility of conducting deafness research. We recently had some success using a gene transfer technique to maybe have cured deafness in a young rat."

"So why do you think your business partner was poisoned?"

"When my daughter and I got to the hospital after Charly notified us, we were directed to the family waiting area for surgery patients. Charly was in a state of rage. She said that the nurse who admitted August to the E.R. had been told by the young woman who delivered his wallet and car keys, that August was supplying her with medical grade cocaine when he passed out and she called for an ambulance. She also said that August's car was parked at a hotel and then, she quickly disappeared.

"Finally, after waiting more than two hours, the neurosurgeon came and told us that surgery was successful. He had been able to clip a bleeding artery. He explained that sometimes, a big dose of cocaine causes such severe spasm of arteries, that a weak spot in an artery wall can rupture due to back pressure. If August's vital signs stayed stable overnight, he had a chance of surviving, and we might be able to see him the next day.

"Then, a nurse asked us to provide some medical history. Did he have any drug allergies? Was he taking any prescriptions? Stuff like that. She told us that August's drug screen was positive for cocaine and benzos. We, no I, was surprised. August tried to avoid any drug besides caffeine. He is a caffeine fiend.

"But then, Charly told this nurse that August was occasionally using a benzo to sleep. That was news to me. In the thirty some years I slept with the man, he hardly ever had insomnia. He could read himself to sleep in less than ten minutes on the rare occasion that he couldn't just fall asleep. So, I wasn't suspicious of the benzo in his system then, but I was mortified if he was pilfering cocaine from the lab supply. That would be catastrophic for our licensing.

"However, my daughter Elsie refused to believe that her father was abusing cocaine, and she asked August's doctors to check him for a knockout drug and that test came back positive for the date rate drug, Rohypnol, which is also a benzo.

"Now, we believe that someone knocked August out with Rohypnol and then contaminated his system with cocaine, maybe to kill him, maybe to embarrass our lab or disable our research. I think my daughter is right. I don't believe that August would have done this to himself."

"Was your husband having any kind of disputes or conflicts with anyone?"

Jenna's eyes shot from the screen to Toby who was sitting on a couch behind the computer. "You mean my business partner. August is my ex-husband. But I have to say, August is a congenial guy; he gets along with people really well."

"What about family, his siblings, his kids?"

Again, Jenna hesitated before telling the detective that August was orphaned at a young age by a single mother and raised by his grandparents. Most of his people were either elderly or gone. "He has no siblings, just some cousins, a few years older. There's no one I can think of that he's been in touch with except his great aunt who he calls a few times a year, like on Mother's Day and her birthday.

"August is absolutely devoted to our daughter Elsie who also works in our lab, so they see each other almost daily. Of course, I haven't been living with August for the past year, so I no longer actually know who he's in touch with.

"However, I have to tell you that as a research scientist, August's funding is enviable. With many researchers currently losing funding for their life's work, a competitor could be desperate enough to have sought to knock a well-endowed researcher out of the competition."

"So how many competitors might your ex have?"

Jenna's shoulders heaved as she sighed. "I placed an ad calling for research proposals in a widely read journal about addiction some eight months ago. Hundreds, maybe thousands of scientists could have seen that ad. It was big and eye-catching, and the journal has international circulation. Research proposals started coming in immediately and they are still coming into an online account I established for recruitment purpose."

"Hundreds, maybe thousands?" C.C.'s skimpy eyebrows went up and down as she echoed those numbers. Then she became wordless while Jenna chewed on her lower lip.

"Okay Ms. Laudren. I'm going to take a look at your husband's research and learn how cocaine is supplied for research, and what grade of cocaine we're currently seeing in police labs, and I'm going to get back to you before I can even start to figure out how to pursue such a potential crime."

As Jenna clicked off her Zoom connection, Toby audibly exhaled. Jenna guessed they were both going to have difficulty sleeping.

<h1 style="text-align:center">23</h1>

<h2 style="text-align:center">October 8 - Morning</h2>

Neil and Marcy, the E.R. triage nurse, went back and forth through the security tapes of the entrance corridor several times, but the only image Marcy thought might match her memory, showed the back of a small person with long dark hair wearing dark clothes. She carried a shoulder bag that looked like a briefcase.

She only appeared in a few frames and even with enlargement, there was nothing very identifiable about this person. Maybe they were just assuming she was female because of the small size. Focused on faces, the camera didn't capture feet, sometimes more useful for assessing gender than hair.

When Neil got to August's room to begin his shift, he was greeted by both Nurse Lorrie and Elsie. Jenna had dropped Elsie off early on her way to get her arteriogram. Elsie had been excited to see her father awake, but he was sleeping peacefully when she arrived. She put the cup of coffee close to the head of the bed.

Lorrie informed Elsie that her father had to be sedated a second time since his awakening. At about four in the morning, he awoke again and became very agitated.

"It's just a short-acting drug. The last thing we want to do is keep him sedated, but with the brain monitor still in his skull, we can't let him get rambunctious. We're hoping to get that bolt out of his head as soon as he shows some appropriate sleep-wake cycling or wakes up more coherently."

Lorrie put her hand over her mouth. "Oops, I wasn't supposed to tell you any of that."

"Thank you, but I didn't hear you say anything other than good morning and good morning to you too. Thank you for taking care of my father."

Lorrie signed out and Elsie turned to Neil who was signing into the computer. "I won't hear anything you tell me about my dad either, but I'm delighted to tell you he woke up yesterday when my brother was here, and a nurse named Marshall was on duty. Apparently, he woke up to the smell of coffee. My father is an absolute coffee addict. Should I stick this coffee under his nose now?"

"So I've heard. Marshall called to tell me last evening. We're all very amazed. Based on his brain imaging, none of your father's care providers would have predicted that he would come this far this fast. Yes, give him some whiffs of the coffee. How we under appreciate the sense of smell. But here in a man who can't see or touch, the nose may be working."

August's nostrils twitched and after a few seconds, he opened his eyes. It appeared that he was trying to move his mouth.

"I'm here, Dad," Elsie said as she reached for her father's hand. "I knew you'd come back to us."

Neil heard a deep sound coming from August, apparently too deep for Elsie to hear, but she sensed him trying to move his fingers as she held his hand. She brought the coffee to his nose again and Neil said, "yeah! That's it, August. Smell that coffee and try to swallow and you won't need that tube in your belly. You can do it, August. Try to swallow!"

With a syringe, Neil put a few drops of sugar water on the tip of August's tongue. "Now please don't gag, cough or choke on me, August. Let me see you try to swallow." He put another two drops on August's tongue and August moved his tongue but didn't manage to swallow. Neil turned to Elsie.

"If he wakes up a little more, I'll check his gag reflex. We can't let him try to drink or eat until we know his gag is working. Aspiration of anything into the lungs leads to pneumonia, so we have to be diligent in protecting his airway.

"And of course, I didn't tell you anything about your father that you didn't see for yourself. What I did tell you was just some information about the early stages of recovery from unconsciousness, which may or may not apply in your father's case.

"Elsie, do you know why Charly has placed a gag order on our communications with you? It's inappropriate. If it wasn't for you, we may never have realized what actually happened to your father. Do any of you have any ideas about who might have victimized him, other than all of those competing researchers you told me about the other day?"

"My family hasn't even had time to look at the proposals from scientists who have shown interest in accessing our lab. My mother shares my concerns about professional jealousy though, and also thinks it could be someone from the research community. Investigating science researchers could be a challenging job for a police profiler. My mom says scientists think differently than most people.

"I can't speak for why Charly would have done that. Maybe she knows something the rest of us don't. Maybe she just wants to cut the rest of us out of his life, even though my mother is the one who's providing his care.

"You should know Neil, my mother called the police last night. Like me, she doesn't believe that my father did this to himself. I think we were misled by what Charly initially told us about August's hospitalization.

"You may hear from the police. A Detective C.C. McAllister is handling the case. She's an older woman and she seemed to have a lot of medical questions that my family isn't going to be able to answer, now that we've been cut out of the information loop. I think we'll have to refer her to you.

"We only saw this police person on a Zoom platform. She asked something that implied that the chemical signature of the type of cocaine that was in my father's system could tell us something about the source, but wouldn't it be too late to get that information?"

"As far as I know," Neil said, "It's probably not still in the blood or urine, but maybe it's in hair follicles. I don't know how sophisticated the police lab is, but cocaine metabolites can hang around in hair follicles for about three months."

Elsie and Neil were suddenly interrupted by a noise coming out of August. He appeared to be staring at them. Elsie waved the coffee cup in front of his nose again. It had grown cold, but there was still a coffee smell. August appeared to try to inhale, and his nostrils twitched. Again, an indecipherable sound rattled inside him. He shook his head just a tiny bit, closed his eyes and appeared to go back to sleep.

Then, Jenna came into the room with a steaming hot cup of coffee. She waved it under August's nose and once more, he opened his eyes. His mouth muscles quivered. He lifted his left index finger ever so slightly, but Neil caught the motion. "Your people are here, August. Lift that finger again to say hello to Jenna and Elsie." It looked like August was trying to lift his fingers.

24

OCTOBER 8 - MORNING

When C.C. McAllister showed up in August Rincade's hospital room, Neil hoped he was prepared. The policewoman arrived with a subpoena for the medical records, just after Elsie and Jenna left. She was accompanied by a young man identified as Detective Garrett Towser.

The pair went directly to Neil's computer and asked him to enter his password. Detective McAllister seemed to know the system and she quickly scanned August's chart. She identified particular screens and used a pointer to highlight things while Officer Towser snapped pictures. When they were done with the computer, C.C. McAllister briefly looked at the sleeping patient. Then she took a chair next to Neil while her sidekick sat at the foot of the bed.

"I was once a nurse," she told Neil. "But I never took care of the living dead. I switched from nursing to police work after six years of night shifts in a big city E.R. where we regularly took care of gunshot and knife wounds, rape victims and drug overdoses.

"Now, the precinct sends me out on medical cases and you, I'm sorry to say, are on top of the witness list in this case. Please tell me about your background and experience in coma care and your relationship to August Rincade."

As Neil spoke, Detective Towser speedily typed into a laptop.

"Neil Joseph Jonson. I was born in 1988 in Sioux City, Iowa. My father had a stroke when I was eleven and I spent my teen years helping him. Then I lost him when I was about to start college, so I went to nursing school instead and got a B.S. in nursing and a master's degree in neuroscience nursing, six years of training. I did some general hospital nursing, I spent some years doing private duty nursing for disabled persons, and I've been doing hospital coma care for the past seven years.

"Here in this unit, we not only monitor vital signs, but we continuously monitor patients for six levels of function. At the lowest level, they may demonstrate intact hearing with a reflexive response to an obnoxious sound. Next, we look for signs of visual function like pupillary response to light, eye opening and visual tracking. We look carefully for any other voluntary muscle movement such as opening the mouth or lifting a finger.

"The ability to swallow without choking is a major breakthrough. The next signs of consciousness are seen with attempts to communicate with facial or hand gestures if not speech. Some cognitively aware persons never regain speech, though they can communicate in other ways. Ultimate emergence from a coma requires the person to become awake, alert and in touch with their environment, even if their ability to move is severely limited."

"Thank you, Neil. So, where is your patient on the coma recovery scale? I'm talking about the 0–23-point scoring system to be precise."

"Umm, so you're familiar with our assessment tools. August is just coming up from the bottom. The first two days we only used a brain reflex scale before we switched to the recovery scale. He initially scored in the vegetative range though we believe he can hear.

"Then we started to see improving attempts at eye opening and mouth movement and his sense of smell has definitely come alive. He only just awakened last evening, and he came up disoriented and agitated. It's taken some sedation to stabilize him, so we need at least another 12-24 hours to have meaningful scores. At this point, we believe that August is minimally conscious."

"And what do you think his prognosis is?"

"He's already outperformed his prognosis, so nurse to nurse, I don't even want to venture a guess. Prior to last evening, I would have said his outlook was awful, but what we've seen in his recent responses to family is now giving me hope. Some part of this man seems conscious.

"As you may know, levels of consciousness can be variable and unpredictable at this stage of recovery. I've been his primary daytime nurse, and I am amazed that he's come this far this soon. So are his other two primary nurses. Lorrie, his night nurse, has done coma care for four years and Marshall, the evening nurse, has been at it for almost ten years."

"Who are his visitors?"

"His wife, ex-wife and his daughter and son."

"He has a son? His ex-wife didn't mention a son."

"Toby looks just like him too. Visitation is mostly limited to immediate family, but this family is so entangled that the ex-wife Jenna has been included. This patient and his ex-wife own and operate a neuroscience laboratory together.

"The current wife Charly is August's research partner and an employee of the ex-wife Jenna. August's daughter Elsie is a disabled young woman who also works in the lab, and August's son Toby is away at veterinary school."

"Hmm, so one big happy family? Please tell me about the son."

Neil was never good at lying but he had already decided to keep his remote suspicions about Toby to himself. The way the kid had broken down and cried had plucked at Neil's heartstrings. He knew what it was like to lose a loving father to a neurologic catastrophe. From what Toby had told Neil about his sister Elsie's development, Neil suspected that it would be painful to lose as devoted a father as August.

Whatever their differences had been, Toby had come to see and to apologize to August. Too often, Neil had taken care of patients whose children didn't care about them at all or even wished them dead. He had to give Toby the benefit of doubt.

"The son visited twice. Like the others, he talks to August and tells him to come back to them. The daughter comes three times a day. They only stay briefly, not only because it's too sad for them, but also because we recommend only brief periods of stimulation. We think August may have responded to his family members but especially to his son and daughter."

"What's this daughter's disability?"

"Elsie's got hearing, visual and vocal impairments, but I suspect she's also a genius. She's the one who requested testing for knockout drugs."

"How often do the others visit?"

"The ex-wife, once to three times a day along with the daughter. Sometimes the daughter comes with one of the lab workers named Renée or with a lady named Maya, introduced as a family friend. Both Maya and Renée say hello to August and tell him they're praying for him, but then they leave Elsie alone with her father."

"And the wife?"

"Charly came on the first day after surgery, one other time and twice yesterday." Neil felt his mouth go dry as he considered revealing Charly's apparent hostility to August's family. But maybe she was right to do that if Toby was a suspect.

"Yesterday, to my total surprise, the current wife exercised her power of attorney to deny my patient's other immediate family access to information about his medical status."

"Really?" Detective McAllister said. "That's illegal. The Privacy Rule of the Code of Federal Regulations, (CFR), 45/164 blah blah blah, permits a health plan to disclose protected health information to a family member or close patient associate if it's directly relevant to that person's involvement with the patient's care or payment for care. And from what you've just told me; these immediate family members may be essential to this patient's recovery. So how did Mrs. Rincade execute such a gag order?"

"She told us the hospital attorney sanctioned it. I guess I should have questioned that."

"Don't sweat it, Neil Joseph Jonson. I know this hospital attorney. He's a bit of a jerk, but I'll take care of this gag order. Thanks for letting me know about it. You just keep taking care of this patient and maybe he'll solve the crime for us. He needs a nurse like you. Thanks for your time.

"And please empty your patient's urine bag and give Detective Towser a sample along with a blood sample and a specimen of scalp hair roots.

"Here's my card. You and I need to stay in touch. Please notify me if there are any significant changes in this patient's status."

25

OCTOBER 8 - AFTERNOON

C.C. McAllister liked reading medical research, but she didn't have enough time or energy to tackle all of August Rincade's publications. That's why she'd chosen to work with rookie Garrett Towser on this case. The kid could scour the web to find the info she needed in a fraction of the time it took anyone else, and he was more accurate than AI. McAllister had scanned two of August's articles just to glimpse into his world and then she turned the job over to her protégé.

Detective Garret Towser was also tasked with compiling a list of all of the U.S. researchers whose research funding had recently been cut and who had been working on projects similar to that of August Rincade. He'd also need to get clearance from the medical school library to access the research journals, or he'd have to pay an exorbitant price for each article.

Additionally, C.C. wanted profiles on all of the researchers that had sent proposals to Jenna Laudren, so Garrett would have to gain access to her files. He was also tasked with constructing profiles on all the Laudren/Rincades and Charly Swift. His boss also wanted records of any and all lawsuits against the Laudren NeuroScience Foundation and the Laudren Retail Plaza.

Detective Garrett Towser had been warned by others in the department. Working with Chelsea Cole McAllister was both a privilege and a curse. C.C. was as famous for her investigative prowess and diligence, as she was for abusing her assistants. But Garrett Towser had set out to become an extraordinary detective, so he volunteered to work with one of the best, C.C. McAllister, a renowned, obsessive-compulsive slave driver.

~ ~ ~ ~ ~

Detective McAllister showed up unannounced at Jenna's lab at three in the afternoon with Garrett Towser in tow. Renée let them in when she was shown their credentials. They were given the option of having the people they wanted to talk to come out to the reception area, or they could suit up and Renée would escort them back into the lab.

C.C. opted to suit up. She wanted a peek into this rat-infested facility. She had been to an animal research lab once before and it shocked her sensibilities to the extent that she wound up sending donations to several animal welfare organizations after the experience. While her career choice wasn't conducive to taking care of a pet, C.C. was an animal lover at heart, and she hated seeing man or beast suffer.

Renée told the detectives that neither Jenna or Charly were in the lab this afternoon and that she didn't know if Toby had returned to vet school or was still at home. Jenna had left a short time ago to go see a doctor and Renée didn't know where Charly was, but Elsie was in the breeder lab. C.C. was eager to speak with all of them but especially Elsie, the one who inquired about the possibility of a knock-out drug.

The two policepersons were shown to dressing rooms where they removed their street clothes and donned scrubs, masks, surgical bonnets and booties. Renée gave the detectives the standard visitor tour. Through observation windows, they were shown the high-tech equipment areas, the animal facilities, and then they were taken to the breeding lab to meet with Elsie who had a rat pup in each hand while Freyja was sitting on top of her head. Renée had to suppress her amusement.

"Elsie Rincade, this is Detective C.C. McAllister. She'd like to speak to you."

"Certainly," Elsie whispered. She took the two babies back to their mother's nest, signaled for Freyja to climb down to her left shoulder, and she put on her cap with the earpiece and microphone."

"Pleased to meet you, Officer 'Galliver.' And this little rat pup is Freyja."

As was the case for most people upon first seeing the unusual appearing Elsie, even without rats in her hands and on her head, C.C.

McAllister didn't quite know what to say, until she blurted out, "no cages. Wow!"

As McAllister gaped at the screens which showed live videos of the rat residences, she exclaimed, "your rat housing is nicer than my apartment. Private bedrooms with plush nesting material, comfy little hammocks hanging from the rafters, art on the walls, toys everywhere, an exercise room and a backyard swimming pool. Is this for real and how do I sign up? I wouldn't mind living in a resort like this."

Elsie took a little bow and offered seating to the two policepersons. Detective Towser got out his laptop and started to take notes.

"It's essential to study addiction in populations that do not suffer from deprivation. If you confine a highly social, intelligent mammal in a wire cage with no companionship and no stimuli, why wouldn't it prefer to stay high on cocaine, or heroin, or whatever other psychoactive alternative is available. That's what most addiction research has proven.

"There's already ample data to show that deprivation is a risk factor for addiction, so for most of our research, we use rats whose lives are comfortable. We're trying to isolate and combat other risk factors for addiction that have the potential to be treatable. It's up to society to combat deprivation. The rats can't remedy how miserable some humans' lives are."

"Well, that's refreshing," C.C. said. "I'm delighted to see your rats treated so kindly. And yet, despite living in the lap of luxury, you're saying that some of these creatures will still become addicts. Do you know why?"

"That's what we study, the chemistry and currents that drive addiction: hormones, neurotransmitters, nutrients, environmental factors like temperature, light exposure and electrical fields, and the genetic formulas for stress responses and resilience."

"What do you do to stress rats?"

"There's an awful lot of awful ways to stress a rat: noise, bright lights, cold temperatures, erratic feeding schedules, confinement, anything that you wouldn't like.

"We sometimes use a technique whereby a well-cared-for rat is entrapped in a small plexiglass cylinder for a few hours a day. The rats aren't hurt in any way, they can see all around them, but they can't escape. The animal's experience could be analogous to a driver getting caught in a traffic jam every day for two hours.

"After a few weeks of the cylinder treatment, rats have been found to show swollen adrenal glands from pumping out excessive stress hormones. Their thymus glands shrink which compromises their immune function and they develop stress ulcers in their stomachs.

"If we have to do a deprivation trial for any of our studies, we typically use social isolation, but we try not to do much deprivation research. It's already out there."

"Okay, Miss Rincade, got it. But can you also please explain why there's a rat sitting on your shoulder?"

Elsie's crooked smile spread across her face. "This is Freyja. She's just seven weeks old. I'm her trainer and she's my star student, the most amazing I've ever had. The other babies I just put back in the nest are also seven weeks old, and I won't even start their training for maybe another two or three weeks. Right now, I just take them out of the nest a few times a day, so they become accustomed to human handling.

"But Freyja here showed readiness to train at four weeks, and she's learned more in her first two weeks of training than most rats will be able to learn in their lifetimes. She's also helping me to train the other pups. She seems to understand the process.

"And by the way, did you know that rats actually have excellent facial recognition skills and just look at how intently Freyja is studying you."

"Oh my! Yes, she is. Who knew anyone here would be this interested in me, let alone a baby rat? It even looks like she's following my words with her little ears. This is ah, um, quite remarkable. But Elsie,

I'm here to ask you some questions. I understand you're the one who concluded that your father was a victim. May I ask you how old you are?"

"I'll be nineteen next month."

C.C. McAllister and Garrett Towser exchanged furtive glances at each other. There was something unreal about Elsie Rincade that was amplified by the behavior of the rat sitting on her shoulder. Elsie seemed to have such an old soul and now her little rat was looking directly at Garrett. It was watching his hands on the keyboard and its ears seemed to move with the soft sound of keystrokes. C.C. had encountered many unusual people in the course of her careers as a nurse and as a police detective, but interacting with Elsie and her rat pup was starting to make her feel like she had entered an unfamiliar realm.

C.C. asked Elsie why she had come to suspect that her father was victimized, and Elsie recounted how she had heard her father's phone call to set up the appointment because the conversation was transmitted through the car speaker while they were on the road.

When asked about the nature of the person her father spoke with, Elsie explained that the speech of others had to be amplified and have its pitch altered through the apparatus on her cap for her to be able to hear it, and even then, she had to extrapolate some of what was said.

"My impression of the speaker was that she was female, and she had some kind of a foreign accent. I couldn't tell you from where.

"It now strikes me though, that this person was much too specific as to where my father should park his car before going into the science building. There are big parking lots all around those buildings. Why should it have mattered where he left his car unless they were planning to do something to the car, like leave it in a hotel parking lot after knocking my father off?"

Elsie also informed C.C. of her observations about someone other than her father having driven the car. She had also calculated the mileage, beyond that fifty-thousand milestone she had witnessed, and she concluded that whoever drove the car from the college to the downtown hotel took the highway, while her father would have saved six miles by taking the side streets. He always tried to avoid the highway.

Elsie also told the detectives that her father was far too dedicated to his research goals to have sacrificed his commitments. She told them about her father's early history with addiction and his devotion to conquering cocaine. Her eyes teared up as she talked about how great a father he had always been.

That's when C.C. decided to end the interview. This young woman wasn't going to give her objective information about anyone in her family. Obviously, she was too dependent on all of them. She was also exceptionally smart. It was always challenging to deal with brilliant criminals who got their kicks from outsmarting law enforcement.

At this point, C.C. produced a subpoena to obtain a sample of the lab's cocaine supply, and Renée recruited Elsie, Celia Fromme, and one of Celia's grad students to open the drug vault and measure out a sample.

Then Renée was warned as the police were leaving, that Detective Towser would be back to see Jenna's files on the scientists that had submitted research proposals. He'd return with another court order.

26

OCTOBER 9 - MORNING

It was August Rincade's ninth post-operative day and his second day of minimal consciousness. Physical therapists would be working his legs, occupational therapists would work his hands, and a speech therapist was trying to coax his swallowing muscles into action.

August was opening his eyes more frequently and moving his tongue more effectively, but his responses to commands like 'blink your eyes' or 'lift your finger' were inconsistent. Between frequent brief therapy sessions he was mostly sleeping, but his brain wave patterns were continuing to improve.

As Nurse Lorrie had warned when signing August's care over to Nurse Umberto earlier that morning, August had made some attempts to move his left fingers. They'd have to keep his hand restrained. If he could get through another sleep-wake cycle, the neurosurgeon might take the bolt out of his skull. The brain swelling had continued to resolve, and they wanted him to be able to freely move.

The placement of a tube into his stomach had also been postponed, but the nasogastric feeding tube was definitely becoming an issue. August needed fluids and nutrition but giving it all intravenously was never the best option. However, if August started to recover hand function before becoming cognitively aware, he could also pull a surgically implanted gastrostomy tube out of his belly. Surgeons weren't comfortable with that possibility, so they were continuing to feed him through his nose.

Umberto had heard quite a bit of gossip about Mrs. Charly Rincade over the course of the week since August's admission to the coma care unit, but this morning was the first time he had seen her. He was disappointed. She was wearing white sneakers and a white lab coat over baby pink scrubs. Her hair was pulled back in a bushy ponytail. The now infamous rat tattoo was concealed, and she sported round, green framed eyeglasses. Still, she was a very pretty woman.

Charly asked Umberto if the other family members had been there and if they were seeking information about August's medical status. Umberto replied that since it was Neil's day off, he was only covering for the day, and he didn't know anything about August's other visitors. Charly was the first to have shown up on his shift.

Umberto explained that he was one of several floating neuro nurses who picked up dayshifts and occasionally evening shifts from patients' primary nurses. The hospital tried to keep neuro patients and their nurses paired as much as possible, but Neil needed some personal time. Today, Umberto was going to do both a day and an evening shift and spend all of it with August. He told Charly that he always liked to attend to patients in their waking up phases, so it was a privilege for him to be taking care of August at this point in his recovery. Sometimes waking up patients did very remarkable things.

"So, do you actually think he's going to recover?"

"I'm so sorry, Mrs. Rincade. I've only been taking care of your husband for an hour, besides the evening shift I did on his second night here. His coma was deep then. I'm excited to see him opening his eyes now, and I know that his other nurses are becoming optimistic that August has a chance to wake up.

"I also know that chances for complete recovery are limited for patients in circumstances like your husband's. I'm sorry to say, Mrs. Rincade, that the statistics aren't favorable. However, I've seen too many comatose patients deviate from their predicted potential to have much faith in statistics. And I haven't spent enough time with your husband to have any gut feelings about him. I just don't know.

"I can tell you that every case of neurologic injury and recovery is unique. I like to believe that most patients have a chance if we can give them the care they need. I will also tell you that human contact may be the most critical element for recovery. Too often, I've seen that when loved ones give up on a comatose patient, it decreases that patient's chance of waking up, and I've been doing coma care since I'm twenty-six. I'm now forty-two.

"For me, nothing is more satisfying than watching someone come alive, be reborn, so to speak. It doesn't happen often enough but when it does, it makes my career worthwhile. That's what I'm hoping is happening to your husband."

Charly didn't like Umberto's preachy little speech. She took it personally. She hadn't been very supportive of August. She had immediately assumed the worst about him. She was the one who had been harshly judgmental, and now it appeared that Elsie was the one with good judgment. But then, Charly consoled herself with the rationalization that for the Jolenes of the world who steal other women's husbands because they can, distrusting their straying husbands is just a natural instinct.

"Okay." Charly conceded. "I'd like to know what your gut tells you, when and if it speaks to you. But I'd also like to know that you know that the rest of August's family is no longer permitted to access his medical records. I have an exclusive power of attorney."

Umberto had heard all about the war between Charly and the rest of August's family and her attempt to keep the ex-wife and his kids out of the information loop. He had also heard that the gag order probably had no teeth and didn't have to be adhered to.

Lorrie had also told him about the police investigation that Neil had told her about. She'd also told Umberto that the hospital attorney might be caught between the wife and the ex-wife, and that August's nurses should maybe try to avoid the whole issue. Since the ex-wife was paying for August's health insurance, she had rights that the wife shouldn't have been able to block. It was the talk of the nurse's lounge. August's nurses worried that any or all of them could get drawn into a legal conflict, a criminal investigation, a courtroom drama, and/or an emotional mine field that would impair their ability to provide objective care.

"I haven't encountered any other family members, Mrs. Rincade. My shift only just started, but I will be here with August all day and evening. What is it that you don't want me to tell who, should such persons come to visit?"

Charly looked irritated and her eyes darted between August and Umberto. She furrowed her brow and then puffed up her cheeks before she exhaled and said, "you don't need to tell them anything.

"Jenna Laudren is not an immediate member of the family. She's his boss and she's violating August's privacy. He's just an expense to her and she's actively trying to replace August as the lead researcher in her lab.

"Toby Drew Rincade is an ungrateful son who could care less about his father. And Elsie Jean Rincade is a dependent, adult daughter who wants her daddy to take care of her forever.

"August's well-being isn't the priority of any of these people. I intend to protect my husband from his former family members' dependency and exploitation. None of them have his best interests at heart."

Umberto struggled to keep a neutral expression. "As you wish, Mrs. Rincade. And I intend to ensure that Mr. Rincade gets the best coma recovery care possible. Thanks for being here and for giving August your support."

Umberto turned his back on Charly and started to prepare a sponge bath for August. Charly sat down at the foot of the bed as if to supervise. August suddenly opened his eyes and started to cough, and Umberto jumped into action, adjusting the position of the nasogastric tube in August's throat.

"He's getting his swallowing reflexes back," he said. "That's great. If we can get him to swallow today, we can get that tube out of his nose. Did you hear that, August? Start swallowing, Buddy, and we can say bye-bye to that nasty NG tube in your schnozz."

August opened his eyes and protruded his tongue for a few seconds. Umberto put two drops of sugar water on the tongue tip. August's cheeks fluttered and then he fell back to sleep.

Charly got up and walked out of the room without saying another word.

27

October 9 - Morning

Detective Garrett Towser showed up at the Laudren NeuroScience lab unannounced with his subpoena for the research proposals that Jenna had told C.C. McAllister about. Renée told him that Jenna would be back in about an hour. She was at a doctor's appointment.

Garrett said he had plenty he could do on his laptop while he waited, if he could connect to the lab's WIFI network. Renée gave him the password, but instead of signing on to his computer, the policeman asked if Elsie was in her lab and could he speak with her again. He had learned a lot about rats since visiting twenty-some hours ago and he wanted to learn more.

Renée checked with Elsie who loved visitors almost as much as she loved rats. People touring the lab gave her social experience she didn't get elsewhere. Charly could ensnare people with her looks, but Elsie had learned to do it with her artful way of sharing her knowledge and her ever evolving wisdom. Once a visitor had been to Elsie's lab, they often wanted to come back and learn more.

Renée had Garrett change into lab attire, and she accompanied him to the breeder lab where they found Elsie with Freyja perched on her shoulder. Elsie had another tiny rat running through a simplistic maze.

"Welcome back, Detective Towser. How can I help you today?" Elsie said as Renée retreated back to her reception area, and Elsie delivered the young maze-runner back to its residence, after it successfully found the route to its reward. The rat on her shoulder remained there, looking at him.

Before he could answer, Garrett watched Elsie's rat stand up on its hind legs, put its hands against her ear lobe and squeak into Elsie's ear as Elsie tilted her head towards it. Garrett shook his head in disbelief.

"Yes, this little rat is trying to tell me something. How I wish I knew what she was saying. I think she might be telling me she knows you, but that's a wild guess. However, she doesn't make that sound when she encounters an unfamiliar person. She just studies them. She's always intrigued by new people.

"May I take your picture? I'm trying to separate her visual recall from her sense of smell, so when I have a gallery of facial pictures, I'll maybe be able to tell if she recognizes the people she knows from the pictures. Rats are very good at complex pattern recognition and recall, even if the patterns get turned upside down. They're actually better at it than most humans."

As Elsie maneuvered Garrett into her photo-shoot setup, he forgot what it was he originally came to ask her. But then, his rapidly expanding interest in her research and her remarkable little rat flooded his brain with questions. "Do rats have language?"

"Most certainly they do. Humans have been trying to decipher their ultrasonic vocalizations for some forty years. It's difficult because their squeaks are out of the range of human hearing, so we have to use amplifiers and lower the pitch by slowing down the frequency of their sounds. That means if we record five hours of rat squeaks, it takes a human listener more than a hundred hours to wade through the tapes and try to interpret a complex matrix of sound.

"A computer program called DeepSqueak can now convert ultrasonic input into visual images which may accelerate our ability to understand what they're saying. This program is getting continuously upgraded. So far, DeepSqueak has revealed that mice use about twenty different whistle-like sounds that get repeated in their conversations in different orders. It's also been observed that two male rodents conversing may rely on some monotonous phrasing, but if a female rodent enters the room, the sounds they make become more lyrical, similar to birdsong.

"We also don't know if rats, like bats, who not only vocally speak but sing, might have different languages or regional dialects. And then there's the problem that we've mostly been studying language in domesticated lab rats whose life experiences are limited.

"Maybe country rats have names for the farmers' fields that they dine in, and for the predators that they have to hide from. Perhaps city rats have special words for things like pizza crust and the sauce on the bottom of the Chinese food containers that they feast on in dumpsters. Maybe city rats use urban slang or have gang passwords.

"Most researchers and pet rat owners believe that rats make happy sounds and sad sounds appropriate to their situation. The hope of researchers who study mood and substance abuse disorders, like my parents, is that we'll ultimately be able to monitor the animals' response to treatments by understanding their language, instead of trying to interpret their behavior.

"Currently though, humans seem more interested in communicating with dolphins and monkeys than with rats, and these species definitely have vocal language. But for now, animal language interpretation is too underdeveloped for practical application. Artificial intelligence may change that.

"Maybe so will Professor Freyja over here. I believe she's trying to teach me her language. And, since eighty-five percent of the twenty-five million animals being used in research right now are mice or rats, we owe it to them to learn their language. They undoubtedly have a lot to tell us."

"Detective Towser," a speaker over his head said. "Jenna Laudren is back and Elsie, can you please escort the detective to your mom's office. She also left a message asking you to not have Freyja with you, now that she's been out and about, even if she's only been on your shoulder."

Elsie pushed a button on her head gear and said, "I should have known that was coming. Okay, Renée. Tell Mom we're ninety seconds away." She put Freyja back in her residence and walked the policeman to her mother's office in the center of the building.

As they entered, Elsie said, "I completely decontaminated Freyja when I brought her back to the lab. The only places she's been outside of my unit is in her travel cage and on my head, hand and shoulder. What's the difference if I handle her in the lab or in my bedroom? It's not like she's running around on the furniture or the floor."

"Elsie Jean Rincade! Are you kidding me? You had that rat in your father's car and in his hospital room, on your person throughout our house, and outdoors on the way into and out of all of those places, even if she was in a travel cage. Are you going to tell me this baby hasn't breathed in different environmental contaminants than the others? You can keep her, but I want her out of the lab."

Elsie's face grew red, and she fisted her hands. "Okay, Mom. You're right, my bad. But she's already back in the lab, so she's already contaminated her roommates and everything else anyway, so please, can't she stay? She's a phenomenon. She's actually helping me to train some other pups. I promise, I won't take her out again, even though she deserves to know the world. I promise. Please?"

Jenna Laudren's face was also getting red which looked healthier than the pallor that Garrett had noticed when they first walked into her office.

"Later!" Jenna barked. Then she turned to apologize to the policeman for this little family dispute as Elsie stormed out of her office.

Garrett hadn't missed this argument, but he was trying hard to appear to be preoccupied with observing the video screens that lined the wall behind Jenna's desk. There were sixteen screens. Apparently, Jenna could observe what was going on in every corner of the lab, even the hallways. Maybe studying a controlled substance like cocaine required this level of surveillance. Or maybe, Jenna Laudren was a control freak. Garrett planned to start looking around for the cameras. What was it that she was trying to capture?

~ ~ ~ ~ ~

Jenna ran the subpoena through a scanner and sat the policeman down at a terminal. "I've opened some files for you. I don't know about the legalities of your downloading all of these files, but I guess the subpoena covers it. I'm deferring that to you. I need the police to help solve this crime.

"Please notice, I've divided the proposals I've received into five categories. The first consists of valid proposals by worthy scientists. Then, there are proposals that have some flaws, but they still deserve consideration, The third folder consists of proposals I might want to sponsor, but they come from researchers who I have doubts about. The fourth and largest category is proposals not worth considering. And the fifth folder contains proposals I haven't reviewed yet. Proposals still come trickling in, but I've been too busy to look at them in the past few weeks. Between August's hospitalization and other pressing issues, my professional time has been compromised.

"The tagged files are the people I've already interviewed, mostly remotely. I've only met with a few in-person. I had two such interviews scheduled for this past week, and I went ahead with them in spite of August's hospitalization. It was very awkward, but finding the right person has proven to be exceedingly difficult, and these researchers had made considerable effort to get here."

"Well, this is very helpful, Ms. Laudren. Tell me more about the ideas you like from the people you don't like. Actually, just tell me why you don't like some of these researchers. I see six files in that folder."

"It's not necessarily that I dislike the people. Three of those researchers are just too inexperienced. I'm looking for someone with a proven track record. Some researchers peak early in their careers. They come up with one brilliant idea and then they never progress beyond that. I'm looking for someone who isn't going to outlive their creativity.

"One of the people in that unfavorable researcher group, who I actually interviewed, looked fantastic on paper, but he came with a hard-to-understand foreign accent. I worry that my hearing-impaired daughter and another employee or two who do animal care here, would struggle trying to communicate with this person. One of our animal care workers also can't read but he's a tremendous asset to our lab. I need to accommodate the people I'm already invested in.

"On the phone, even I couldn't understand most of what this researcher said. I've been conflicted about not following up with him, because aside from the language barrier, he might be a good fit. But now, I'm also wondering if any foreign-born scientist would choose to relocate to the U.S. when many of our scientists are leaving.

"Then, there's a researcher in that file who recently had a prestigious university position pulled out from under him because of a scandal over some erroneous data. It was a big news story for a day or two. This scientist is renowned because his research designs are very ingenious, and he's produced numerous concepts that have garnered widespread acceptance. But I cannot allow my lab to be associated with a tarnished name, even if the guy isn't actually guilty. I've worked too hard to build my lab's reputation for legitimacy.

"The sixth person in that file is someone I actually did not like. He was too arrogant relative to his young age. I think he's got a creative mind, but his narcissistic personality turned me off, which is a shame because his proposal so closely aligned with August's work."

Garrett typed speedily as Jenna described why some ideas weren't worth consideration. Her prime example was a proposal to use rats' willingness to jump longer and longer distances as a measure of how much they craved cocaine.

Jenna then showed Garrett a YouTube video of someone's three pet rats doing tricks, one of which involved jumping. Two of the three rats jumped without hesitation, but one was clearly dismayed by the challenge.

Then, using a tight rope for access to a favorite treat, one of these three YouTube rats ran on top of the rope like a skilled circus acrobat. The second rat hung upside down and used his hands and feet to quickly scurry to the other side. The third rat hung from the rope by both hands, persistently grimaced and used a slow, laborious hand over hand method to barely make it to the other side.

"Measuring rats' confidence and capacity for jumping would only separate them by their innate levels of athleticism and courage," Jenna said. "Like humans with whom rats share ninety-seven percent of their DNA, some rats are exceptionally agile and quick, and some are slow and klutzy. Some are bold and adventurous; some are reserved and timid.

"However, both the confident, athletic types and the self-doubting, clumsy types can lose their souls to drug addiction. There are safer and less discriminatory ways to measure a rat's craving for a drug than to make it perform a risky athletic feat. The person who wrote this proposal doesn't belong in a lab, not in my lab anyway."

Garrett Towser was impressed with Jenna's approach to this monumental responsibility of wisely investing in research. He was starting to appreciate how science-dedicated these rat people were. Even young Elsie was an inspiring scholar. He had also found the YouTube rat videos intriguing. Some of the rats were unbelievably cute and clever.

Garrett was also grateful to see that all of these proposals that Jenna was reviewing contained the researchers' personal data and summaries of their professional backgrounds. Jenna's application form had made Garrett's job easy. He downloaded all of the files onto a thumb drive and left Jenna to resolve her rat restriction issues with her daughter.

Personally, Garrett was rooting for Elsie and Freyja. He was also starting to wonder whether he had more to learn about the victim's family members than he did about rats and addiction research. Interacting with Jenna, Elsie and Freyja was more enlightening than any encounters Garrett had ever had.

28

OCTOBER 10 - MIDDAY

Charly headed for the hospital cafeteria for some lunch and a cup of coffee to take to August's room. She'd changed from her lab outfit into fuchsia palazzo pants and a billowing, shimmery white blouse, the neckline of which contoured perfectly to show off Riki the rat.

Her tattoo was adorned with a necklace of tiny white pearls, around a delicate chain encircling Charly's neck. The rat's necklace matched Charly's dangling earrings. A string of little pearls also encircled the red waterspout of curls dancing on the crown of Charly's head. She had chosen to wear what she thought was a conservative outfit to demonstrate to nurse Umberto that she was there to be supportive of August.

Maybe her being there could actually be of help to August, though she had grave doubts that he could recover to the extent that she'd still want to be his wife. Charly was only forty-two. Between her traumatic childhood and her previous marriages, she'd had enough hardship. There were still a lot of things she wanted to do, and being the caretake of an on old, disabled guy wasn't one of them. She hated to admit it even to herself, but that's how she felt. She was starting to realize that maybe, she had loved August more as a conquest than as a husband.

As she turned into the cafeteria, she was confronted by an elderly woman calling her name and displaying a police shield. She accompanied the woman to a table in the corner where a young man in a poorly cut sport jacket was typing on a laptop. Garrett Towser was gaping at her in a way that she knew she could cash in on, but clearly, it was the old woman who was in charge.

Garrett Towser and C.C. McAllister had driven in circles trying to catch up with Charlotte Swift-Rincade. After missing her in the lab twice and at her townhouse twice, C.C. had sent Garrett Towser to tail her early this morning.

Garrett got to Charly's place at 6:30, but she was already gone. She returned to her townhouse at 7:30 and left for the hospital at 8:30. Then she went to the lab.

While waiting, Garrett went into the lab and asked Renée if he could talk to Elsie. He was kind of relieved when Elsie told him that her genius rat Freyja had not been kicked out of the lab after all, though she was now imprisoned within.

Elsie was inviting Garrett to come back to visit her unit when he spotted Charly coming down a hallway. He recognized her from a thumbprint size picture that had appeared in one of August's publications. It was probably that picture that made most researchers look at the boring article.

Though Charly didn't know who Garrett Towser was at that point, he ducked out of sight into a dressing room. He then hustled out to his car to tail her again. He followed her back to her townhouse and when she came out, she had changed clothes again, and she started on her route towards the hospital. That's when Garrett notified C.C. that there could be an opportunity to intercept her.

Charly's instincts told her that she'd do better playing on the old woman's sympathies than on the young man's fantasies, but damn if Detective Garrett Towser didn't look like the hungry, nerdy type that she could so easily charm the pants off.

"So how can I help you, Officers? I'm so glad my husband's boss reported this. They learned about the date rape drug before I knew anything about it. What someone did to my husband is so horrific, I'm relieved that you're investigating. I was just about to bring a cup of hot coffee to his room. His nurse said the smell of coffee triggered his brain to start to recover. Isn't that remarkable?"

"Yes, it is, that he might be able to recover. He is getting very good care here. I've been in more than a few stroke recovery facilities and your husband is fortunate to be where he is.

"So, do you also believe that your husband is a victim?" C.C. asked, while Garrett was working hard not to stare at Charly's tattoo embellished cleavage.

Charly closed her eyes and shook her head. "I cannot believe my husband did this to himself. We were happily married. We've spent the last seven years working long, long hours to come up with a cure for the scourge of cocaine addiction. We are, we were almost there. Everything was going well.

"August was also totally committed to abstinence. He still went to Narcotics Anonymous meetings once a week. Occasionally he went twice a week. He was healthy. He has a daughter that he absolutely adores. No, I cannot believe that he did this to himself."

"So, when did you start to think that your husband was a victim, Mrs. Rincade?"

Charly felt as though she was trapped like a rat. She also felt guilty. When she had received that phone call from the hospital eight days ago, she hadn't even considered the possibility that August was a victim. She had continued to blame him for his situation right up until the moment she learned about the positive test for the date rape drug. Her pharmaceutical analysis had confirmed that August had been given a monster dose of Rohypnol.

A lot of Charly's life had been about not being able to trust people, and when she got that call from the hospital, she had transferred that distrust to August. But, Charly rationalized, August had brought the distrust unto himself by cheating on Jenna, the mother of his children.

"Well," Charly offered, "when someone from the hospital called to tell me that my husband was undergoing brain surgery for a cocaine-induced stroke, they definitely made it sound like August was the bad guy. I was told that his personal belongings were brought to the E.R. by a young woman who claimed his car was parked at a hotel.

"I was cheated on by my previous husband, and August cheated on his first wife, and I've only been married to him for a year, and I guess I just thought that he was cheating before I thought about him being a victim of a crime. The suggestion that he was cheating was painful for me, so I guess I wasn't thinking clearly. I was too angry and hurt.

"In retrospect, August was too devoted to too many causes to have done this to himself. His daughter was right to be suspicious and his boss was right to call the police. So how are you looking into this?"

"We're interviewing those who know him. August's son is out of state at vet school. What can you tell us about him?"

"Toby? He's a really smart kid and an animal lover. He's also an animal rights activist who doesn't like the animal research that his family does. He's hardly been around since he left for college six years ago, but he did come home to visit his father."

"And what's your relationship with August's ex-wife Jenna? We understand she's been your boss for the past seven years."

"And she's a very good boss, smart, generous, fair. I have the greatest respect for Jenna as a scientist, philanthropist, businesswoman and an employer. She just didn't have enough bandwidth left to be a wife, or to have been able to stop her husband from falling in love with me. All things considered; we get along okay."

"What's your relationship with your husband's daughter, Elsie?"

"You've met Elsie?" Charly asked.

"Yes, we interviewed her yesterday."

Charly's lips pressed tightly together for a few seconds. "Then you know. Part of what makes my husband a great person is having a miracle kid like Elsie. There are simply no words to describe Elsie other than brilliant and devoted to her father and to science. There's nothing else in life for that poor girl. I see her in the lab almost every day and I marvel at how she fits in and belongs there, but I don't know where else she could be. Like her father, I admire and adore her."

"I have a question," Garrett interjected as it looked like C.C. was about to conclude the interview. Garrett suspected that C.C. wasn't buying into Charly's overly sugary descriptions of her husband's ex-family members. He certainly didn't feel that she was credible. Charly came across as a manipulative shrewdie. "Where do you go so early in the morning?"

Charly smiled broadly. "To the ice rink. I play in a hockey league, and the rink offers league members an hour for stick and puck drills at six in the morning, three days a week. I try to get there when I can. It's a great work out on great ice. The women play our games on Thursday nights because the men have the rink on the weekends. I play forward and we have a big game next Thursday.

"Did you know that this past summer, the U.S women won the 2025 Women's World Ice Hockey Championship? They beat Canada. Did you know the U.S. Olympic Women's Ice Hockey teams have medaled in seven Olympic games straight since 1998?"

"Well, thank you for that information, Mrs. Rincade. Why don't you go get your husband a cup of coffee," was C.C.'s final remark.

29

October 10 - Afternoon

Charly hated to perspire, and the police interview had left her sweaty and anxious. She thought about going home to change, but she decided instead to just chill in the cafeteria for a while. She sipped at an iced tea for about three minutes, lost patience, and got back in line to get August his coffee.

Watching for Umberto's reaction when she entered August's room, Charly was stunned to find Detectives C.C. McAllister and Garrett Towser at her husband's bedside. She was so surprised she almost dropped the coffee, but her quick reflexes saved her.

"August," she called out from the foot of the bed where there was still room to stand, "I brought you a cop of steaming hot java. Wake up to the smell of fresh coffee, Sweetheart."

Then, Charly noticed that August was already awake, sort of. He appeared to be looking directly at her. His upper lip twitched. She maneuvered next to Garrett Towser and held the coffee under August's nose. For a few seconds, it looked like he was trying to smell the coffee. Then his eyes rolled back, and it appeared that he'd gone back to LaLa land.

"You missed it," Umberto said. "He was awake for almost an hour. Elsie was here for most of that time. He made some more purposeful tongue movements, and Elsie reported feeling the muscles of his left hand twitch a few times. This is the first time he's gone back to sleep since Elsie left, about twenty minutes ago. That's the longest we've seen him awake and looking at things."

"Would you consider that significant progress?" Detective McAllister asked.

"Absolutely. His body isn't cooperating, but I sense some awareness in this patient, even in the short time I've been with him. I can't give you objective evidence of that beyond what you just saw. It's something I see in his eyes. Have you ever looked into someone's eyes and seen determination or defeat?"

"Absolutely," C.C. McAllister agreed. "You just did a pretty good job of describing 'it,' but it's impossible to describe to someone who's never noticed.

"Thanks for the update, Umberto. Please keep us posted if August shows a significant change. And goodbye again, Mrs. Rincade. We're rooting for your husband's recovery. We may come back to you for more information in the next day or two. Thank you for helping us out."

Charly bowed her head to C.C. McAllister. When C.C. turned to walk out of the room, Charly met Garrett Towser's lingering gaze with an alluring smile.

Garrett mimicked a little hockey stick action, waved, and then ran to catch up with C.C. She walked surprisingly fast for a little old lady.

~ ~ ~ ~ ~

"What about his being able to swallow?" Charly asked Umberto. "I have to make a decision about the feeding tube surgery, so where are we on that issue?"

"When he's awake, he responds to sweetness on his tongue by retracting it more proficiently than he was able to do yesterday. The facial nerve, the trigeminal nerve and the glossopharyngeal nerve respectively power taste, touch and movement of the tongue. Along with his sense of smell, his apparent ability to hear, and his pupillary responses, there's great improvement from his admission status. Most of his cranial nerves are starting to work. We are allowing ourselves to hope.

"The attending neurologist plans to temporarily resort to intravenous hydration and nutrition for a few days to give his throat function more time to come back, before having the surgeon sew a tube into his stomach. That's the best option for now. They're coming to start another intravenous line in the next few minutes, and then, we'll get that nasal tube out before he winds up with ulcers in his nose."

Umberto turned to his patient. "Did you hear that, August? We're going to get that big bad booger out of your nose today, very soon in fact. You're on your way there, Cowboy. Let me see you swallow."

August opened his eyes and appeared to be trying to move his mouth. Then he seemed to see Charly. She put her face close to his and it looked as though he was staring at her. His left cheek muscles fluttered ever so slightly. His tongue seemed to move. Then he closed his eyes and went back to sleep, or whatever stage of consciousness he was in at the moment.

Charly sat back down. "Wow, August. They say you're beating the odds. I know you're trying. If anyone can make monkeys out of the doctors, Sweetheart, it's you. They can't keep you down, you're way too tough. You have to come back. You have to help us find who did this to you. I know you didn't do this to yourself, Sweetheart. Please come back to me, August. I miss you. I love you."

August's eyelids fluttered but his eyes remain closed.

Charly watched him for a few minutes and then she left without saying goodbye.

30

October 11- Morning

Renée welcomed Detectives C.C. McAllister and Garrett Towser back into the lab, though they had arrived unannounced. Renée advised them that Jenna, Elsie, and Charly were all currently present.

The policewoman said if there was a way to meet with them all simultaneously, it could save a lot of time. Renée contacted Jenna and within a minute, Renée escorted the police people into a small conference room next to the reception area. They were allowed to remain in their street clothes.

While they waited, Garrett Towser started perusing the framed documents on the walls. Some were diplomas and licenses. Some were the front covers of research journals featuring articles by August Rincade. Some were local newspaper articles about the Laudren NeuroScience Foundation.

One photo showed August at a podium in front of a packed audience Behind him was an enormous banner for the Laudren NeuroScience Foundation. Garrett was struck by what a handsome man August had been, not very long ago.

Some darker spots on the walls indicated that some pictures had been taken down. The dark spots supported Garrett's suspicion that all was not well between the principals of this enterprise.

Jenna entered the conference room wearing street clothes. Her tailored beige slacks looked baggy. A light tan cashmere turtleneck made her look so washed out that the old nurse in C.C. McAllister surmised she was ill. Jenna Laudren also looked like she had been beaten down, but she spoke with the voice of authority. "Charly and Elsie have some things to finish up and they'll be along shortly."

Garrett Towser told Jenna that he'd read some of August's research articles, and he was wondering how soon they might be bringing this promising new treatment to market.

"Wouldn't that be nice?" Jenna responded, nodding up and down. Then she shook her head back and forth and snickered. "But I understand why you would think that we are creating a pharmaceutical product here. Let me explain how this actually works.

"The Laudren NeuroScience Foundation provides resources for scientists who've devoted their careers to finding a cure for a cruel and costly human affliction. If our research produces solid results, and if we can attract the attention of other investors, we might be able to get a pharmaceutical company to partner with us and develop a human treatment based on our animal model. That's how most pharmaceuticals get started.

"If we succeed in connecting with a pharmaceutical company, it will then have to petition and maybe even lobby regulators to allow us to construct and implement clinical treatment trials for a population of human addicts.

"Assuming initial trials are successful, it then takes an average of twelve to fifteen years for a new drug to go through more trials and the many regulatory steps required to prove that it's both effective and safe. Only then, does such a treatment become available to the people who have been anxiously awaiting a remedy for their disease.

"Meanwhile, all of what I just told you is based on how pharmaceutical products were developed and approved when regulators were primarily committed to public safety, in an era when government was supportive of science. If the approval process for new drugs is now based on who stands to profit, you can be assured that the pharmaceutical industry will come up with an amazing array of toxins.

"Big pharma has been doing that anyway, even when government watchdogs were still on guard. Just look at the history of the heartburn drug ranitidine, (Zantac). Between its 1981 licensure and 1987, it became the all-time best-selling drug in the world. Thirty-three years later, it got pulled off the market for its cancer-causing potential and instability at varying temperatures. Dozens of other major blockbuster drugs also bit the dust after their unanticipated side effects were ultimately recognized.

"When I was a kid in the 1980s, we had an old-time family doctor who used to say: 'New drugs. I prescribe them to the people I don't like for the first five years. If there are no problems after five years, the rest of my patients might get prescriptions. If no one's died after ten years, I might prescribe them to my family. As for myself, I'll take the drug if it's still available without major lawsuits fifteen years after coming onto the market.'

"I've now lived long enough in the age of modern medicine to be able to appreciate the wisdom of that old doctor. And the number of drugs on the market has exploded since then, new ones almost every day.

"Even if I hadn't just lost my primary researcher after so many years of investment in a potential therapy, seeing the fruition of this research has always been both a long shot and a very prolonged process. You could say, I'm a gambler, but I believe in this cause and my lab's approach to a horrible human illness."

"But don't some drugs get fast-tracked for approval?" C.C. asked.

"Some do, like when tens of thousands of people, or a few very influential people, who are dying from COVID or some other killer disease, manage to push past the approval process. And why shouldn't they be allowed to do so if they're dying?

"Humans should have the right to be lab rats if they're capable of making informed decisions. The state should not be regulating how humans confront terminal illness if there are no conventional cures. Human lab rats are the heroes of medicine. These brave, altruistic people should be celebrated, not judged or harassed based on others' beliefs about morality and mortality.

"Meanwhile, the rapidly rising rate of cocaine addiction and cocaine fatalities, especially amongst young men, apparently doesn't warrant society's sympathy, let alone a fast-track drug approval process.

"There were almost 16,000 U.S. deaths involving cocaine in 2019, and more than 28,000 in 2022, an almost 75% increase in just three years. According to the National Institute on Drug Abuse, more than forty million people had a substance use disorder in 2020, but fewer than 7% received treatment. Now, resources for treatment have been further reduced.

"Cocaine deaths have actually exceeded heroin deaths in recent years, at least in the cases that are reported and tallied. Opioid deaths have recently declined, in part because an antidote for opioid overdoses is now available over the counter as a nose spray. There's no such convenient antidote for a cocaine overdose. A bystander just has to helplessly watch as the afflicted person strokes out or dies.

"I'm sure your narcotics police people know about this, but currently, the hot ticket in drug culture is pink cocaine, which is cocaine laced with a variety of other drugs: ketamine, MDMA (Ecstasy), fentanyl, benzos, hallucinogens, caffeine, bath salts, whatever. If you can think of it, some basement chemist is probably mixing it up right now. Users often have no idea what they're actually snorting. Nor do users realize that the process of extracting the drug from the coca plant usually involves the addition of kerosene, ammonia, acetone, and other toxic substances.

"Some of this pink cocaine, called 'tusi,' may not even contain cocaine. It could be a mixture of fentanyl and powdered sugar. But this indiscriminate mixing of drugs ensures that cocaine related deaths will continue to be undercounted, and therefore, prevention and treatment of cocaine addiction will continue to be underfunded.

"If the the C.D.C.'s website for health statistics hasn't yet been taken down by the those who fear science, you can see the tragedy of how many young Americans are dying from drug overdoses year by year. It's also now estimated that one out of every four children in the U.S. lives with a parent who has a substance abuse disorder.

"But the numbers don't reflect how costly substance abuse is when addicts survive, or die leaving dependents behind, or end up brain damaged and needing total care for the rest of their lives, like maybe will be the case for my ex-husband."

Jenna paused. She swallowed hard and then she asked, "from a police perspective, how big a problem is cocaine in our region?"

C.C. felt like she was getting immersed in a rarely encountered display of genuine altruism. Jenna Laudren seemed to operate on the premise that it was her duty to give a gift to mankind. Jenna had also managed to awaken the academic alter ego embedded in Detective Chelsea Cole McAllister.

"Well, we know that nationally, a whopping 80% of crimes leading to jail time are associated with drugs and alcohol abuse. Polydrug abuse is so common that it's difficult to sort out which drugs have the worst impact. Desperate for their next dose of these costly, addictive drugs, many resort to robbery, burglary, and larceny. Their despair also generates child neglect, domestic violence, motor vehicle accidents, public-order offenses and other crimes that largely keep police forces, courts and prisons in business.

"Some addicts resort to prostitution to pay for their drugs, which also becomes the domain of police departments, while our entertainment industry continues to propagate the idea that prostitutes are the unsung heroes of society. Interested customers can currently view more than a hundred movies about heroic prostitutes.

"So, while our precinct funds a wide-reaching vice division, the rest of our police force is too poor to solve a lot of the crimes that actually have victims. But I don't work vice, so I'm not sure what our local statistics would show," C.C. admitted. "They'd probably be similar to national statistics. Maybe we have a little less violent crime here. Maybe we have more white-collar crime.

"With the college in town, we might have more designer drugs than heroin. But we probably suffer from similar rates of addiction and cocaine abuse that you'd encounter in most suburban regions and on most college campuses. Substance abuse disorder is the number one disease for a large portion of the population."

"Besides that," Jenna added, "the government might be able to stop some of the imported drugs from getting to the vulnerable, but domestic chemists and suppliers will quickly fill the gap until society finds a way to slow down the demand. What do you think some of the more desperate expert chemists who recently lost their research funding are going to do with their skills in order to pay their bills? Home grown designer drugs will undoubtedly replace the foreign supplies."

"I agree with you, Jenna. The good people of the world spend a lot of their resources trying to police and contain the messed-up people of the world. It would be far less costly to help them not be so messed up.

"I must say, I admire you and your foundation's dedication to this unappreciated cause. If what was done to August Rincade is a crime, then I want to solve it."

31

OCTOBER 11 - MORNING

Elsie, and a minute later Charly, entered the conference room wearing lab coats over their scrubs. They greeted the police people, and each gave a deferential nod to Jenna.

Elsie watched as Detective Towser took in the sight of Charly. Her lab coat was open so that her rat tattoo was peeking out from the V-neck of her fire-engine-red scrubs, and Towser was having trouble averting his gaze.

C.C. McAllister also observed Garrett Towser's reaction to Charly, and she detected a flash of jealousy in the squinty little face of Elsie Rincade. If one could overlook his premature balding and strangely scarred nose, and maybe add twenty pounds of muscle to his slight frame, Garrett Towser wasn't too bad looking for a nerd. The receding hairline did make him look older than twenty-four.

Once they were all seated, C.C. said, "I wanted you all to know that the initial cocaine analysis indicates that what was in August's system was not the legal form of cocaine hydrochloride that came from this lab.

"We understand that medical grade cocaine is still stocked by hospitals because it's still the most effective topical agent for uncontrollable bleeding, as well as being a quick-acting anesthetic. There aren't too many independent laboratories that are licensed to do cocaine research like this one is. We understand that there's high security expense and risk involved in doing the kind of research that you're doing.

"Our police department did not know about the supply of cocaine that you stock here, and now we're a little worried about it. We're glad you keep your doors locked and that you so carefully screen the people who work in and visit this facility. We appreciate your diligence in exercising these security measures.

"The government's Drug Enforcement Agency (D.E.A.) has a highly specialized lab that now uses a chemical analysis system that can identify the soil signatures of plants. With a rapidly growing data bank, the source plant that a particular batch of cocaine has been extracted from, can pretty much be pinned right down to the valley it was grown in. Then, another data base can tell us if the farmers in that valley are selling their crops to the legal buyers who process the plant into medical grade cocaine, or to the highly competitive black market. Being able to recognize regional soils variation has become a useful tool for fighting international drug trafficking, as well as for agriculture and the study of history.

"But even as we wait for the more definitive analysis, I can say that it appears that your assumptions are correct. The metabolites found in August's system were compatible with what is typically seen with the local urban strains of cocaine, most of which are cut with corn starch, baking soda, or talcum powder. The drug in his system definitely did not come from your lab.

"That evidence, along with evidence of the knockout benzo in August's system, strongly supports your suspicions. We are going to pursue this as a crime. We are currently looking at a population of recently displaced researchers for a potential suspect.

"We greatly appreciate your cooperation in this investigation, and we may continue to need to stay in touch with each of you, especially because of your expertise in matters of scientific research. Please let us know if any of you have travel plans.

"We also want the assistance of all of you in keeping us informed about August's medical condition as it could be relevant to our investigation. We have advised the hospital attorney of the legal need to know for each of you as well as for August's son Toby. It is our understanding that August's wakefulness has correlated with visits by both of his children.

"Please, if you can think of anyone or anything that might be relevant to this investigation, contact us as soon as possible. We'll do our best to also keep you informed. We know things are tough for all of you right now, so we thank you for your time."

As the detectives got up to leave, C.C. noticed that Charly was glowering at Jenna and Elsie. She could see it in her eyes. This was the kind of police work that C.C. was especially good at that could not be replicated on a Zoom call.

Maybe it was the cancellation of her gag order that had infuriated Charly, but there was little doubt in C.C.'s mind that Charly was trying to cast shade onto the rest of August's family. That was starting to look like her game plan and it left C.C. suspicious of her motives.

32

October 11 - Afternoon

Charly Swift-Rincade was struggling to hang on to hope. She had visited August every day for the last three days and she wasn't getting to see the wakeful periods the others seemed enthused about. Even though she had visited at different times of day, August always seemed to be going back to sleep when she was there.

Charly had signed consent forms for surgical placement of a PIC (Percutaneous Intravascular Catheter), for the administration of fluids and nutrition, now that they had taken the feeding tube out of his nose.

The speech therapist was working with August three times a day and she was optimistic that his swallowing muscles were coming back. Maybe in another couple of days, August would be able to tolerate some liquids, but for now, the intravenous line was critical until oral or gastric feeding could be safely implemented.

Neil had reported that August was continuing to try to occasionally lift his left fingers, and the occupational therapist had been rubbing all kinds of textures across his hands and feet, several times a day. August's fingers didn't show much activity when pressed against glass, metal, silk, satin or a warm or cold thermal pack, but he seemed to respond to the feel of faux fur. Elsie said that the furry fabric felt a little bit like rat fur and her dad had always enjoyed petting the rats.

Elsie also informed August's therapist, that female rats have softer, smoother feeling fur than male rats. Hormones could do things for hair, and petting or being petted could do things for hormones. Elsie had repeatedly pestered the hospital staff about using a therapy rat for her father. Contact with pets had proved to be a valuable intervention for comatose patients in several recent studies. However, Elsie's rat still hadn't been granted permission to visit, not by the hospital administration and not by Jenna who didn't want this potential breeder anywhere out of the lab.

Still, Elsie believed that petting Freyja could help her father. Before suffering a stroke, August had been as excited about this baby rat's precocious development as was Elsie. And baby Freyja had also liked to sit on August's shoulder.

Since the pressure measuring apparatus had been removed from inside August's skull, both Neil and Marshall had noticed that their patient was occasionally making some effort to move his head when they played certain songs for him. In particular, he seemed to respond to the song "Once in A Lifetime" by the Talking Heads.

August's neck muscles were also getting workouts from the speech therapist, who was trying to get him to protrude his tongue by putting sugar water on his lips. Caregivers were using his olfactory function to try to induce increased wakefulness, and so far, the smell of coffee was most effective. He also stirred a bit if they put coconut or mint scents under his nose, but it was coffee that opened his eyes.

The smell of Maya's sancocho stew had also impacted August's level of awareness. The blend of garlic, cloves and cilantro in a steaming hot mug, made August try to lick his lips. His olfactory lobe seemed to be the most awake part of his brain, but even when Charly put a hanky with her 'essence' under his nose, August hadn't responded.

According to recent research, a preserved sense of smell correlated with consciousness in people who otherwise appeared to be vegetative. However, none of these wakeful responses to smell seemed to be occurring when Charly came to visit, and Neil was starting to wonder why.

August's family was grateful for the little lounge the hospital provided for visitors to comatose patients. They were using the microwave to heat the coffee and Maya's fragrant stew. They were also grateful for the accommodations provided by their non-profit health care system. Its revenue seemed to be dedicated to benefitting people who were sick and injured, as opposed to providing riches for the investors who saw the misfortune of others as a profitable commodity.

But unfortunately, in another two weeks, August's health insurance benefits for intensive care would be exhausted. Where he'd wind up and who was going to cover the cost was becoming a looming issue that Charly had yet to bring up with Jenna, whose company policy was paying August's medical bills. It would be extremely costly for August to be transferred to a rehabilitation facility, and August and Charly didn't have that kind of money.

The probability that August was not going to walk out of the hospital I.C.U. in another two weeks was one more thing keeping Jenna up at night, along with her worry about her laboratory's future, her Toby issues, the police investigation and her own health problems.

Meanwhile, Charly was first grasping the gravity of her situation and realizing how unprepared she was for what lied ahead.

33

October 11 - Evening

It had been eleven days since August had suffered a horrific stroke and Charly couldn't imagine him ever coming back as her husband, let alone as her brilliant researcher partner. It would be miraculous if he even regained the ability to walk and talk. Yet, Jenna seemed willing to wait.

Charly thought that was crazy. Even if August could recover, it could take years. A competing researcher would publish data long before August was going to be able to write up their results. Waiting for what probably was never going to happen seemed stupid. Charly needed to start thinking about herself. She was still diligently doing follow-up hormone analyses on August's last treatment group of rats, and she was still collecting paychecks, but how long could that last?

Besides, she was becoming aware of Jenna having some kind of a medical problem. There had been some buzz about it in the lab when Jenna kept leaving for doctor appointments. It was actually Pearson who had been blabbering that, "Mizz Boss Lady went to the doctor again." Pearson tended to repeatedly say whatever he thought he had last heard, at least three times. Echolalia was this good-natured man's most conspicuous imperfection.

Charly was starting to fret that neither August nor Jenna would be able to run the lab anymore and she couldn't envision either Toby or Elsie taking over. If August wasn't going to recover, Charly's gig was up, and she needed to find her next one in the not-too-distant future.

Charly was one hundred percent certain she could get a good lab job almost anywhere she wanted to live, anywhere in the world. Finland offered a great ice hockey culture for women, but Charly had heard that the language was hard to learn. The Netherlands seemed like a good alternative and surprisingly, Argentina had produced some great women's hockey teams.

But what was she going to do about August; just leave him behind for Jenna and his kids to take care of? Even if Jenna wasn't going to be around, his kids weren't such a terrible option. Maybe all it would amount to was visiting him in a nursing home, though even that would be difficult for Elsie.

As for the supposition that someone had tried to kill August, Charly remained suspicious of everyone in his family. They all had motives. They all had the means. Maybe Toby wanted to destroy the lab so his mother could share her wealth with the animal rights interests he was all hyped up about.

Maybe Elsie was seeking revenge for what she perceived as abandonment. Maybe she wanted to take control of the direction of the research. Even August had recently been awed by Elsie's grasp of research design. Maybe Elsie's ultimate goal was manipulating her mother while Jenna was too involved in too many things to keep a step ahead. Charly realized she was maybe even fearful of Elsie's ability to subtly exercise control over whatever she set her insight on.

One way or another, Charly was afraid that August's big project was history. With so many scientists having recently been booted out of their labs, Jenna should have already been able to find a respectable researcher to replace August. Jenna had made it known to August that she was done with him at the completion of his current project. Maybe he had been finishing up this project too slowly for her liking, and she had decided to finish things for him, and finally get rid of Charly.

Those detectives were probably wasting their time. When Charly had spoken with Officer Towser yesterday, he'd told her that they were currently focusing on some academic researchers whose funding for addiction studies had recently been cancelled. They had identified sixteen possible suspects from this list, four of whom were of particular interest. Towser asked Charly if she knew any of the names, and she admitted knowing Merle Nobakov.

"He was my lab supervisor more than two decades ago when I was a college freshman. I also know he got caught up in a scandal and lost his job, so I guess that could make him a suspect. But if Jenna even thought of hiring him, I'd be out of this lab in a heartbeat. Merle Nobakov was a letch back when I first met him, and I wouldn't want to work with him now."

Charly had heard of one of the other people the police were looking at, but she didn't know anything about him. She felt like the police were just trying to make it seem like their suspect net had been cast far and wide, but to her way of thinking, Jenna or Toby were much more viable suspects. A too comprehensive police investigation could take forever, and Charly wanted a resolution a lot sooner than that.

~ ~ ~ ~ ~

As she mulled over her situation on her way to the summer league hockey final play-off game, Charly spotted a media van from the local TV station in the ice rink parking lot. That was a surprise. The hockey league she had been playing with for the past six years had never garnered an iota of media attention, even though some of the ex-college players in the league were professional level. Moreover, for the past five years, Charly's team had defeated every other female hockey team in the region. No one but the players seemed to care.

That media crew was probably only there because the national U.S. Women's Ice Hockey team recently won the World Cup. Big deal. Most media outlets hadn't mentioned it. There was even less interest in women's hockey than there was for a newly created spectator sport called Ice Wars, which essentially amounted to ice skaters fighting while wearing hockey garb, without there being a hockey game going on. It seemed that sports fans didn't have much of an appetite for the game of ice hockey unless there were fights.

Also, there was probably a paucity of other sports stories this week-night evening, and these news people were just grasping at straws. But perhaps, Charly speculated, she could give them some visuals that would promote women's ice hockey.

Suddenly, the thought of seeking publicity about her situation hijacked Charly's consciousness, and if she knew how to do anything, it was how to put on a show. Maybe August's story going public would invite more intense police investigation. Maybe it could bring in some tips. Maybe someone had seen the person that August was with on the night he wound up in the E.R.

Perhaps media attention would also put Jenna on the hot seat. She'd have to explain what she was going to do with her lab, now that her lead researcher was down and out. Maybe the publicity would even bring her lab down and she could go fritter away her precious trust fund on some other cause, like paying for someone to chauffeur Elsie around while Toby was busy vaccinating buffalo.

The idea of exploiting her situation publicly got Charly excited. She lived less than ten minutes from the ice rink, and she had left herself an extra hour to warm up on the ice before the Zamboni prepared it for the game. She dashed home, put on her most attention-grabbing skating garb, and dashed back to the rink in less than thirty minutes.

Then, in a neon green bodysuit with yellow feathery plumes streaming at her wrists and dancing around her cobalt blue hockey skates, she exhibited her slick skating and stick skills amidst two dozen other women who were wearing jerseys and bumper pants. She could steal a puck like a master thief. There was no question that the news team reporter and cameraman were paying due attention. The cameraman couldn't get enough of her.

When the game finally began, Charly returned to the ice in a helmet, mouth guard, neck guard, shoulder pads, a chest protector, elbow pads, heavily padded shorts, shin pads and protective gloves. Normally, she would have pinned her hair up inside her helmet, but tonight she left her ruby ringlets out to fly around the arena. Even if you couldn't see her jersey number, you knew which player was powering the puck.

Charly's emotional misery had her stoked. After a few minutes of play, she noticed that the goalie was slow to move leftward and up, and every time she got a chance at a shot, that's where she sent the puck. A genius at manually controlling pressure and direction, she knew exactly how to angle the blade to get the perfect flight trajectory. She scored in four out of six attempts and her team won, five to two.

The TV sports world went wild for her. The few seconds of tape showing Charly during warmups in her flamboyant outfit and then scoring goals during the game, had been solicited by national news networks.

"Charly Swift-Rincade, a wielder of a scalpel by day and a hockey stick by night," read the caption of the photo the TV news team had sold to the local newspaper the day after the game, along with a clip of a brief interview with Charly.

The next day, Charly's tearful interview about August's catastrophe and her personal story was being played by every news network in the country. Charly was a consummate natural in front of a camera, and who could ignore the story of a ravishing amateur athlete crushed by a profound and mysterious crime?

Reporters started showing up at the lab and Charly agreed to another interview.

34

October 13 - Evening

Charly was loving the attention to the extent that she seemed to have forgotten about August. Since having achieved national celebrity status, she had only been seen on television. Everyone in the hospital was waiting to see her in person.

Once when August's eyes were open, Marshall showed him the now infamous YouTube video clip of Charly's ice rink spectacle, and August appeared to be looking at the screen. But there were no signs that he recognized Charly or even knew what he was looking at. His visual tracking efforts were definitely improving, but none of his care providers could identify what it was that he could see. He would look at objects as intently as he'd look at people, while he remained more responsive to voices than to other sounds.

An hour before Marshall's shift ended at midnight, he used his phone to tune into the eleventh-hour news. He didn't even have to wait for the sports segment. A celebrity anchorwoman had conducted an exclusive interview with Charly Swift-Rincade, and it was getting top billing. *How An Orphan Became an Ice Hockey Sensation* was the headline the network used to rein in the viewers. Marshall propped his phone up on pillows so August would be able to see it if he opened his eyes.

~ ~ ~ ~ ~

While Jenna was preoccupied with a water line break at the Laudren Retail Plaza, Reneé and Charly had granted a well-credentialed TV news team admission to the lab. The cameraman had posed Charly against the white screen in Elsie's photo-shoot set-up, but the clip was ultimately photoshopped to show an ice-rink in the background. It looked like Charly could have been standing rink-side at a pro hockey practice in New York's Madison Square Garden.

A costume designer had her outfitted in a full-body, metallic silver leotard and a red satin varsity jacket that sparkled with rhinestones at the shoulders. Her skates were enveloped in glittery silver boot covers. A hair stylist and a make-up artist had made the most of her already attractive features. The costumer added diamond earrings in the shape of two crossed hockey sticks surrounding a ruby puck. A diamond dog collar with a big ruby in the middle was fastened around her neck.

The director nixed the rat tattoo. "You might like those creatures, but the rest of the world isn't too fond of them. Just pull your leotard up so the tattoo doesn't show, and America is going to eat you up. Perhaps some time in the future, I can get our science reporter to come out here for a story about these rats living in luxury resorts, but this story is about you and women's ice hockey. We've got to enjoy this meal while it's hot."

They propped Charly up on a tall stool and positioned her to show off her long, shapely legs. Then, the beautiful blond sports anchor-woman began: "So we heard that you had a rough start growing up in foster care. How did you learn to play ice hockey?"

"I started out roller skating on the street when I found an old pair of clamp-on skates in one of the homes I lived in."

"But, how did you know how to skate?"

"I don't know, I just did. I had seen other kids skate and once I figured out how to clamp those skates on, I just got up and skated. Actually, I think it could be something you're born with. For all the years I've worked out in ice rinks, I've seen newbies show up when some other activity got rained out, and it's 'hey, there's an indoor rink here. Let's try ice skating.'

"I can pretty much tell within a minute which of these folks will succeed, regardless of their age. Some warble for a few seconds and then, they bend their knees, push off with one foot and skate away. But most of them tend to stiffen their knees, shuffle their feet and hold onto the siderails for dear life. They can't seem to embrace the idea that you can only balance on the thin blade of a skate the same way you balance on the thin tires of a bicycle, by being in motion."

"So, how did you learn to play hockey?"

"That was actually the best thing that ever happened to me as a kid. When I was eight, they assigned me to a caseworker who had two sons that were hockey players. I asked her about their equipment in her car one day, and when she found out I liked to skate, she arranged with my foster family to take me skating with her kids.

"It came naturally to me and then, she gave me her kids outgrown equipment in a duffle bag that was about as big as I was. She'd pick me up on Saturday mornings and take me to the rink along with her sons. She was my caseworker in a few different homes until I was around eleven, and then they assigned me to another caseworker. I didn't get to skate again until my adoptive family got me rink time when I was fourteen."

The anchorwoman's voice continued as the network played the tapes. "So, as we can see in this video of your local championship game and practice session the other night, your control of the puck and your shots are masterful.

"As a golfer, I know how hard it is to perfectly angle the blade of the club in order to shape a shot, while everyone around me is quiet and I'm standing perfectly still. Hockey players do it while skating between people coming at them with sticks and everyone making noise. Hockey is such a difficult sport. How did you become so skilled?"

"I had some coaching. There were no girls' leagues back then, but I worked out with the boys' league at the local rink, and one of the kids' fathers had played college hockey and he taught us a lot. I don't know why I was a better player than most of the boys, but there was no room for girls in competition then. Now, I choose to live only in places where there's good women's hockey."

"Cut. Perfect," the director said. "We'll finish this up in the studio."

The newscaster concluded the story with videos of the U.S. Women's Ice Hockey World Cup win before the network cut to a commercial.

~ ~ ~ ~ ~

During the broadcast, August appeared to be trying to tilt his head in the direction of Marshall's phone, though his eyes remained closed. When Marshall turned his phone off, August's head position seemed more neutral and relaxed. Marshall had the distinct impression that August had been trying to listen to Charly's interview, even if he couldn't see it.

35

October 13 - Evening

Elsie was getting increasingly anxious about her mother and her own future in the lab. She was also bitterly disappointed in how slowly her father was coming around, even though the hospital neurologists were using many of the available sensory stimulation techniques that were known to benefit brain injured patients.

Elsie could appreciate that the demands of vet school were taxing for Toby, but in despair, she finally opted to call him. He didn't answer. After a few more tries, she was totally fed up with her brother.

Their family was in shambles and Toby had continued to close his eyes and ears as though his own future wasn't inextricably connected with what was happening to the rest of them. Thirty hours had gone by before Toby returned Elsie's call. He claimed he had left his phone in a friend's apartment, and he only just got it back. "How's Dad?" he sheepishly asked.

"Nice of you to inquire after a week? Do you even care?"

"I'm sorry Elsie. I have major exams coming up. This is a make-or-break semester for me, and I've been so busy studying, I haven't even bothered to eat today. I'm sincerely sorry, Elsie. So how is Dad?"

"Well, he's still alive if you actually want to know. He's started to develop a swallow reflex, and sometimes, he can keep his head from flopping forward or sideways if they elevate the head of the bed. That's about all of the progress I can report, Toby, though his caregivers think these are very significant signs of his potential to improve.

"They'd really like to get him sitting up more, but he still drifts in and out of that place he seems to go to when he closes his eyes. I guess there is progress, Toby, but I'm not so sure it's looking too hopeful anymore. Dad looks horribly old, thin and lost. I'm terrified that he's going to come back to us as a profoundly disabled man if he comes back at all."

Toby sort of grunted his concern, or at least Elsie was going to give him the benefit of the doubt for the sound she thought he might have made. Her amplifier wasn't proficient for grunts and groans.

"Dad's neurologist has been treating him with amantadine. There are reports of patients who've had cerebral hemorrhages waking up with this drug, after being in a vegetative state for five months. Those people were also treated with hyperbaric oxygen therapy, so the doctors are looking into how they can make a case to treat Dad this way. They're also considering whether or not to use transcranial magnetic stimulation.

"I've looked at this research, Toby and I don't know what to think. Those people on amantadine who woke up from unconsciousness were still profoundly disabled. Maybe Dad will do better since he's not vegetative, and he's only been unconscious for two weeks. That's if they can get the hospital ethics committee and some other regulatory body and Charly to approve of off-label treatment.

"I don't know if you saw Charly's big publicity stunt, but maybe all the media attention will help Dad's doctors get approval for experimental options."

"What publicity stunt?"

"Hmm, I guess you have been studying. It's only been on every local and national TV news network for the last two days. Charly did one of her bombshell exhibitions at the ice rink where she plays hockey. Some newsman caught it on camera, and now, video clips of women's ice hockey are the eye candy of every sports newscast.

"As of this afternoon, we've also had journalists from major media outlets calling the lab to try to get interviews with Charly, and Mom is furious with the situation."

"Yikes! I'll have to check out the news. How is Mom?"

'So, when did you last speak with her, Toby? Do you have any idea what's going on with Mom?"

"Well, I know she was supposed to get some more studies to confirm whether or not it's really MALS."

"And you haven't called her since? I know, you've been studying. Well maybe you ought to start studying for taking over the trust, Toby, because neither of our parents are in very good shape at the moment, and it doesn't look like either of them will be back to normal any time soon.

"Mom is still in pain and she's wasting away. She can barely tolerate eating more than two mouthfuls. They did the celiac nerve plexus block to see if it would eliminate the pain and we're still waiting to see if she can notice any difference.

"When I initially called you, we had just gotten the results of the ultrasound arterial blood flow velocities. It confirmed that every time Mom exhales, her celiac artery and nerves gets crimped by the median arcuate ligament.

"Now, Mom is spending all of her time trying to find a surgeon who can fix it. There are only a few in the entire country who have any experience with this very difficult procedure, and they seem to be hard to access. Moreover, it's reported that recovery from the surgery can take as long as six months."

"Yeesh. That's pretty awful. How have you been getting around, Elsie?"

"Maya takes me if Mom can't. I'm beginning to think that Maya is the only family I've got."

"Well, thank heavens for Maya. She has always been your savior. I'm sorry I'm not more available, Elsie, but I'll try to get home right after these exams."

"Yeah, you do that, Toby." Elsie abruptly hung up. Then, she felt badly about it, and she texted Toby good luck on his tests. As angry as she was with her brother, she couldn't afford to alienate him.

~ ~ ~ ~ ~

Within seconds after Elsie hung up on him, Toby received a call from Detective Garrett Towser. Garrett told him that Detective C.C. McAllister would be interviewing him on Zoom tomorrow at ten a.m. and they'd be sending him a link.

"I have a major exam tomorrow at ten in the morning in comparative anatomy, and another big exam in mammalian physiology at three tomorrow afternoon. Isn't there some way this can be postponed until after tomorrow?"

Garrett told Toby that Detective McAllister had a really tight schedule, but he'd see what he could do.

36

October 15 - Midday

Toby was stressed out. He feared he had blown his exams. As his high school buddy Owen used to say. "I went into that test *hot* because I knew the subject matter *cold*, but I *burned* 'cause I *froze*."

Yet somehow, Owen had managed to graduate, get a degree in mortuary science from the local technical college, serve an apprenticeship, and in three years, he'd become a gainfully employed undertaker. Here Toby was after four years of college and two years of vet school, and he had years to go before he could hope to earn a living.

While C.C. McAllister had been kind enough to postpone the Zoom interview until the day after his exams, Toby still didn't feel like he was prepared to answer for his failed relationship with his father. Ever since the prospect of a police investigation had come up, he'd been riddled with angst. Regrets about how he had behaved towards his father for years, and guilt over having been avoidant of his family's problems since his father's stroke, were undermining his academic effort.

Since visiting his father in the hospital, Toby had been over-indulging in junk food, sleeping poorly, studying with difficulty, and he was probably also losing ground in his budding relationship with fellow vet student Liz Wojcik.

Liz shared Toby's veganism and animal rights interests, but she was even more of an academic than he was. She was also toying with the ideas of becoming a herpetologist, (a snake doctor), or an ichthyologist, (a fish doctor). Like Toby, she also seemed befuddled about her options and her life's purpose.

Although Toby hadn't revealed much to Liz about his deep-seated despair over his family issues, she had recently suggested that he needed to 'get his act together' regarding his father having suffered a stroke and his mother having this weird MALS thing.

Liz really liked Toby, but being a vet school student was hard enough without having to play the additional role of therapist. Like their mutual friend Brigham, Liz couldn't comprehend why her handsome, gifted, wealthy friend/potential boyfriend, was running away from his storybook opportunity. To have a guaranteed career as a researcher was an unfathomably great gift.

Liz hadn't met Toby's remarkable sister Elsie or his philanthropist mother or his brilliant scientist father, but she was starting to think that there was something wrong with Toby for not embracing the phenomenal options that were within his immediate grasp.

Based on what Toby had told her about his sister Elsie, Liz also worried that Toby wasn't a caring enough person to be a good partner. Even if he had to lose a semester, it seemed like he could be a whole lot more altruistic than he was being, considering that the rest of his immediate family seemed to be dealing with profound difficulty. Liz was starting to wonder if the best thing she could do was to tell Toby that she'd be happy to resume their relationship after he figured out what to do about his family.

Of course, Liz didn't know that Toby's biggest conflict regarding his situation was trying to get over Charly. He had finally made a commitment to himself to do it.

~ ~ ~ ~ ~

"So, please tell me about your relationship with your father," was C.C. McAllister's first inquiry after their brief conversation about Toby's status as a vet school student.

"My father is a great guy, but as you've probably heard from the rest of my family, my father and I just don't see eye to eye when it comes to the rights of animals. We're on the opposite ends of that spectrum."

"I read your newspaper opinion piece from when you were a high school senior. It was well-written and thought provoking," C.C. said. "You claimed that what was done in your parents' neuroscience laboratory was unnecessary, cruel and immoral. So, what do you think should be done for people whose lives are consumed by addiction?"

Toby had dozens of examples in his head about what should not be done to innocent animals, but he didn't have any good answers for what should be done with human addicts.

"Animals shouldn't have to suffer and die because humans make stupid choices. People with drug problems can be treated without rooms full of caged animals having to be subjected to addictive drugs."

"Do you know how many humans actually beat their addiction with current treatment options?" C.C. asked.

"I've seen a lot of numbers thrown around, but it's hard to believe that anyone actually knows. And it also doesn't appear that the animals are providing any good answers to the problem, since it's getting worse. So why are we continuing to torture defenseless creatures?"

"Well, you're right about the inadequacy of treatment, Toby. Maybe three out of four humans can get through a rehab program clean, but the relapse rate could be just about as high. For some tormented souls, rehabbing and relapsing and rehabbing and relapsing becomes their entire existence. Addiction is a lifelong disease. Few can remain abstinent.

"And then there's the problem of shame. Earlier in my career I was a nurse, and I once worked for a doctor who became motivated to treat people suffering from addiction because it happened to his wife. She was this smart, healthy, responsible person who wound up with multiple pelvic fractures due to a car accident; and then she wound up so addicted to opioids that she liquidated their life savings buying drugs on the street.

"This doctor was the first in the area to train and become licensed in outpatient treatment of opioid addiction. Prior to that, addicts had to be hospitalized or spend their mornings waiting in line for their daily methadone maintenance dose, which wasn't very conducive to being able to also hold down a job.

"The office-based program this doctor initiated allowed people suffering from addiction to discreetly receive treatment in privacy, instead of in a humiliating public assembly. And wouldn't you know? The first people who came to that doctor seeking help for their carefully concealed opioid problems included a dentist, a bank president, a minister, an elementary school teacher, a construction engineer, and a city councilor. They were all law-abiding citizens doing important jobs, who inadvertently got hooked on painkillers.

"Addictive drugs overtake some of society's most functional people who often don't get counted in addiction statistics because they have the means to hide their problem. Addictive drugs also take out a lot of creative celebrities whose losses are mourned but not remedied. The stigma of being addicted keeps most from seeking treatment.

"But even if we take the shame out of addiction, office-based treatment costs money which many don't have. Insurance coverage for addiction treatment is also hard to come by. What insurance is most likely to cover are drug therapies, if only someone could invent a drug that could remedy the terrible disease of addiction?

"You're a scientist, Toby, and you're studying to be a doctor. How would you propose we help some tortured human being beat his or her addiction? Do you still believe that what your parents do is immoral?"

"I do, but so would be drugging or killing my father. That would be far more immoral. My father is a good person who was trying to do something good. I just can't partake in the way he goes about it."

"Would experimenting on humans be more or less immoral than animal research?"

"But humans would have a choice. The rats do not and that's the difference. Humans show up for clinical trials of their own free will all the time. They may even compete to get accepted into trials. They're willing to risk the possibility of unknown harm in order to try to recover from the lousy disease that they already know. Besides, some people are risk-takers and gamblers by nature.

"Giving people a choice is what pharmaceutical companies do. They would rather experiment on humans than animals anyway. You see their ads in local newspapers regularly. Wanted: Men with enlarged prostate for drug trial. Compensation for time and travel provided to those who qualify."

"I see, Toby. You're not okay with a rat living in a luxury condo and giving his body and life for research, but you are okay with some impoverished, incapacitated human having to sell his diseased body for money.

"Your views are very divergent from that of your parents, but in that newspaper piece that you wrote and now, it seems to me that your animosity is not directed at your mother who funds this research. Is there some other reason that you and your father don't get along?"

Toby couldn't think of anything to say to these painful accusations. Like his old friend Owen the mortician, on this test, he had burned because he froze. He had witnessed the dumb look on his own face on the Zoom screen, and he feared it was the look of guilt.

"I just can't live with what they do to innocent, defenseless animals," was all he could manage to say.

37

October 15 - Evening

Doctor Maximillian Siegle was an acclaimed neurologist in the frustrating field of coma care. He had witnessed the dramatic awakening of a comatose patient early in his training, and he had spent the rest of his career trying to awaken others.

Having grown up in Canada, Doctor Siegle was also an avid ice hockey fan. His interest in the sport introduced him to the story of Charly Swift-Rincade and her brain injured, scientist husband. After reading about August Rincade's research, Doctor Siegle called the lead neurologist at August's hospital to get the inside scoop. He then became persuaded that August could be a good test subject for the application of transcranial magnetic brain stimulation and other protocols he was developing that he believed would be more successful than treating comatose patients with amantadine.

Amantadine for treatment of unconsciousness had become accepted practice, though not without controversy. While improved outcomes were reported in some studies, other researchers saw no difference, and one observed worse outcomes in patients given this drug when compared to a placebo.

Doctor Maximillian Siegle had a colleague who chaired a national medical board that had the power to authorize experimental treatments for certain conditions. While it would have taken most neurologists weeks to obtain permission to implement an investigational treatment protocol, Austin Rincade's doctors were granted permission within an hour of Max Siegle making a phone call to his old friend.

Now, August's chance to be a lab rat was in Charly's hands. All of the experts felt that the sooner the treatment was started, the greater the chances that August's recovery potential could be boosted. The hospital attorney was currently getting advice on how to draw up the consent forms and if Charly could get there to sign them, they could arrange to start treatment.

Charly was conflicted. She looked at as much information as was available in order to learn about what August's physicians wanted to do, and it was truly experimental. But what disturbed her the most, was the possibility that the treatment might be just a little bit successful.

If August were to become more conscious, but still profoundly impaired, it would be more difficult for Charly to make her escape. If he stayed in his semi-vegetative state, she'd have a clearer conscience about abandoning him. With his condition as it currently was, she had very little guilt regarding her plan to divorce him and be free. That was all that she had thought about during her last few visits, as August laid there motionless with his eyes closed, seemingly unaware of her presence.

At five-thirty in the evening, nurse Marshall called Charly to tell her that the hospital attorney had finalized the consent forms. They were ready for her to sign. If she could get there this evening to formalize consent, they'd begin the treatment as soon as the equipment was set up. The neurologist on call would be glad to help her review the forms and the plans.

Still in a quandary about what to do, Charly decided to go back to the hospital and take another look at the man whose life she held power over. She was depressed and she didn't even feel like bothering to dress up for this visit, but then she remembered that her celebrity status had some reporters hanging around the hospital for the chance of snapping a picture of her. She had avoided them so far, but maybe she should take advantage of them.

Her appearance could make August's experimental treatment into another national news story. Everyone would come to sympathize with her if the story turned out badly, or perhaps, she could become the face of a medical TV show about people coming out of comas.

Charly decked herself out in a flowing white pantsuit and a wide brimmed white hat that embellished her cherry tresses. Taking the director's advice from the last video, she kept the rat tattoo concealed under a white silk scarf. Dangly earrings had her camera ready, but she didn't notice any photographers on her way to August's room.

At seven p.m., Charly found her husband propped up in a semi-reclined position with his eyes open. Sitting next to him and holding his hand was Elsie. On the other side of the bed sat Toby. He had just flown in from school.

"It's a miracle, Charly," Elsie said. "When Toby and I got here about a half-hour ago and Toby said hello, Dad opened his eyes, and he looked right at Toby, and he was trying to move his mouth. Marshall raised the head of the bed and Dad has continued to hold his head up and keep his eyes open. We've been talking to him, and I think he's trying to follow the conversation."

Charly avoided looking at Toby. She came to the side of the bed where Elsie was sitting and leaned in to give August a peck on the cheek. His eyes closed for a second but then reopened and it seemed that he was watching her as she retreated to the foot of the bed. Then he turned his head ever so slightly towards Toby.

"Here's the consent, Mrs. Rincade," Marshall said, with a wad of papers in his hand. "The forms are dense, but August's doctors are very optimistic about his potential to recover. They're excited to have this expert physician, Doctor Max Siegle, guiding them through the protocol. The equipment arrived by express delivery a few hours ago."

Charly felt like she was being cornered, and she was having a really hard time with the fact that August seemed to be more responsive to his estranged son than he was to her. She had not seen him in this more wakeful state until just now, and it jolted her. The vegetable had been replaced by a person. It was astonishing how different August looked when his eyes were open. It put a dent in Charly's guilt-free abandonment plans. In distress, she lashed out at the most convenient target.

"So, what brings you to town, Toby? I thought you were too busy with your studies to help your family out in a time of crisis. Do you think we should be giving your father amantadine when there's a possibility it could make him worse? And do you actually care whether or not your father recovers?"

Charly's kick below the belt was exactly what Toby needed to wake up from his seven-year stupor. For the first time ever, he saw Charly for who she was, besides the goddess of hormone-driven bliss. She was a psychologically scarred, selfish temptress and homewrecker. She wasn't worthy of his father's love or his own.

Now, Toby hated her for having crushed the love he once felt for his father. But he had also read the research about new treatment options, and he shared Charly's reservations, especially in view of the possibility that August might be recovering without experimental treatment.

"I want my lawyer to review this consent form," Charly announced. Both Toby and Elsie were struck by Charly's statement as she was never known to be associated with any lawyers. Why did she need one now?

While Charly and Toby glared at each other, Elsie felt her father's fingers trying to move in her hand. Elsie turned her microphone up to loud.

"Look at him, Charly! He doesn't want to be like this. I fear he's locked in. He knows what's going on, but he can't respond.

"Of course, he would volunteer to be a lab rat if there's even a chance he could regain some function. How could you not give him that chance? Look at him, Charly! How much worse off could he be?"

38

October 16 - Morning

C.C. McAllister had asked Jenna to set up an interview with Adrien Kysilia as soon as possible. Garrett Towser had identified this foreign-born, tech-savvy neuroscientist as the leading suspect on the list of researchers whose proposals Jenna had rejected and who might be looking for a new job.

Jenna had rejected Kysilia's proposal to study hormonal influences on addiction due to his inclusion of brain and adrenal gland dissections in young animals. In recent years, August had largely replaced dissection with implanted electrodes and chemical sensors. Inserting these tiny instruments into the tiny organs of their tiny research subjects was another physical skill that Charly was especially good at. August could not have done it without her.

Only after the natural deaths of their research animals would the Laudren scientists look at brains and other body parts under a microscope, and then, only if the anatomic changes were related to understanding the disease or the treatment. One didn't need to take apart an adrenal gland if imaging had already indicated that it was tremendously swollen from pumping out excessive levels of stress hormones.

Law enforcement didn't like Adrien Kysilia for another reason. His name had come up on some semi-official government list of potentially dangerous scientists. Garrett Towser had managed to dig up this list from deeply buried documents.

Before immigrating to the United States two decades previously, Kysilia had reportedly worked on the development of a weapons-grade neurotoxic gas for a foreign government. It was unclear how he had managed to gain U.S. entry. His history in U.S. laboratory research was clean, but he had moved around a lot.

Kysilia had been working on a project that had recently lost funding, and he was only a few hours away from Jenna Laudren's lab in drive-time. He was surprised by Jenna's call after not having heard anything about his proposal for several months, and he was very agreeable on the phone. His English was excellent, and his voice was in a range that Elsie would be able to hear. Jenna was able to set the interview up for the following afternoon.

Somehow suave in a sweatsuit and sneakers, sun-tanned, silver-crowned and smiley, Adrien Kysilia showed up ready to change into the customary lab scrubs. Jenna was glad that Charly wasn't there. She didn't think she'd like how these two beautiful people might have reacted to one another. Jenna had been around Charly long enough to have learned how to recognize the smell of the pheromones that this woman could set off. If she was anything other than a manual marvel, she was a testosterone tonic.

Nurse Neil's comment a few days previously about Charly having not broken through to August's olfactory awareness, had sparked some sense of vindication for Jenna. Even Maya's sancocho stew had awakened her ex-husband at the primal level. Charly hadn't. Maya had joked that August's comatose reactions to his relatives was like footwear: After spending some time in the prettier new shoes, the old broken-in ones felt so much better.

Detective McAllister played the role of Jenna's assistant as they guided Adrien Kysilia around the lab. Garrett Towser had been assigned to track down evasive Charly and was elsewhere.

As was the case for most all visitors, Elsie's unit would be the highlight of the tour. C.C. was actually looking forward to getting back to Elsie's unit herself; not only because Elsie and her rat Freyja were fascinating, but because C.C. hadn't yet written Elsie off of her suspect list. There were things about Elsie that were hard to comprehend.

Before they arrived at the breeding unit, Jenna informed Adrien about Elsie's hearing and vocal impairments and about her special abilities. Adrien responded that he had a son with cerebral palsy and the reason he had moved around so much during his career, was to find better educational opportunities for his kid, who was now a college student studying to be an entomologist, (an insect specialist). C.C. started to think about all of the horrific things a mad scientist could do if he cultivated the right insect. Science fiction wasn't so fictitious nowadays.

Jenna, C.C. and Adrien arrived in Elsie's lab as she was testing some rats for their level of compassion. Adrien said he had read studies about that but hadn't partaken in one.

Jenna explained that they briefly used a confinement cylinder to stress their rats, a plexiglass tube that the rat just fits into and can't escape from. Once a rat has learned that the tube is unpleasant, it's trained to push a lever to free another rat that it can see has been entrapped in the tube.

"After it's determined that a rat knows how to release another rat, it's put into a situation where it can choose to push a lever to free another rat, or a different lever that provides it with a favorite treat. Most rats will free the trapped rat before they'll go for the treat.

"Once we know that a particular rat is compassionate, we can use that trait as a measure of addiction. Will the rat first free the trapped rat or will it first push a lever that gives it another dose of cocaine?"

"So how compassionate is the litter you're working with right now?" Jenna asked Elsie.

"There are seven pups in this litter. They're three-and-a-half months-old. Three show strong levels of compassion for both their litter mates and unknown rats. They become very distressed in the presence of other distressed rats and would go hungry until the rat victim is rescued. Two of these pups are a little slower to rescue an unfamiliar rat but they'll release their friends quickly. One is somewhat slow to rescue both the familiar and the unknown rat, but he still shows a sense of compassion.

"And one of these boys would probably eat his brothers and sisters before he'd rescue any of them. Both his testosterone and steroid levels measure above the normal range and he's quite the little alpha bully. Would you care to guess which of these rats might have the worst addiction tendency based on their innate sense of compassion?"

Both Jenna and Adrien shook their heads no. "Neither would I," said Elsie. "Addiction can overtake the most noble among us. Our research has convinced me that addiction has nothing to do with the levels of our intellect or the kindness of our hearts. It is a disease that can strike the best of us as readily as it does the worst of us."

Jenna was starting to tell Adrien about the longevity of the Laudren rats when Elsie suddenly jerked her head, jumped up, and ran over to a rat condo.

"What's the matter?" Jenna asked.

Elsie turned back to face her visitors looking tearful. "It's Piper, the matriarch of this family. She just died." Elsie put a glove on and put the little black and white rat out on the rear patio of the housing complex.

"The other rats need to say goodbye for a while. Rats seem to know the difference between unconscious and dead, perhaps through scent. Rats sometimes groom their deceased loved ones like little morticians. Some will bury their dead, but usually not until several hours after death. Some will forever avoid the place where their rat friend died.

"I'll get Piper out of there later today and expect that her older relatives will show mourning behaviors for the next few weeks. They'll eat and sleep less. I don't know what to do about Freyja, but her mother and aunts will teach her what she needs to know. With their limited lifespans, rats are all too familiar with death and grief.

"Piper was three years and nine months old, and she passed a hearing test just last month. My dad would have wanted her inner ear studied. That's why he wanted the OTC equipment.

"Piper was the great, great aunt of Freyja, the little rat genius that I am now training. She gave our lab more than four dozen babies and when given the choice, she opted for motherhood over cocaine. She was also super quick to rescue another rat in distress. She was like you, Mom. She was a rescuer."

Jenna's pale face flushed, and she flashed a painful smile.

"What did you hear when you jumped up, Elsie?" Adrien Kysilia asked. C.C. McAllister was wondering the same thing.

"There's a rat pup in this condo that has learned to make a sound that I can hear and recognize. I think I heard her shout and then when I came close, I could hear some rats crying."

~ ~ ~ ~ ~

Adrien Kysilia left the interview after expressing intense interest in working with Jenna's foundation, with August's hypothesis, and with the most remarkable Elsie. Jenna found herself really liking this man and wanting to take another look at his research. He seemed flexible and easy-going, and she was impressed by how he had reacted to Elsie's astonishing behavior.

When the interview was done, C.C. McAllister instructed Garrett Towser to reconstruct his list of suspects. Checking out Adrien Kysilia had proved to be fruitless for the police, although it might have proved fruitful for Jenna Laudren.

39

OCTOBER 16 – OCTOBER 18

Not only wasn't there light, but even the end of the tunnel wasn't coming into focus for Detective C.C. McAllister. All of August Rincade's significant others were capable of committing crimes that they could cleverly conceal. They were all also cunning enough to create ruses that could readily send the police investigation in the wrong direction.

C.C. also perceived that both of August's wives and his daughter were being protective of his son, Toby. She decided to put the housekeeper on the hot seat. One morning after Jenna and Elsie had left their house, C.C. made a surprise visit to Maya. The woman seemed distressed by the questions C.C. asked and she wore her family loyalty like a logo.

Maya became emotional when she spoke about what a wonderful father August had been to both of his children. When she had arrived in their household, Elsie was six and Toby was twelve and August was always there for both of them. Jenna was forever preoccupied with managing the trust, the retail plaza and the lab, but being a devoted parent was August's number one priority.

However, Maya admitted, as Elsie was still learning to understand spoken language at that time, attention was so focused on her development by both parents, that Toby undoubtedly felt left out. He started to pull away from his family and hang out more with friends. Maya made a point of saying that that's what adolescents are supposed to do. It wasn't until his mid to late teens that Toby started to openly rebel against being involved with the lab.

C.C. asked Maya why, if Toby had become so strongly opposed to his parents' use of animals, that it was only his father and not his mother that he had become alienated from.

Maya hesitated. She looked down and then she started to frequently blink. Finally, she said, "I think because Toby blames his father for breaking up the family."

"But wasn't that just last year?" C.C. said. "Toby expressed anger with his father's research more than five years ago when he wrote about it in the local newspaper. Weren't the Rincades an intact family then?"

Maya rubbed her eyes as if trying to remember. "Yes, you are right. The family was together then, and both Jenna and August were angry with Toby for sending that letter to the paper. As that letter reveals, Toby was going off in a different direction."

"How so?" C.C. persisted.

"Toby was getting ready to leave for college then, and Jenna was extremely busy as she always is. August's research was starting to get a lot of attention around that time, and he was frequently away at conferences. Also, Elsie was starting to work in the lab around then and she quickly surpassed Toby in her knowledge and dedication to her father's projects. I think Toby just felt left out and resentful."

"But if neither parent was available to Toby and both were angry over the letter, why didn't he also come to resent his mother who funds this research? What am I missing here?"

Maya shook her head and shrugged. "I don't know, but Toby's a good kid. He may not have appreciated his father or his parents' research, but I cannot believe he would ever hurt anyone, let alone someone in his family. Toby wouldn't even hurt a mouse; he's a kind-hearted, sensitive person.

"Actually, Toby is very much like his mother in that he's driven to do good. Also, when I think about it, Jenna was far more forgiving than August was after Toby wrote that letter. Like Toby, Jenna has a tender heart. August continued to be angry with Toby, but Jenna quickly let it go."

C.C. came away from Maya's interview with the same impression she had going into it. Everyone in this family seemed hellbent on protecting Toby, which had only served to make him a more likely suspect on her list.

C.C. couldn't even cross Charly off of her list. If it had been planned all along that Jenna was going to bounce both August and Charly out of the lab when their current project was finished, they both would have become jobless.

That notion made C.C. wonder if there could be some sugar daddy lurking in the background that had more to offer Charly than August did. Maybe Charly was getting rid of August so she could have a more financially secure future, while also getting revenge on Jenna for cancelling them and their income.

~ ~ ~ ~ ~

Garrett Towser was assigned to tail Charly, after they had gone looking for her at the lab and found out she'd been fired. She also hadn't answered her phone when Towser had repeatedly tried to call.

During three days of surveillance, Charly had grocery shopped twice. She went to the liquor store once. She went to the ice rink early one morning. She made daily brief visits to the hospital and two visits to a salon. On the third afternoon, just after a lengthy salon visit, a woman and a man with camera equipment were welcomed into her townhouse. They stayed for almost four hours.

Charly hadn't gone out in the evenings, and her lights stayed on until almost midnight. Her voice mailbox remained full. On the evening of day three, she answered a text saying she was sorry she hadn't realized that her ringtone had been silenced. She was catching up with missed messages.

~ ~ ~ ~ ~

The tailing task hadn't been all wasted time for Garrett Towser. The computer hookup in his car had allowed him to do lots of research and entertain himself. Another candidate from Jenna Laudren's file of rejected researchers had caught his attention, but after further investigation, suspicions evaporated.

Garrett had spent some of his time watching videos of pet rats performing tricks, and other rats training to do search and rescue work in the crumbled buildings of war-torn Ukraine. Then, Garrett read about an academy in The Netherlands where rats were being trained to sniff out drugs and gunshot residue on suspects' skin and clothing. Others were being trained to sniff out bomb-making materials.

The rats were as technically accurate as laboratory tests, and with far fewer people handling evidence, the chance for error was further reduced. The rats were also much faster; a sniff or two and the arresting officers instantly knew that they had nabbed the person who had fired the gun, or that a boxful of an unknown substance was dangerous. Sometimes, results from labs would come back days after the crimes, keeping suspects, police, and jail cells on hold.

The rats were also much easier to handle, train, feed, and transport than were drug-sniffing dogs who worked with just one handler. Another concern with canines was that highly trained police dogs too often got shot in the chaos of crime scenes. Rats didn't scare criminals the same way that German Shepherds did. They were also much smaller targets, so their risk of being shot was reduced.

Moreover, the Dutch detection rats cost only a tiny fraction of what it costs to build and maintain sophisticated laboratories and pay highly trained lab technicians.

In his dreams of becoming a super detective, Garrett Towser was starting to wonder if his police partner could perhaps be a rat like Freyja. He really wanted to visit Elsie's lab again.

40

October 17- Morning

Toby was relieved to see that his mother looked less lean than when he had last seen her. She was still experiencing nearly constant pain, but it had become less intense. She could now tolerate eating more than a few bites.

Jenna's doctor thought the nerve block might have calmed down the celiac plexus, or she had developed enough collateral circulation from the big mesenteric arteries to compensate for the lack of blood coming from the pinched celiac artery. The body's ability to grow new blood vessels is one of nature's wonders, though it takes time, patience and some suffering.

Jenna was still sitting with a heating pad on her abdomen when she allowed herself to relax at the end of her long days, but she seemed less ill than she had been.

Charly had finally agreed to sign the consent for investigational treatment, two days after the forms had been drawn up, and only after August's neurologist, Doctor Iris Wittel, had put considerable pressure on Charly.

Doctor Wittel threatened to call the local reporter who had kindled Charly's rise to fame and tell him that the exhibitionist wife who publicly cried about her husband's calamitous condition was now standing in the way of the most promising treatment doctors could hope to offer.

Doctor Iris Wittel also claimed to have a son-in-law who worked for a major network and who'd be interested in August's story. Besides, what did Charly have to lose? Why would she deny this exceptional person a chance? In his current state of existence, August was profoundly impaired and on his way to chronic care at an enormous cost.

Charly finally became persuaded that she didn't want to become the public face of the terrible wife. Maybe this Doctor Iris Wittel didn't really have media connections, but the old doctor did have lofty credentials and a certain presence. Besides, August's case was already news because Charly had publicized it herself. She couldn't expect privacy now.

In the meantime, August was continuing to show responsiveness to the presence of his son and daughter and the more often they visited, the more time August showed some wakefulness. Since they had started the transcranial magnetic treatment, August's effort to swallow was also progressing.

~ ~ ~ ~ ~

Maya had taken Elsie to visit August for a third time that day, and Jenna and Toby were left alone. "Are you still trying to get in with a surgeon?" Toby asked his mother.

"No and yes. I actually found a surgeon who provided me with a telemedicine consult. He has as much experience in treating MALS as almost anyone in the world. But by the time I got to speak with this doctor, I was starting to improve. He suggested I give it more time if I could tolerate the symptoms. The development of collateral circulation could be the best cure.

"Then, I had three relatively good days in a row, and I thought, hooray, I'm getting better, and I don't need surgery. The next day, the horrible pain returned and after just having had a taste of life without that misery, the pain seemed harder to tolerate. At this point, I don't know what to do except that I need to get back to a normal life."

"What are you going to do about the lab, Mom?"

"Well, Toby, if you're not interested in picking up where your poor father left off, I might go ahead and hire someone. I just had a good interview with a researcher and I'm seriously considering bringing him on board, though I still have a lot of vetting to do. Turning our lab over to someone is a monstrous decision for me, so I'd really like to know if you think you could be interested. And if you're not, I'm going to turn the lab and the trust over to Elsie.

"I'm so sorry I have to put you on the spot like this, Toby, but if I have to go for this surgery, I need to know that the Laudren NeuroScience Foundation will carry on. It's been my life's work for almost three decades.

"I had always hoped that you would be my successor, but I understand that your heart isn't in it. You have other goals. You're an adult. I'm not going to tell you what to do with your life and I'll continue to finance your education if that's your choice. But I can no longer delay in re-establishing ownership of the lab and operation of the foundation in the event that I'm not going to be around much longer.

"My other question to you now, Toby, if you're not interested in taking over the lab, is this: will you be available to help Elsie? Will you back her up if she has a health crisis? As you suggested when we previously discussed this, I'm thinking of turning the trust over to Elsie.

"Again, I know I'm putting you in a tough spot, but I need to know where your loyalties are. If your life plans can't intertwine with Elsie's and mine, I will make Maya the secondary trustee to Elsie. I'm sorry, Toby, but that's where things are at. You don't have to answer me this minute, but next week, I'm meeting with my attorney to update the trust and lab ownership. I have to do that before I even consider surgery.

"Please also let me know if you have any interest in meeting the scientist I may replace your father with before I make my final decision.

"And, oh, by the way, I fired Charly yesterday. Maya's son José has become quite competent, and he can finish up the hormone analyses. I can interpret and write up the results, and the scientist I'm interested in hiring likes to do his own dissections."

After a minute of stunned silence, Toby asked, "But who's going to pay for Dad's care, Mom?"

"Your father's wife will have to purchase private health insurance. I can't keep either of them on the payroll anymore. Hopefully, they have some savings that Charly hasn't spent on facial rejuvenation. I warned them months ago that they better find themselves a new lab to screw around in when their current project was finished, and at this point, it's finished."

"But Mom, Charly doesn't have the means to provide Dad with good care. He'll wind up in some substandard nursing home with neglectful care. I can't believe you would do that to him. You're too kind a person. He was your husband for twenty-eight years."

"Well, Toby, after twenty-eight years, I can't believe what your father did to me, to Elsie, and to you. I've wanted to forgive him, but I haven't been able to. The deception was too devious. The hurt is too deep."

"I believe you, Mom, but I know you. The hurt will be deeper if you allow Dad to rot in some crappy facility."

"So, what would you do, Toby, to prevent your father from facing an unfathomable fate? He's not my partner anymore but he's still your father.

"And what will you do, Toby, if Charly somehow persuades the police that you or I orchestrated your father's undoing? Do you have any idea about the magnitude of the crises that we are all facing, or is your head just buried too deeply in your textbooks?"

41

October 17 - Afternoon

It wasn't Doctor Iris Wittel who put Charly back in front of a camera. Charly's new-found celebrity status was about to be boosted by a hungry free-lance photojournalist looking for an enticing interview that could win over an editor. Kristy Findalson hadn't produced a salable news piece for weeks, she wasn't getting good tips, and she was in desperate need of a hot story.

The major network producer who most often bought Kristy's interviews didn't give a fig about ice hockey, but he certainly seemed to favor stories about attractive women. Pretty females in awful situations seemed to be especially newsworthy. Stories about ordinary women in desperate situations or doing magnanimous things, rarely resulted in robust ratings.

The ice hockey clips of Charly Swift-Rincade were still occasionally flashing across screens, and the skater's story about growing up in foster care seemed alluring. Kristy suspected that there could be some juicier details embedded in that history, and maybe she could squeeze it out of this jezebel while public interest in the skater was still fresh.

Charly had already been terminated from her position when Kristy Findalson showed up at Renée's reception desk at the Laudren NeuroScience Laboratory. Renée buzzed her in after checking out the journalist's press credentials. Kristy was devastated to think she wouldn't be able to get the story when she was told that Charly didn't work there anymore.

Renée felt some sympathy both for Charly and for this reporter, and she decided to call Charly and ask her if she would want to meet with this person.

Charly didn't hesitate for a second before agreeing to do an interview with Kristy Findalson. She'd never heard of the reporter, nor had she ever seen any of the celebrity athlete interviews the reporter boasted about having done, but Charly figured any publicity she could muster right now might be the best solution to her suddenly devastated life.

Out-of-work with no new prospects for employment, and tethered to a semi-vegetative husband, Charly didn't have enough resources to even stay in her townhouse beyond the next two months. She had never been a saver. Her childhood had left her with a fatalistic attitude and whenever she had had some extra money, she'd spent it on herself.

Before marrying her, August had lived a privileged life on Jenna's wealth, and he had no savings of his own. If he had ever squirrelled away some assets, Charly had no knowledge of what or where. Charly regretted not having gotten out from under Jenna's thumb when August finally sought a divorce, when they still might have been able to take their project to another lab.

Even before Jenna had given her the axe, Charly had started to realize that finding a new position wasn't going to be nearly as easy as she had initially anticipated. Research labs were being shut down throughout the United States as an anti-science administration withdrew funding from universities and other research facilities. Funding for the study of many human afflictions had either been reduced or outright cancelled.

Leaving the U.S. would be a better option, but Charly hadn't yet figured out how to escape her marriage. What if August had debts she didn't know about in addition to all of the medical bills? She could be in debt for the rest of her life. Maybe she needed to sneak off somewhere and change her identity. She wondered what she'd look like with short, spiky black hair.

Charly called several former colleagues hoping they could direct her to someone who would be eager to hire a person with her skills, only to learn that these people were also looking for work. One was emigrating to Scotland. One of Charly's old colleagues said she had established a dog walker service, and she was earning the same income she did as a lab tech. However, without the company's health insurance benefits, she was unable to afford health care.

Charly feared that she was going to have the same problem, and she was starting to panic about what she was going to do with all of August's medical bills when Jenna stopped paying them.

It was now apparent that Jenna was no longer waiting for August to recover. She had actively been trying to hire someone to take his place even before August had a stroke, and she was probably about to actually do it. On her last day at the lab, Charly had heard Pearson prattling about the interviewee who had recently been given a tour of the lab and had been introduced to Pearson. "Mizz Boss Lady has a new ratty doctor. New ratty doctor. Ratty doctor."

It was all too distressing and Charly turned her thoughts to what she should wear for the upcoming interview. She needed to present herself as a dedicated worker that any employer would be eager to hire, but that caused her conflict. She didn't know if she should present herself as modest and serious, or whether she should flaunt her sexuality.

What she did know was that she needed to find a source of income in a hurry and get the message across to someone out there that she was for hire.

42

October 17 - Afternoon

Toby had surprised his mother when he offered her his opinion of Adrien Kysilia's research. He had apparently read most of it, and he liked its creativity and its direction, except for the dissection part. But he also realized that Kysilia hadn't had access to the latest generation of the higher-level imaging tools that Jenna had invested in. The gold standard of dissection was losing its luster as technology continuously improved, though the cost of keeping up with the technology was beyond the reach of most scientists.

While Toby hadn't yet addressed Jenna's plan of turning the trust over to Elsie and Maya, he was paradoxically showing some interest in the future of the lab. Jenna sensed her son was suffering from all kinds of internal conflicts and probably wasn't in an appropriate state of mind for making monumental decisions. But in times of crisis, who is?

Jenna had been hardened by having tragically lost almost everyone in her family and by her disastrous reproductive history. She had always counselled herself that a competent human learns how to cope with whatever's thrown at them: disease, disability, deceit, divorce, death and darkness. Like Elsie, you have to generate your own light. You carry on and make the best of what you've got. Of course, it helped to not also have to be dealing with poverty or war.

Jenna hoped that like Elsie, Toby was also resilient. According to science, there are genes for resilience which unfortunately not everyone inherits. Jenna believed that she, August, Elsie, Maya, and even Charly were all especially resilient people. They had all outplayed the deck that life had delt them.

At least Toby was interested in meeting his father's potential replacement. Perhaps, he could see himself winding up in the lab some time down the road, and that gave Jenna a little bit of hope. Maybe her son was beginning to look beyond the dark filters he had come to view his parents' research with. Maybe he was starting to see what was at stake.

To Jenna's astonishment, Toby volunteered to come with her and Elsie to meet Adrien Kysilia for a continued discussion of August's research.

Adrien was very interested in Toby's veterinarian school curriculum. Did vets learn dissection as part of their surgical training? What percent of vets were becoming specialists? Were most young vets trying to stay independent or work for corporations? What were they teaching veterinarians about widely used research animals like rats and mice? Did sick or injured research animals ever show up in veterinarian offices?

Toby pointed out that there were options for veterinarians that did not require cutting animals up. There was radiology, infection control, acupuncture, reproductive technology, public health, education, and of course, clinical research as opposed to laboratory research.

Since attending vet school, Toby had also come to believe that it was absurd that all capable human beings aren't educated in important life skills, like how to set a broken bone, drain an abscess, repair a laceration or deliver a baby. Many of Toby's fellow vet students who had grown up on farms seemed to know how to do these important things. Some even knew how to remove foreign bodies from goat guts and perform emergency caesarian sections on sheep.

After Adrien and the Rincades exchanged more ideas about the direction of August's research, Jenna was again surprised by how much Toby knew. He had apparently been reading August's publications. Jenna wondered if he had just started doing that, or had he been doing it all along?

"How is your father doing?" Adrien asked as they all became more comfortable with each other.

"We have some hope that the transcranial magnetic stimulation is helping," Toby said. "He's not drooling anymore when he's awake. His throat muscles are working to the point that he can swallow some Jello. Maya, our family's guardian angel, made him some blobs of Jello infused with coffee, and that seemed to get his mouth going. Today, they'll try some liquid, like a teaspoon of the sweetened water they've been putting on his tongue. 'Baby steps,' but at least we can see some progress.

"But it's not all progress. Even though they work his muscles daily, he's just wasting away. It's stupefying as to what sixteen days of debilitation can do to a man. I asked Nurse Neil where things stand with Dad's nutrition. He said the doctors have recommended that they go forward with the gastric tube placement, but Dad's wife wants to give the swallowing issue more time."

"I'm so sorry that it's that bad," Adrien said, "but maybe he'll improve if they can boost his nutrition. Why would the wife wait if he's just wasting away?"

"I asked Dad's nurse what we can do about this because Charly, Dad's wife, has power of attorney. He said we can contest her power of attorney in court if there's evidence that she's not acting in his best interests. However, with his swallowing starting to improve, Nurse Neil thought a judge might rule in Charly's favor if we were to take this to court right now. Dad would probably have to be even more emaciated before a court would rule against her."

Toby turned to his mother and sister. "You've seen him every day, so you probably don't appreciate how seriously Dad has shrunk, but I was alarmed when I visited him yesterday."

Jenna gulped. "Things could be even more complicated than a decision about the feeding tube. Based on the agreements August and I had when we were still each other's power of attorney, August probably declared that he would not have wanted for his life to be sustained if he were to be in a persistently vegetative state. But how are the courts supposed to decide about this when the family and the professional caretakers don't even know what to make of his level of consciousness? When we made those declarations, we never considered whether or not we would want to be kept going if we landed in a minimally conscience state."

"Yikes," Adrien remarked. "You and probably everyone else who thinks they would know what they would want in such a situation, without even realizing what the situation could be. This is scary."

"Dad would want to keep going," Elsie interjected. "I'm sure of it. He's never been a quitter, he's a fighter. He's been a fighter his whole life. He's trying to wake-up. I can see more effort every day. He wants to come back to us."

"I'm not so sure of that, Elsie." Toby argued. "After seeing him yesterday, all I could think about last night was that Dad would not want to exist this way, not in the state he's in. What makes you think that he would, Elsie? Would you want to be in Dad's situation? Do you really think that he would choose to be so disabled that he's a burden on others? I doubt very much that's what Dad would want for himself or for us."

Adrien was distressed to find himself inadvertently immersed in this intimate family discussion. He could see that Jenna was holding back tears and Elsie was letting hers flow. He felt guilty for being there, but it was because of this family tragedy that he was there.

Although Adrien was a total outsider, as a father of a disabled son he could relate to these people. It seemed that August's kids were each projecting their own feelings onto their unfortunate father. The sad truth was that no one could really know whether or not August Rincade wanted to stay and fight. In this undefinable situation, even those closest to him could not know.

Adrien pitied the healthcare professionals who had to make such decisions, and he couldn't fathom how a judge could do so, let alone some activist in a statehouse. Adrien was reminded of the Washington leaders who had once decided that Teri Schiavo, a young woman whose cardiac arrest left her in a persistently vegetative state, should be artificially kept alive, in spite of what those closest to her thought would have been her wishes.

After seven years of politicians capitalizing on this horrific family dilemma, and overburdened courts trying to intervene, braindead Teri

Schiavo was finally granted peace when her feeding tube was removed in 2005. Adrien Kysilia had paid attention to this story because it had been in the news at the same time that he had first arrived in the U.S., seeking better care and opportunities for his baby with cerebral palsy.

Adrien was also aware of a current controversial case in the state of Georgia, where a pregnant woman who was braindead was being artificially kept alive to preserve the life of her fetus. This mother-to-be stroked out in her second month of pregnancy. Without consent from her family, she was connected to a ventilator and a feeding tube was surgically placed in her stomach, so that her surviving organs might continue to support a motherless fetus with a seriously questionable future.

Adrien surmised that there were people in power who believed that it's within their rights, as the American phrase goes, to beat a dead horse. Would mandatory organ donation come next?

Although he hadn't admitted it to the Rincades, Adrien had seen those ice hockey videos of August's wife Charly. He hoped there wouldn't be any more journalists or politicians jumping in on the case, but he worried. In the new scenario of U.S. scientists being shut down, a crafty journalist could run August Rincade's story through the wringer.

Adrien Kysilia feared background checks and journalistic scrutiny. He had once been forced into working for a bad cause for a government that he had risked his and his family's lives to escape from. He knew first-hand how powerful people could exploit science and scientists in extremely evil ways.

Adrien didn't need to be immersed in publicity of any kind.

43

October 14 – October 18

As a detective for the U.S. Drug Enforcement Agency, (D.E.A.), Spencer Parrow had been tracking the sources of cocaine in college populations for the past three years. With the experience of a forty-year-old, but an exceptionally youthful and unimposing appearance, he was a successful undercover agent on campuses.

Laboratory analyses had recently identified a particular cocaine signature in multiple student deaths. Now, this strain of cocaine had just shown up in a criminal case at the same time that the story of the crime appeared on the national news because of an ice hockey performance by a strikingly attractive woman.

Abuse of amphetamines, cocaine and other stimulants amongst ice hockey pros had been a problem for decades. Hockey players ranked high amongst athletes who suffered serious injuries, wound up on painkillers, and slid into the culture of recreational and performance enhancing drugs. Anabolic steroid abuse by an array of athletes was a persistent issue for law enforcement and sports regulators. Random drug testing by the hockey leagues was now helping to curb these problems, so Spencer hadn't been screening hockey players for cocaine deaths. Now he was wondering if he should be.

The D.E.A. lab had determined that the strain of cocaine identified in August Rincade's case was associated with an especially high level of lethality. This drug was frequently causing fatal and disabling heart attacks and strokes in college kids who wouldn't normally be dying and becoming crippled like this.

The D.E.A. scientists were also concerned that the soil source of the plant was being doctored, or that the plant itself had been genetically altered in order to thwart the technology that law enforcement was using to identify the plant's source. They wondered if genetic manipulation of the plant was what was making this strain of the drug so deadly? Who knew what schemes angry, demoted, inventive geneticists might come up with, if they no longer had legitimate jobs?

Spencer put on his student attire and showed up on the campus where August Rincade had been knocked out. After the first day of observation, he had scoped out where some of the drug deals were likely taking place. On a grassy central plaza, crisscrossed by stone pathways and benches, and surrounded by historic buildings, hundreds of students passed through and congregated between classes in the too warm autumn weather.

The presence of more than a few alarmingly skinny kids suggested that stimulant abuse was part of the scene. The semaglutide class of weight loss drugs like Ozempic and the popular stimulant Adderall didn't suppress appetite as much as methamphetamine and cocaine did.

In addition to very thin people, Spencer paid attention to little, brief congregations. He'd managed to snap a photo of a guy in a black leather jacket and oversized sunglasses who kept appearing in two-person meetups. An anorectic looking girl had also registered on his internal radar but had eluded his camera.

On the second day of surveillance, a young kid caught Spencer's attention when he locked a high-end bicycle into a stanchion. He was wearing the same orange sweatshirt that Spencer had noticed the day before. He looked like he might be in middle school, not college.

The kid stood next to a shrub that bordered the steps to the college library. It appeared that he was texting on a phone. A minute later, a man wearing a university logo sweatshirt appeared and the cyclist kid gave him something out of his pocket. He then put something into his pocket, retrieved his bicycle, and rode off in the direction of town, while the package recipient disappeared into a throng of passersby.

Spencer had managed to snap photos of the deal with a camera concealed in his smart sunglasses, which transferred the pictures to his phone. On day three, Spencer saw the cyclist kid again. He jumped on his rented moped and tailed him to the other side of town where the kid disappeared into an old, small house along with his bicycle. It was the sort of neighborhood where the kid's bike might have been more valuable than the shabby house in which he was stowing it.

Spencer suspected that one of the residences on this street was home to a basement chem lab. Spencer had spent the last few years working with a canine unit including a German Shepherd who could identify a meth lab and a Labrador retriever who could locate a lab that was producing Ecstasy. But traveling with these dogs was logistically difficult.

Some of the dogs, whose sense of smell is a thousand times more sensitive than that of humans, could hit on a person whose pocket had recently contained even a few grams of cocaine. Spencer especially liked working with an English springer spaniel named Shirley, who was irresistibly adorable in her bejeweled pink collar. When she smelled cocaine on a person, she would sheepishly approach them wagging her tail and then lie down at their feet. The suspects would never deduce that they were being fingered for cocaine possession. Most of them just wanted to pet Shirley. But once word about a drug-sniffing dog started spreading, people avoided Shirley like she was the COVID virus.

Spencer returned to the campus where he'd seen the drug deal. It took until late in the afternoon, but he finally spotted the recipient of the cyclist kid's package walking towards the dormitory complex. As he walked up alongside of him, Spencer showed the guy his identification and advised him that the federal Drug Enforcement Agency was trying to track down the source of a lethal strain of cocaine. Then, Spencer showed the guy the video and photos he had taken of him in the exchange with the cyclist in the orange sweatshirt.

The package recipient froze at first. Then he walked along side of Spencer, trembling, sweating and stammering. He was probably high on meth. He identified himself as Joshua, a pre-law student from a family of lawyers, and he'd already been accepted into a prestigious law school for next year.

Joshua also admitted that he had a penchant for methamphetamine which he blamed on having been treated with amphetamines for attention deficit disorder with hyperactivity for most of his life. After all, Joshua explained to Spencer, he had been academically gifted, but he had also been that little boy in the back of the classroom who was either wriggling or rocking in his chair, tapping his foot or pencil, making clicking noises with his tongue, or blurting out test answers.

A Ritalin prescription helped at first, but Joshua had less anxiety when they switched him to Dexedrine (dextro-amphetamine) in third grade. Then they changed him to Adderall in sixth grade because of persistent academic anxiety. He'd also been put on benzos for generalized anxiety, and he was still taking those, too often he confessed.

Joshua readily admitted to his addictions and rationalized that at least meth was cheaper and easier to produce and access than cocaine. As if Spencer didn't know the pharmacology, Joshua recounted that meth is at least three times more powerful than coke, and it lasts much longer with each dose. Joshua couldn't figure out why cocaine was some peoples' drug of choice, but he also knew that his rapidly accelerating meth addiction was the road to hell.

Joshua actually felt somewhat relieved to have been caught and to be forced to try to reverse course. He stopped shaking as soon as he decided that he'd just tell Agent Spencer Parrow absolutely everything he knew, so long as doing so could keep him out of jail. He'd been part of the campus drug scene for three years and while he stayed away from cocaine, especially the pink stuff, he knew where to get it.

Agent Spencer Parrow could not have found a more willing and helpful informant. His next step was to coordinate with the local police to see what they might know about the campus drug issues and August Rincade's case. He contacted a Detective C.C. McAllister who had sent Rincade's specimens to the D.E.A. lab.

C.C. had expected and hoped that someone from the D.E.A. office might move in on the case and she welcomed the assistance. So far, she had no evidence of anything beyond what the D.E.A. lab had confirmed.

C.C. informed Spencer that the college had its own police force that worked cooperatively with the local police. However, the narcotics people on her force were rarely called in for campus drug issues. Or perhaps, the campus drug issues weren't really issues because the college admin chose to ignore this all-too ordinary aspect of student life.

C.C. also told Agent Parrow that there was a canine in her precinct, a Jack Russell terrier named Winston, who could smell a meth lab from a block away. The narcotics team could jump on the cyclist kid's address as soon as the weather improved. The forecast was for rain and high winds for two days and little Winston's nose needed dryer air.

Detective McAllister also told D.E.A. Agent Parrow about August Rincade, the nature of his research, and the jilted ex-wife who owned and philanthropically funded a research laboratory. She further informed Spencer about the abandoned disabled daughter, the estranged son, and the celebrity hockey player/femme fatale wife over whom the family had fractured. C.C. was also troubled by the current wife seemingly wanting to pin the crime on the ex-wife.

Then, C.C. told Spencer about the numerous defunded scientists competing for the philanthropic support that this laboratory could offer, a list of potential suspects that was rapidly growing as funding for brain disorder research kept disappearing.

C.C. also told Spencer that the chief of her police force was in a rage about the current wife having taken the case to the media, putting their investigation under the public microscope.

In turn, Spencer Parrow told C.C. McAllister about some of the mob bosses involved in cocaine trafficking who could also be considered as suspects. Some of them were sophisticated enough to be following research that could be threatening to their trade, like the kind of research that August Rincade had been doing. Well-published scientists were especially at risk.

Spencer also informed C.C. that some of these drug trafficking organizations seemed to be actively recruiting scientists whose labs or projects had been shut down. The mob bosses could afford to pay these researchers much better than universities ever could, so it was difficult for some of these out-of-work people to not be drawn to the dark side.

C.C. didn't have the resources that would be needed to effectively whittle down her long list of potential suspects, but Spencer had greater resources. He planned to submit the case to AI to see what it came up with.

44

October 18 - Afternoon

Kristy Findalson was bewildered by the starkness of Charly Swift-Rincade's living room. The walls were white, the furniture was light gray and what little art was on the walls was of little interest. There were no plants, no family photos and the window shade was drawn in the middle of the afternoon. It felt like the sitting area of an old roadside motel, except for an ultramodern sleek desk on which sat multiple computers.

Charly looked gorgeous and she reeked of hairspray. She wore a tailored white jacket opened to show off a skintight knit turtleneck in forest green. It highlighted her green eyes and her red hair, which was piled up into a stately bun with springy tendrils that framed her face. Dangling on a gold chain, a big white moonstone heart landed perfectly at the triangle of her cleavage. Her tops were paired with a white leather pencil skirt with a front slit, white strappy stilettos, and a gold chain link belt that ended in a down pointing arrow over the skirt's center front seam.

Cameraman Blake Findalson opened the window shade and chose the direction of the shoot. He replaced an armchair with a stool from the kitchen, set up some lights and positioned Charly's head and shoulders for a short practice clip. Charly was stunned by how well he had featured her profile as she smiled and spoke. She had never before seen herself in that particular way.

Blake Findalson was born to be a portrait photographer. Growing up with a basset hound, a pug, a Persian cat, and two younger siblings, he had become an astute observer of facial expressions. When given a camera, he somehow learned to capture faces from the right angle at the right moment, and he had an uncanny ability for making them look better than their human owners thought they looked when seeing themselves in mirrors.

Blake started doing photo shoots for babies and pets as a young teen and by the time he finished high school, he had more business than he could handle. Still, he put his mother first when he wasn't contracted to do a wedding. Kristy's interviews sometimes got national attention, and he saw his mom's success as the key to his own future. He also thought that photographing this captivating hockey woman was going to be both joyful art and play.

Charly signed a bunch of release forms that basically said that the film could be edited and presented without restrictions, and that there could be no liability for anyone involved in its creation or use.

Charly watched a prerecorded clip of Kristy starting the interview, which featured the previously broadcast videos of her hockey performance.

"Hi! Kristy Findalson here with ice hockey sensation Charly Swift-Rincade. If you haven't been living under a rock, you've seen her punishing the puck and the opposition goalie. Ouch! Watch her score over and over again and just watch her tear up the ice when she's practicing."

Blake announced that he was starting to film.

"So, Charly," Kristy continued, "how does it feel to have the whole world watching your hockey skills? Do you think female athletes are appreciated for being talented or are they just sex objects?"

Charly just about fell off of her stool. How she wished she had checked out some other interviews by this reporter before consenting to this. She was prepared to try to garner sympathy for her criminally assaulted husband, and to appeal to an employer somewhere out there in the research world. She was not prepared to be the subject of tabloid sensationalism.

The best defense was an offense, Charly reminded herself. That's what hockey had taught her and that's how she had gotten through life. "I think the really skilled athletes, just like some of the most successful female journalists, are appreciated for their abilities regardless of their appearance."

Now it was Kristy on defense. "But would women's beach volleyball ever get the media coverage it gets if the women wore clothing that protects them from the sand and sun? What athlete wants to perform with burnt skin and sand up their butt and crotch?"

Charly laughed. "Well amen to that, but protective clothing is a very different story in ice hockey. We don't show skin because we don't want ice burns. Maybe that's why no one watches women's hockey. No, I doubt that highly skilled volleyball players would get media attention if they wore tee-shirts and shorts. Maybe, nobody would watch them either.

"But now that I think about it, quite a few of the women sportscasters I see on TV also seem to have to dress in uncomfortable clothes. They also often have to sit with their legs bared, while the male sportscasters' legs are concealed in pants and are behind counters. Why? I like looking at men's calves.

"It also looks like the female judges on some of the popular talent shows are made to wear seductive clothing to a level of discomfort. And look at how the rock stars dress. What about ballet dancers and figure skaters spinning around spread eagle in micro miniskirts? Why are you picking on volleyball players?"

Charly was on a roll and Kristy opted to give her a downhill ramp.

"I think women are treated as sex objects in all walks of life, but athletes sometimes attract more attention because they *are* highly skilled. Still, they probably don't get a fraction of the media attention paid to male athletes. Lately, some prominent female athletes are getting publicity because their salaries are so much lower than are those of less talented men playing the same sport."

Kristy hadn't anticipated being able to spar with this interviewee. Now she was hoping it could get really feisty. The producers loved verbal scrimmage.

"Well, you're not even a pro, Charly. You're just an amateur player in a local women's hockey league and you're getting major media attention. Do you think that's because of your hockey skills or because you're a pretty damsel in distress?

"And by the way, how is your husband doing?"

"Thank you for asking," Charly said condescendingly, while seizing an opportunity to change this obnoxious subject and promote herself. "My husband, a brilliant researcher, remains severely impaired, and the police have no leads as to who tried to kill him. It's my hope that I will be able to continue his research if he can't do so himself. We worked together on developing a cure for addiction for seven years and we were almost there. I pray I will be able to continue his research should he be unable to."

Kristy had done her homework, and she'd previously decided that neither addiction research in rodents, nor a crime against a scientist, were going to excite the sponsors or the producers. Neither story was sexy enough and she had to shift gears.

"I noticed in the state marriage records and news files, Charly, that before you went to work with and married your current husband, you were previously married to someone who went to jail for stealing the drugs out of another research laboratory. You were married to him for two years and before that, you were married to someone else for two years, and seven years before that, you were married to someone else for five months. With your looks, I imagine you have to fend the men off with weaponry, so how come you keep picking the wrong guy?"

Charly was thinking about kicking Kristy Findalson in the groin at this point, but she managed to maintain her composure. *Stay on the offense,* she reminded herself.

"Well Kristy, you left out some of the relationships I had before, during and after those marriages and since you've asked, I was always just looking for the better man. And finally, I found him, and now some monster has taken him from me. And not only have they taken my husband and my professional partner, but they've taken my best friend."

Charly's voice started to quaver, and Blake focused his lens on her watery eyes. Kristy turned to Blake and said, "Cut! Let's take five." This wasn't going in the direction she had planned, and she needed to rethink her line of questioning. Then, she thought of another tactic, and she turned back to Charly.

"Sorry I have to be so nasty, Honey, but it's what the viewers want. You're doing a fantastic job of being the fierce female, but if what you want is some sympathy from the fickle public who watch my interviews, you ought to play up your crappy childhood. People love sob stories, especially from adopted orphans who go on to greatness.

"You *are* the perfect damsel in distress that the public will want to root for. They already love you as an athlete and a beauty; now all you have to do is bare your soul. Just a suggestion, Charly. My viewers need smart female heroes that they can relate to, and you've got the brains to go with the looks and the talent. The puck is in your zone.

"And may I please use your bathroom?"

~ ~ ~ ~ ~

While Kristy sat in Charly's powder room trying to assess how to alter her approach with this manipulator, Charly excused herself to her kitchen where she chugged giants gulps from a gin bottle she kept stowed in her freezer. She only drank alcohol when August wasn't around, and he surely wasn't around now.

Just the thought of publicly talking about her childhood made her want to drown herself. She didn't like remembering it and she rarely talked about it, even in private.

45

September 30 – Afternoon

Spencer Parrow's time on the local campus had been fruitful. His informant Joshua had ratted out three sources of methamphetamine, two of cocaine and one each of Ecstasy and heroin. Spencer had called in assistants to help shakedown these campus drug mules.

Winston the terrier had sniffed out the local meth lab and this fire hazard had been extinguished. Ever since methamphetamine was created by a German pharmacy in 1938 as a nonprescription drug, marketed to soldiers for wakefulness and alertness, it had been both beneficially used and seriously abused. As informant Joshua had put it, "I've lived a privileged life, but nothing compares to that meth level of euphoria."

The meth lab delivery boy had been rehomed and enrolled in school for the first time in three years. His chemist stepdad was in jail, his addicted mom was in rehab and his two younger siblings were in a different foster home.

This thirteen-year-old cyclist, who had been charging a thirty-dollar delivery fee for the first five miles of his reliable service, had also ratted out another neighborhood chem lab that was cranking out a stimulant compound that they were calling 'nice ice.' Lately, Spencer's sophisticated government lab had been seeing more and more of these novel, homemade compounds. The production of synthetic amphetamines was clearly moving from the pharmaceutical labs to the basement labs as chemists found themselves out of work.

One of the campus cocaine dealers that Joshua had put him in touch with, had led Spencer to a tentacle of a major drug trafficking organization that hadn't previously been detected in this region. Now it seemed to be infiltrating everywhere in the U.S. while the feds still hadn't managed to find its brain. These organizations had layers upon layers of distributors and no one at the bottom had any idea who was at the top.

As helpful as ratfink Joshua's information had been, Spencer and his lab scientists still hadn't been able to identify the source of the lethal strain of cocaine that was associated with the bad outcomes of two of this college's students, as well as the cases of August Rincade and multiple students from other colleges.

Spencer was determined to track down the source of this bad coke, but his work on this campus was done. Most of the college drug community was on high alert for an undercover narcotics agent and the dealers were laying low.

There was also the risk that Spencer was being hunted by the security people from the drug trafficking organization that was supplying the campus dealers. These drug traffickers were extremely protective of their networks and territory, and they employed highly competent hitmen. Spencer would never again wear the wig, glasses and clothing that he had worn for this investigation, and he'd bleach his black eyebrows back to their natural light brown.

Spencer's informant Joshua also had to drop out of sight. He withdrew from school and was on his way to a secure, remote rehab facility for government informants. He planned to transfer to another college once he got clean. Joshua and his family were ultimately grateful that he got caught the way that he did, though he sure missed his meth. He knew it wasn't worth throwing his life away for, but he also didn't know if he could beat his addiction. During the previous few months, it had completely overpowered him and cures for meth addiction were of limited success.

Like other addictive substances, methamphetamine could cause profound changes in brain chemistry as well as changes in the expression of genetic traits, all of which made recovery exceedingly difficult. Joshua would have to continue to travel a long, hellacious road if he hoped to get to his destination.

While C.C. McAllister continued to look at Rincade's family and some scientists who might want to gain access to their lab, Spencer was looking at which of the drug trafficking organizations (DTOs) was most likely in control of this region. Although Mexican DTOs were suspected of being the primary source of cocaine in more than two hundred U.S. cities, Columbian and Dominican DTOs were also operating in many parts of the country. Ecstasy had typically been imported from Asia, but now domestic labs were becoming more prevalent as demand for this designer drug was growing.

It was just a fact of life that humans always had been and probably always would be seeking pleasure and euphoria in the most convenient form available, while scientists and other seekers would continue trying to improve on those routes to rapture.

~ ~ ~ ~ ~

Hoping for maybe one more clue from the medical side of the crime before moving on, Agent Spencer Parrow showed up in August Rincade's hospital room. There he encountered Nurse Neil and by happenstance, the victim's daughter Elsie.

August was semi-reclined with a bolster on each side of his head. His eyes and his mouth were open, and he appeared to be watching as Spencer showed Neil and Elsie his credentials. Spencer then turned to August and as if the man was aware, he introduced himself and explained about his mission to find and neutralize the source of a particularly lethal strain of cocaine.

"I understand you have also been dedicated to fighting the scourge of cocaine," Spencer said to an unblinking August. "I lost my twin brother to cocaine on our sixteenth birthday. I'm rooting for you, August, and I plan to find the devil whose distributing this deadly drug."

Elsie and Neil watched tears trickle down August's cheeks as he appeared to be trying to nod his head.

46

October 18 - Afternoon

"Unbelievable," Neil said. "We were so misled. When the surgical recovery team handed August's care over to me, I saw the E.R. admission note that said he was found by an unrelated bystander on the floor of a restroom in the lobby. It was also documented that the escort who brought his wallet to the E.R. told the triage nurse that he had medical grade cocaine and that his car was parked at a hotel."

"That's the only version of the story that I ever heard," Elsie echoed.

Spencer Parrow was glad he'd decided to further pursue this case with direct contact. "You're right about that part," he said, "but August wasn't found in the lobby of the hotel where his car was parked. The ambulance picked him up in a restroom in the lobby of the science building at the college."

Both Elsie and Neil responded to that information like they'd been slapped.

Spencer continued. "I met with local detective C.C. McAllister this morning. She had access to the medical records, and she also obtained the ambulance call report from before the paramedics arrived on the scene. The report indicates that 911 was called from Rincade's own phone five minutes before a second caller found Rincade in the restroom, at which time 911 was called again. The second call was from the second caller's phone.

"Rincade's hospital record included the paramedics report which suggests that the paramedics didn't know about the second call because they were already on their way. When they arrived at the scene, they just assumed that the concerned bystander who was with Rincade was the only caller.

"Detective McAllister interviewed the 911 operator who was covering that day and he indicated that the call from Rincade's phone was not from Rincade himself but someone who said that they had found Rincade passed out in the restroom. The call ended abruptly, and the caller was not identified. The dispatcher called the number back to get more information, but the phone wasn't answered. It hasn't been answered since.

"The first caller probably absconded with Rincade's belongings because reportedly, none of that was found by the second caller or the paramedics. It's also possible that someone else entered that restroom in the five minutes between those calls and took the wallet and the car keys and then decided to unload them at the hospital. Anyone could have looked up August Rincade and found out that he was a scientist working on cocaine addiction, so a third party can't be ruled out.

"There was no cash in the wallet according to the triage desk nurse who went through it to find August's identification. Up until that wallet showed up, August was just another unidentifiable, probably uninsured cokehead on his way to brain surgery."

"Actually," Elsie commented, "my dad never used cash. He used credit cards for everything. At least that was the way things were when my mom was paying the bills. But when he and I went to lunch on the day of his stroke, he paid with a credit card. And all of this confirms that my father did, or at least thought he did, have a legitimate appointment at the college science lab that afternoon.

"So why would someone bother to take his car from the college into town after knocking him out on the campus? By the way, I think it was two people because of the adjustments made to the front seats." Elsie proceeded to tell Spencer about what she had noticed when she went with her brother to pick their father's car up at the hotel.

Spencer was interested in Elsie's observations. "Here's what I'm thinking. The hotel story was a deliberate ploy, as was the escort's report about August being a scientist who could get medical grade cocaine. It worked. That was the kind of juicy information that the ER staff was apparently taken in by. Few people can resist a little scandal here and there. The culprit wanted to make it appear that August was having an affair and stealing cocaine and they did a good job of it. They had all of you believing it too until you, Miss Rincade, cast suspicion on their scheme.

"I can't think of any other reason they would have bothered to transport his car and then take his wallet and keys back to the hospital, other than to make sure that August was positively identified and that he looked like the guilty party. I strongly suspect that they wanted to humiliate him, not kill him, and the stroke was an unplanned complication.

"If they had wanted him dead, they could have just killed him. If he was already rag-dolled from the date rape drug, they could have easily suffocated him and not have wasted a big dose of their precious cocaine. They wanted him to be found alive with the cocaine in his system, or they wouldn't have called for an ambulance. They also wanted to embarrass him professionally by making noise about his being a scientist.

"Unfortunately, everyone was a little too inclined to believe that a cheating, ex-addict scientist did this to himself, and consequently the wallet and keys were never checked for fingerprints, nor was the car. C.C. McAllister wasn't on the case until six days after August was victimized when Elsie's suspicions were confirmed by a lab test. It then took another few days for my lab to receive and process the specimens and confirm that the cocaine in August's system wasn't from the Laudren lab. Only then, was Detective McAllister persuaded that Rincade was a victim of a crime.

"For the past few days, McAllister has been trying to track down evidence with little cooperation from August's wife. Apparently, when Charly Rincade was raging over the erroneous assumption that her husband was cheating on her, she threw away his keychain and his wallet after rescuing his ID, credit cards and keys. She also threw away the clothes he had been wearing when the hospital passed them along with the keys and wallet. She told Detective McAllister that the thought of the other woman on those clothes made her stomach turn.

"It also appears that Charly had August's car cleaned and detailed, which just happened to be observed by a police officer that McAllister had looking in on Charly because they had been unable to reach her by phone. McAllister suspects she's putting the car up for sale."

"Could there still be any evidence in that car at this late stage?" Elsie asked.

Just then, August made a sound, something like a cough. Neil, Spencer and Elsie all turned their heads in his direction. His eyes were open, and it looked like he was trying to move his mouth.

"Is there some clue in your car, Dad?" Elsie said close to August's ear. Blink once if yes."

August just looked at Agent Spencer Parrow and then he blinked a few times. Elsie tried again to get an answer, but his blinking and tongue movements were too random to interpret.

Spencer shook his head. "Evidence in the car might depend on whether or not the detailer did a good job. Most of them just do superficial stuff on the interior, or they bomb everything with chemicals.

"In my experience, a good dog nose can still pick up the scent of cocaine in some of the superficially cleaned vehicles in the first day or two, but it's probably been way too long in the case of August's car for even the best dog nose.

"But first, we have to get our hands on the car and sort out any fingerprints that might still be on the steering wheel, gear shift and door handles, if the detailer or the criminals didn't wipe all of that clean."

47

October 18 – Afternoon

Charly was thinking about making up some shocking phony story to feed this third-rate reporter's stupid audience, but she realized that wasn't going to help her connect with an employer in the research world. Above all else, she needed a job, and she wanted to be hired for her attributes, not out of pity.

Meanwhile, the five-minute break was stretching into a half-hour. Initially the pause was extended because the sun had dropped down to where a tree was casting shadows across the room, even with the shade down. Cameraman Blake was moving the living room furniture and his equipment around to get better lighting,

The pause got longer when Kristy seized the interlude to do some investigating on her laptop. She had already scoped out information about August Rincade's research. She'd also read some stories about the increasing incidence of substance abuse in the U.S. and around the world, especially amongst the affluent.

Wikipedia listed over six-hundred celebrities whose untimely deaths were attributed to drug overdoses, and similar lists could be found on numerous other websites. There was no web mention of the tens of thousands of ordinary individuals who had also died from drug overdoses, except for the statistics. There was no mention of the hundreds of thousands who were left disabled after surviving drug overdoses, or the family members whose lives were also ruined by their loved ones' addictions.

Kristy came across an article about how sophisticated some of the drug suppliers were becoming. Then she saw another journalist's piece about the proliferation of movies and TV shows that were about law enforcement trying to bust drug traffickers. Too often it seemed, the drug pushers were portrayed as the smart, successful people. They were surely becoming heroes to kids who might otherwise have no hope of ever being able to make a living.

Kristy was starting to think that maybe the victimization of a scientist who was trying to fight drug addiction was the more interesting and durable story. She wondered if this week's viewers would be more attracted to news about the takedown of a scientist, or the predicament of a beautiful woman who apparently needed a new job. Maybe Charly Swift-Rincade was attractive enough to stoke interest in any subject.

Then Kristy wondered, what would most likely grab the wandering attention of the news-oversaturated viewership next week? It was getting increasingly difficult to be more outrageous than what was now being reported by the mainstream media. No matter how good Kristy was at her job, and how great Blake's photography was, it was becoming harder and harder to compete with all of the daily national scandals, as well as with all of the other tabloid journalists who were also running around with cameras.

Kristy needed to rethink her approach to this story and to Charly.

~ ~ ~ ~ ~

Charly used the filming interlude to hang out in her kitchen and drink too much gin. She had taken a big gulp before Kristy and Blake arrived and it had helped her to relax. Then, she seemingly forgot that she wasn't as tolerant as she used to be. Since she had been living with August for the past year, she had practiced abstinence at home. She only drank on occasion when she'd hang out with some of her hockey team buddies after practice or a game.

Charly had never drunk excessively, but alcohol had always made her feel good. If she carefully controlled her rate of intake, the buzz made her feel warm and relaxed. Her inner conflicts felt less pressing. Her thoughts flowed more freely. She was more comfortable being social and she could communicate more openly. She could laugh more easily. And miraculously, she hadn't inherited her mother's genetic tendency to addiction. For her, alcohol was just one of life's more easily attained little pleasures.

Momentarily, Charly reveled in the idea that she could enjoy alcohol again without August around. There wasn't anything else going on in her life at present that gave her pleasure, except maybe gliding across the ice when she could get to the rink. Everything else that was going on was downright painful, especially her marriage.

Thoughts of August and all of her losses, along with the alcohol, fueled her sense of victimization. It also reminded her of why she had chosen to participate in this interview. Just then, Kristy called her back to the living room. She took one more giant gulp of gin to brace herself.

~ ~ ~ ~ ~

Kristy immediately picked up on the change in Charly's demeanor. She seemed less angry, less uptight and more approachable. Kristy suspected weed or alcohol was in play, and she was worried that Charly's demeanor might unexpectedly change again. She wanted to get this done quickly.

Blake repositioned Charly and his lights and then he aimed the camera at his mother.

"Hi. Kristy Findalson here with ice hockey sensation Charly Swift-Rincade. She captured the sports world's attention this past week when she led her hockey team to victory, while simultaneously fighting to find the criminals who disabled her scientist husband."

"Thanks for joining me today, Charly, when you are under such duress. Do the police investigating the attempted murder of your husband have any suspects yet?"

Blake focused the camera back onto Charly and she suddenly felt like a goalie without protective gear. She had just steeled herself to talk about her miserable childhood, and now the reporter had pelted the puck right at her throat. She tried to think of a sharp retort, but her thinking had slowed.

"The police are nowhere with this crime. I don't think they have a clue, and my husband has been left severely disabled." Then she squinched her brows and looked angry while Blake backed the camera away.

Kristy quickly jumped in as Blake realigned his lens. "As I understand it, your husband was trying to find a cure for cocaine addiction. Lately it's been in the news that there are monstrous drug trafficking organizations meeting an ever-growing demand for drugs that are being engineered to be more and more addictive.

"Maybe some of these drug traffickers wouldn't appreciate it if addicts could be cured and the demand for their poisonous products diminished. Are the police considering whether some drug lord might have tried to snuff out your husband?"

Charly was slow to respond. She was squinting and wrinkling her forehead as she said, "maybe you should be working for the police." She started feeling queasy. She had spent the whole morning primping for this interview, and she hadn't eaten anything other than a nutrition bar, almost three hours before she started gulping gin. Big mistake. She hoped she could hold it together, but she could feel the gin catching up to her and she feared she was fading fast.

Kristy Findalson was an old pro at handling drunken and drugged out celebrities. The more famous they were, the less they cared about whether or not they appeared sober. However, Kristy rarely saw this level of inebriation in people whose fame was fleeting. She needed to get this over with in a hurry, but she still hoped to salvage something out of it. Then, she took another hard look at Charly whose eyes were getting glassier by the second.

"Cut," she said to Blake, and she turned back to Charly? "Are you okay, Honey? You look like you need to crunch some crackers and chug some water. I want you to tell your story, but I don't want you passing out in front of the camera."

Charly was grateful to have Kristy and Blake hold her up as she stumbled back to her kitchen.

48

OCTOBER 19 - MORNING

Garrett Towser was enamored with the idea that he could improve a detective's efficiency by employing drug sniffing rats. In his rare moments of free time, he was trying to learn more about these highly intelligent animals and how they were trained. The more he learned, the more he realized he didn't know, so he was thrilled to eke out an hour to revisit Elsie.

Though she was still reeling from yesterday's revelations about how her father was victimized, Elsie was happy to have a visitor, especially someone who showed some real scientific curiosity. When Garrett Towser explained that he wanted to learn how to train rats to sniff out drugs or hazardous materials, Elsie was ecstatic. Beyond learning, sharing her knowledge was what she most loved in life.

Elsie was familiar with the information about the Dutch police rat academy that Garrett had read about. The concept had also given her some ideas about what she could do with the lab if ever it became hers to develop. But what she had been able to learn about the police rats was limited. The article had said that it took about nine months and thousands of dollars' worth of classical conditioning for the rats to perform satisfactorily, but it didn't specify the rat breed.

"Apparently, their rats aren't geniuses like my Freyja," Elsie quipped, while Freyja sat on her shoulder and twitched her ears back and forth as if following the human conversation. Freyja had also done her little announcement routine when Garrett had first come into the lab, squeaking something into Elsie's left ear.

"So, what do I need to learn to take my idea beyond fantasy?" Garrett asked. "I don't know how I would even start such a project. I thought about adopting a pet rat to learn more about them, but apparently, they're like dogs that need your companionship. My schedule is too unpredictable, and I couldn't give any kind of pet the attention it deserves."

"Have you ever had a pet?"

"Funny, you should ask, Elsie. This scar on my nose is a souvenir from the only pet I ever had. I was an only child who begged for a dog, but my mother was very resistant to the idea. My best friend down the block had a wonderful mutt, and all I wanted was a dog-brother like my friend's dog, Skippy.

"Finally, when I was nine and a neighbor was giving away adorable puppies, my mother relented, and that precious little dog instantly had us all wrapped around his tail. He was energetic, playful and super affectionate. I named him Bauser, Bauser Towser.

"We knew the mother dog was a miniature schnauzer, but the father was an unknown until the pups came along. Bauser turned out to be one part terrier, one part husky and one part demon from hell. He was a good watchdog, but he barked loudly and incessantly and acted aggressively towards anyone who tried to enter our house.

"Bauser bolted out the door if ever it was left open for a nanosecond, and we spent whole days running and driving around the neighborhood trying to find and catch him. Twice we had to rescue him from the pound when he got picked up by Animal Control, and that cost more than the outrageous vet bills my parents once paid when he got chewed up in a fight with a dalmatian.

"Bauser's furry face was always encrusted with food which he'd wipe on our pillows. He shed like an oak in autumn, yanked like a lunatic on a leash, attacked other dogs without provocation, humped any leg he could get his paws around, chewed up upholstery and shoes, dug holes in the lawn, and claimed the bedroom hallway as his toilet.

"And oh, one day he got his paw caught in a chain-link fence and he was screaming like a siren. When I tried to rescue him, I inadvertently hurt him and he reflexively bit off a piece of my nose, but other than that, he never bit anyone.

"In spite of all that, I think everyone in my family loved that rascal, up until the day he managed to escape out the front door and get run over by a station wagon. My mother cried the most, but I've always wondered if she was crying for joy. I haven't had a pet since."

"Well, Garrett, you're funny but that's actually a bit of a horror story. I'm going to guess that no one in your family ever really trained Bauser. It takes some knowledge and a whole lot of time, effort, patience, and repetition to get an animal who's living with an alien species to understand how it's supposed to behave. They have to be taught manners."

Garrett looked pensive for a moment. "Exactly, Elsie. I never thought about it before, but unless you count goldfish, neither of my parents had ever had a pet. I guess out of ignorance, we just assumed that Bauser somehow understood what we wanted him to do and not do if we told him so a couple of times. Obviously he didn't, so he did what came naturally. Maybe he could have been a well-behaved dog."

"Maybe. Some rats can be hard to train, and we occasionally do get a demon from hell. However, I work with our rats every day and if I'm not here, our other trainers Tara or Alice take over. Some rats take much longer to train than others, but it's a rare individual that's unable to learn how to obtain a treat for desired behavior. Even quicker, they learn to avoid the fox piss spritz they get in their faces if they bite the trainer.

"Almost always, the untrainable rats have some form of neurologic or hormonal disorder, which is also to say that some are cognitively impaired, and some don't like being told what to do. Maybe poor Bauser had a learning disability."

"No, I don't think Bauser was at fault. My family apparently had no idea what we were doing. Bauser probably knew what he was doing. I guess I have a lot to learn. Where do I begin?"

"I think the first thing you would have to do, is figure out the type of rat that would be most appropriate for the type of police work that you want it to do. There are many species of domestic rats and many variations in populations of wild rats, and they can all have different traits.

A lot of domestic rats have been bred because they are docile and easy to handle, but some are easier to train than others. For example, my father likes to work with Long-Evans rats in his addiction studies because they are bolder than other domestic breeds. They are more curious and more likely to explore something new, while many rats are very cautious about anything new in their environment. You might even say that some rats are liberal and some are conservative.

"Bolder rats tend to live longer than timid ones, and that helps to keep the research going. Long-Evans rats also succumb to addiction at a quicker rate than do other breeds, as is the case for some humans. That makes our research more relevant for more serious addiction, while also being less costly because it takes less time.

"Trainability would be very important for police rats. The Laudren breed of rats that my parents created are especially easy to train, even when their lives are comfortable. In many studies, it's been found that rats that are a little hungry will work harder and longer for their rewards than will rats who have all their needs met. Typically, well-cared-for rats become like human trust-fund-babies who never go out and get jobs. Laudren rats, on the other hand, seem to like having jobs, even though we treat them well.

"Another major factor for your purposes would be the rats' sense of smell. Wild rats are much better smellers than domestic rats. Even the olfactory lobes in their brains are bigger. Wild rats are totally dependent on and driven by the smell of food. If people didn't leave crumbs around, the rats' noses would take them elsewhere.

"Lab rats only get exposed to the unnatural smells of their unnatural environments, so maybe we have dampened their sense of smell by not giving them more opportunity to use it. I don't think we really know how well they can smell. It's recently been discovered that rats have the most genes related to olfactory function of all mammals except elephants. I guess that's not too surprising if you consider that rats are the most successful scavengers on the planet and an elephant's trunk is actually a ginormous nose.

"You'll also need to spend some time in a lab like mine to see how we train our rats. It's pretty simple to do, but it requires time and patience. Ideally, you'd also be able to observe how the Dutch trainers are schooling their police rats. I'd like to see that myself."

"I'd really like to observe in your lab, Elsie, if I can find the time, maybe just to see if this is really a good idea for me."

"Of course, Garrett. Except when I'm visiting my dad in the hospital, I'm here most weekdays and you're always welcome. The other trainers would also be fine if you hung out. Tara's a very good trainer."

"Thanks, Elsie. Say, you took my picture when I was here the other day to try to figure out if Freyja recognized people by sight or smell. Have you figured it out yet?"

"I think it's both. I think she also recognizes voices. She amazes me more every day and it's getting difficult to come up with challenges that demonstrate the limits of her abilities. I also think she watches television. Pet rats, dogs and cats have all been reported to watch TV and recent research revealed that some monkeys like to watch videos of monkeys fighting.

"I have that TV on the counter over there, and when I came in early this morning, I turned it on to catch up with some news. There was a story about a rabid raccoon, and the narrator was advising people to keep their pets indoors, while pictures of pets were flashing across the screen.

"For a second or two, there was this close-up face-shot of a scruffy, orange cat. As soon as it appeared, Freyja raced down my shoulder and hid inside my lab coat, trembling. Rats instinctively fear cats, foxes, and raptors. I'm pretty certain she's never seen a cat before and she could not have smelled it on TV. She had to be reacting to something visual that's prewired into her brain.

"Freyja's behavior makes me think that fear levels could be another factor in selecting rats for police training. There are multiple YouTube videos that show wild rats teasing, chasing and actually attacking dogs and cats. Perhaps some rats are naturally fearless, and you have to wonder if that boosts or diminishes their rate of survival. Or, maybe these feisty, courageous rats are just smarter than dogs and cats, and they've learned enough from experience to take advantage of their superior abilities.

"As you know, my mother won't let me take Freyja out of the lab, but I think this little smarty-pants needs more stimulation. I just put in an order for two very tiny video player kits and a tiny screen video converter which will scale down any video. Now I'm looking for film of animals that don't terrify rats, vegetarian animals like cows, horses, deer, giraffes, elephants, kangaroos and pandas.

"I'm also wondering if rat responses to videos could become a research tool. Will a TV-loving, cocaine exposed rat hang out in the TV room or the cocaine room? And will it depend on which video I'm showing? Will rats get addicted to TV?

"I'm going to set one screen up in Freyja's condo and one in a bachelor pad that houses some young male pups and observe what they do. I hope it doesn't compromise their sleep."

Garrett was finding Elsie and her rats captivating. She could be an extraordinary resource for exploring his new idea. He wanted to ask her many more questions, but he had to leave to team up with C.C. Before he turned to go, he asked Elsie, if his boss would give him the evening off, would she go to dinner with him?

Elsie presumed that he just wanted to pick her brain, but his invite had made her heart flutter.

Just then, Freyja started exhibiting mating behaviors, arching her back and wiggling her ears. Elsie wondered if Freyja was picking up on the pheromones she thought she herself might be emitting or could some pheromones have come from Garrett. Whatever it was, it put the adolescent rat in the mood for making puppies. With their short lifespan, rats were fiercely driven by the biologic imperative to procreate.

49

October 19 – Afternoon

The interview with Charly had been exhausting, but hopefully worth the effort. Kristy was spending an inordinate amount of time reviewing and editing the tapes, but she was still struggling with how to merge the images of the frisky athlete with the down-and-out casualty that was revealed when Charly became compromised.

After Kristy had interrupted the filming to deal with the drunkenness, Charly tried to alleviate the problem by purging herself. She was actually an expert at purging, but it was too late. Most of the alcohol had already been absorbed.

Kristy made Charly drink some instant coffee and nibble microwave popcorn. The fridge contained some veggies and packaged ground meat, but there was no bread, crackers or other snacks. Two cans of soup, a jar of peanut butter, and a cannister of coffee looked lost in a big cupboard that reminded Kristy of her college days. This was the pantry of a poor person, not the highly stylized, salon-enhanced sophisticate that they had initially encountered.

Charly was more alert after about five minutes of sitting with a cold pack on the back of her neck. She was slurring her words, but she no longer seemed at risk for falling on her face. Kristy suggested they get her a little more cleaned up and walked her to her bedroom. Charly immediately collapsed onto her bed. Kristy wrestled her out of her jacket and shoes and let her doze off, while she and Blake tried to figure out what they could do with the situation.

Kristy wasn't sure if the release forms Charly had signed covered filming her when she was passed out, but she decided to let the camera roll. She could always erase the tapes if what was captured was illegal.

After nearly an hour of snooze time, Kristy put a cold washcloth over Charly's eyes and forehead. Ten seconds later, she awoke. Sitting up on the side of the bed in her constricting clothes, it took a few minutes for her to orient. When she seemed to have come part way to her senses, Kristy presented her with a hand mirror.

"Let's get you prettied back up, Honey. While you were sleeping it off, Blake got your coffee maker going. We'll get you another cup and pick up where we left off."

Charly sat immobile for another minute while she tried to process what Kristy was saying. Finally, she was able to walk to her bathroom and Kristy told her to leave the door unlocked and call for help if needed. Charly spent almost fifteen minutes within and came out looking reasonably put together. Kristy helped her get back into her jacket and sat her in her bedroom chair which had been strategically positioned.

Blake handed her a cup of the fresh brew. She sipped at it, contemplating her options. She hoped she could quickly rebound from her own stupidity, though she still felt like she was under the influence. This was maybe her only chance to find a benefactor and she desperately needed to take advantage of it. As she thought about how to play the camera, she didn't realize that Blake was using remote control to operate the camera from the other side of the room.

~ ~ ~ ~ ~

"You look gorgeous again, Charly, and a lot better than you did a little while ago when you were collapsing from all the stress you've been under. Thanks for hanging in there so bravely. In spite of the tremendous hardship you've had to face, you're already making a comeback.

"You know, Charly, it takes real courage to be battling drug cartels like you and your husband have been doing all these years. Thank you for being a willing warrior in this vicious war."

Once more, Charly was incensed by Kristy's ploy of attacking from multiple directions. She also worried that Kristy could be inviting more drug dealers to come after people who were trying to stop the devastation and carnage caused by cocaine. She was still too inebriated to play verbal ping-pong, and she closed her eyes and shook her head in defeat. "We're trying to help the victims of addiction, not fight drug cartels," she said with exasperation.

Kristy didn't like where the conversation might be going so she again changed the subject and her tone. "So, Charly, I couldn't help but notice this picture on your nightstand. It has to be your mother; she's gorgeous. How old was she when this picture was taken?"

As Charly took the picture from Kristy's hand, she realized that she hadn't looked at it in a long time; maybe only when she'd packed it up to move and again when she'd unpacked it. As she looked at it now, she felt a heaviness in her heart.

"Maybe twenty, I don't really know."

"What *do* you know about your mother?"

Charly grabbed at her own lower lip and kind of gnawed at the side of her index finger. Then she said, "not much. To me, she was the woman who kept abandoning me, though I know she had troubles of her own."

"How old were you when you were first separated from your mother?"

"I've been told I was with my mother for the first two and a half years, but I don't remember any of that. I remember her from when I was five. I had about a year and a half with her around then, before I went to another foster home. I got to live with her again for a while when I was seven, and again when I was ten and eleven. She was still beautiful then," Charly said as she continued to stare at the picture.

"What happened to her?"

"When I was little, the caseworkers would tell me that my mother was sick, and she had to go away to get better. I didn't know that 'sick' meant in jail or in rehab until I was about nine, when I overheard my foster family talking about it.

"Do you know how old your mother was when you were born?"

"Not quite sixteen."

"Where did you live when you lived with your mother?"

"Once when I was little, I remember being in a house with two other mothers with little kids, but I'm not sure when that was. I remember one of the other mothers because she stunk of cigarettes. I still despise that smell.

"Sometimes we lived with my mother's friends. They all smoked cigarettes too. One time we lived with some women and a man who was probably my mother's pimp. He was very nice to me. That's when the caseworker sent me back to foster care."

"Do you know why your mother fell into such a murky lifestyle?"

"Not too long before my mother died from an overdose, she told me that when she was fourteen, she ran away from home. Her father was an abusive alcoholic and that turned her mother into a closet alcoholic. She also had an angry, violent older brother who she was afraid of. Once, he pushed her down a staircase.

"She had been living on the streets in Seattle when a smart pimp saw her and apparently recognized her as a lucrative commodity. He rescued her with shelter and food but then, he got her so addicted to heroin that she became a willing prostitute to pay for the drugs. I only know some of that because that's what the caseworker told my adoptive parents, and when I was about thirty, my adoptive mother shared it with me.

"I do believe that in her prime, my mother was more of a high-priced call girl, maybe the most valuable commodity in that pimp's stable. When we lived with that man, we were in a nice, big house with lots of rooms and a barroom in the basement. I don't know where it was exactly, not in the city but close to it."

"Hmmm. What do you know about your father?"

Charly pouted. "Um, yeah, well, …. He must have had red hair, and he probably didn't suffer from addiction. Those are the genes that I most obviously didn't get from my mother's side of the family."

Charly's frown morphed into an almost smile. "I also like to think that my father was some kind of a smart, athletic, and successful person who could afford top-of-the-line prostitutes. I'm grateful for the genes that both my parents gave me."

Kristy gestured to take the picture back and Charly handed it to her. As Kristy angled it towards Blake's lens, she said, "your mother was certainly everyman's fancy; truly sad that she had such a tough life.

"So, after all of those foster homes, Charly, how did you come to be adopted?"

"I was just lucky. Most foster kids never get adopted and when they turn eighteen, they're turned out into the world with maybe just a few belongings in a backpack. They can either face life alone or try to reconnect with the families that they were taken away from. It's a disgusting system. I was more fortunate.

"A few weeks after my mother died, a caseworker learned about an older couple that had lost their only child, a fifteen-year-old daughter. She was killed in a car accident involving four teenagers including a sixteen-year-old drunk driver. A therapist convinced my adoptive mother that giving another young girl a chance would help to relieve her grief, and that therapist was an associate of my caseworker.

"The Swifts fostered me for about two years, and I did whatever I could to win them over. Their offer to adopt me was a dream come true. They were great people, and I was ecstatic to change my last name to Swift. Before that, I was Charlotte Hufnogel. Had they not adopted me, I may have wound up like my mother."

"Where are your adoptive parents now?"

"My adoptive dad died about six years ago. He was a Viet Nam vet, and he had a bad back and a bad heart. About three years ago, my adoptive mom who was younger, met her second husband and got swept off her feet. She moved to his home in New Zealand. I haven't seen her since."

"So, you're very alone in this world, aren't you, Charly? No kids of your own? What will you do if your husband doesn't recover? With so many science labs shutting down and artificial intelligence taking over everything else, how will a biotechnologist like yourself make a living?"

Charly was starting to accept that Kristy was truly talented at throwing rocks, and she needed to catch them or duck. "I'm primarily a micro-dissectionist in addition to having advanced biotech skills. Most countries are embracing instead of beheading scientists and I'm looking at some possibilities in New Zealand where my adoptive mother lives. New Zealand has very good women's ice hockey."

"So, will your husband be able to go with you if you emigrate?"

For a minute, Charly appeared dumbstruck. Then she burst into tears. Kristy handed her a tissue and let her cry for a minute while the camera continued to roll.

Finally, Charly blubbered, "no one knows if my husband can recover and I have no idea how I will be able to pay for his care. I don't have a job, and I don't have health insurance for either of us. Do you know if we can get any assistance for my husband for being a crime victim?"

Kristy knew that a federal law required states to provide compensation for victims of violent crimes, but each state had its own criteria for what was criminal and what was covered. Lawmakers didn't want people stabbing and shooting themselves so they could collect benefits.

Kristy didn't know how the law was applied in this state, and she also didn't know if Charly's husband would be eligible for such benefits. She did know that it took almost a week for law enforcement to be called in on the case of August Rincade, which made her think that the family didn't initially perceive his condition as being the result of a crime.

"States determine what benefits victims are eligible to receive depending on the nature and outcome of the crime. Didn't you initially suspect that your husband's stroke resulted from an accidental overdose? How did you arrive at the conclusion that someone assaulted him?"

Charly's upper lip curled into a sneer. Her anger squelched the lethargy the alcohol had induced, but she forced herself to squash the anger.

"That's what the doctors at the hospital believed and that's what their misinformation led me and my husband's family to believe. It was both a gross misunderstanding and a terrible deception. We should have suspected foul play immediately, but the person who called from the hospital to tell me that they had taken my unconscious husband to emergency brain surgery, told me an erroneous story about how he came to suffer a cocaine-induced stroke. And that's what I believed and that's what I told the rest of his family.

"After the shock wore off, my husband's daughter, who is also a scientist and a very insightful person, started to question what the hospital staff had reported. She was the person who requested that August be tested for a knock-out drug, and when that test came back positive, we knew that the story from the hospital was wrong.

"Someone lured my husband to a meeting with false information, knocked him out with the illegal date rape drug Rohypnol, contaminated his system with bad cocaine and then showed up at the hospital for the specific purpose of providing false and misleading information about what had happened to him.

"The federal and local law enforcement people believe that my husband was the victim of a crime, so why are you questioning that? Are you conducting this interview to contaminate his case? I think we're done here. Please get out of my house, now!"

Kristy and Blake had had enough anyway. This was not the interview that Kristy had planned. She said, "good luck to you, Charly, and thanks for your time," as they promptly packed up and skedaddled.

Now, Kristy was feeling unsatisfied with the tapes and most of the interview. It was exciting to watch this beautiful woman wield a hockey stick. It was depressing to hear her story and watch her try to cope with losing her husband, her job, and maybe her profession or her country.

50

OCTOBER 19 - EVENING

C.C. McAllister had misgivings about Garrett Towser's plan to have dinner with the victim's daughter in order to learn more about the Rincade family. C.C. was adamant that Elsie, already disadvantaged and maybe vulnerable, should know up front that this invite represented a police encounter, and not mistake it for romantic intentions.

Garrett said that Elsie was incredibly smart and perceptive and that she probably understood everything that was going on with their investigation. He assured C.C. that in spite of the fact that he was a nerd, he was also socially competent. He'd have to play it by ear in his interactions with someone as intuitive as Elsie, and Detective C.C. McAllister was going to have to trust his judgement.

C.C. was getting too motherly from Garrett's point of view. He wondered if that was why she chose to work with the youngest of detectives. She liked to nurture them, but she was also abusive. She wanted her sidekicks to be available at all times of the day and night.

That was the way that it was when C.C. trained in police work some thirty plus years ago, but people of Garrett's generation had come to believe that a little more tender loving care was better nurturance. It was now well-known that keeping people up all night caused them to have increased risks for diabetes, cardiovascular and gastrointestinal diseases, cancer and other health problems.

Of course, things like blood clots and criminals didn't care too much about the hands on the clock. The middle of the night was prime time for most of the things that plagued humankind, requiring the police to keep the peace and the hospital night shift to save lives. But there was no good reason for C.C. to be keeping Garrett working day and night in the case of August Rincade.

Garrett was also bothered that Rincade's case seemed to be going nowhere. Garrett hoped that he could be the one to change that. His mother, an elementary school secretary and a small-town mayor had always told him that things can only change if someone sets out to change them. Most people are more comfortable with constancy.

Garrett told C.C. that he wanted to see if he could figure out if the rest of the Rincade family was covering for Toby, and if any of the family members that were still considered suspect could be crossed off the list.

Garrett didn't tell C.C. that he wanted to take more control of the case and figure out how to set some boundaries with his boss, but she probably knew that. What he hoped C.C. didn't know, was that he was just ever so slightly smitten by Freyja and Elsie, and that he was even more infatuated with the idea of making police work safer and more efficient by capitalizing on the amazing abilities of rats.

Garrett had to develop his concept to a much greater degree before he could reveal it to C.C. or anyone else in the precinct. His colleagues might start putting dead rats in his locker, and he didn't want his idea to become a joke. He wanted to do something innovative and productive. Garrett's grandfather had been a policeman and Garrett had dearly loved the man. He had always wanted to honor his grandfather's memory and avenge his death. Grandpa Towser had been killed in a police raid on a drug cartel's warehouse when Garrett was twelve years old.

C.C. gave Garrett her blessings. Between Spencer Parrow's long list of drug traffickers and her own long list of defrocked scientists, a family member was still her best hope. She needed to look more into extended family. Who might be hoping to get their hands on the Laudren family fortune by taking the trust away from Jenna? And who else could have known that August was interested in checking out a piece of lab equipment?

"See what else you can find about other relatives on Elsie's mother's side of the family."

~ ~ ~ ~ ~

When Garrett arrived to meet up with Elsie at the lab, she was wearing jeans and a Mickey Mouse sweatshirt. Her face was partially concealed by her hat, microphone and long brown bangs which brushed the frame of her glasses.

Garrett was wearing his ill-fitting sport jacket with a stain on the sleeve. They walked from the lab to the Laudren Retail Plaza where they were seated in a booth in the back of a sports bar. Elsie and many of the lab employees were regular customers in this eatery with its diverse menu.

Elsie ordered the house special salad with grilled chicken and sparkling water. Garrett ordered a steak sandwich with fries and a beer. It was noisy and Elsie had to turn her speaker and her hearing aid up. She advised Garrett that the fries were sinfully good, and she planned to steal some. They talked about how unseasonably warm it was for October.

Garrett shared his dream of doing something important in police work and told Elsie that he had been enchanted by Freyja and by rats in general. He had worked on several police cases where he could see how a police rat could have been an asset. He wondered if the Laudren NeuroScience foundation would be interested in funding a project like training police rats.

Elsie didn't think so if her mother was in charge. However, she said that if she were in charge, she would consider it only if such a tool wasn't used to put addicts in jail.

"Sorry, Garrett. I'm not a big fan of how society treats drug addicts. They suffer from a disease that we need to learn how to prevent and cure. The cost of prosecuting and incarcerating these people is enormous, useless, and downright stupid. Resources would be far better spent on developing a tweak of the gene that makes some people become addicted to substances that most people can use judiciously."

"So, would you legalize the use of cocaine?" Garrett asked.

"I'd decriminalize the misuse of all abused substances. The war on drugs has cost billions and done nothing to reduce drug abuse. Overdose rates have quadrupled since the turn of the millennium and more than a million arrests a year for possession has become a huge burden on the courts.

"Then, if and when addicts do recover, they are saddled with criminal records that can leave them unemployable. Also, drug laws are often abused to discriminately persecute certain groups of people. Only prison owners benefit from the criminalization of drug abuse, while all of the expense is borne by us taxpayers."

Garrett was skeptical. "From what I've learned, not all of the places that have legalized drugs have seen reduced overdose deaths. In some cases, the demand for drugs increased and fueled more black-market production,"

"True perhaps, if the statistics aren't stilted, but it's also been shown that when the state takes over production, offers safer products and undercuts the illegal suppliers, the state's coffers are fattened, and the black market goes bust. And when people don't have to steal to support their addiction, crime rate drops dramatically."

"Elsie, are you saying the government should support addiction?"

"No, not at all. I am merely recounting that experts around the world believe that revenue would be far better spent on finding ways to prevent and cure addiction than on turning impaired people into criminals.

"Look, Garrett, you're drinking a beer right now. Ninety percent of the human population can enjoy alcohol without becoming addicted. I don't drink alcohol for fear I might have my father's genes for addiction. The few times I tried it, I liked it too much, so I'm going to avoid it. But most of humanity has been enjoying the mood-altering effects of alcohol since the first caveman ate a fermented berry. Many animals also enjoy alcohol, especially elephants, monkeys, and hornets.

"Hallucinogenic plants have long been used by humans in spiritual searches and religious traditions in cultures around the world, as well as by birds and other animals. Reindeer love magic mushrooms, big horn sheep go for psychedelic lichens, wallabies sneak into poppy fields to get high, and cats covet catnip.

"Modern man has built an entire industry out of mood-altering drugs. It's in the DNA of humans and other animals to like to explore and alter their state of consciousness. Why do we punish people for it? What are we gaining by condemning the ten percent of humans who can't control their use of psychoactive substances? Why haven't we figured out a way to help them?

"In the 1930s, the temperance movement tried to stop alcohol consumption and prohibition spawned more alcohol abuse than there ever had been. Bootlegging produced stronger brews. Social drinking became secretive. A sense of rebellion fueled binging, and reports of alcohol-related health issues and deaths dramatically increased. And let's not forget that prohibition also spawned violent crime. Mankind should have learned its lessons about forbidden fruit by now.

"Life for most people is hard and why should anyone be denied access to life's little pleasures by those who equate pleasure with sin? Addiction is an illness, not a sin."

Garrett closed his eyes and shook his head. He was thrown off balance by Elsie's arguments. Decriminalization of drugs would put a lot of police out of work, but he suspected that she was right. "So, does my idea of police rats seem ludicrous to you?"

"Not at all. The olfactory ability of rats demands far more appreciation and exploration. They could help find the illegal sources of bad drugs. Maybe they could help track down pollutants. Perhaps they could find contaminants in the food supply. Maybe they could detect termites. Possibly they could find rare elements in the earth.

"African poached rats have been used to sniff out people infected with tuberculosis, as well as land mines. Dogs, whose noses may be inferior to rat noses, have been trained to smell lung cancer on someone's breath, predict seizures in people with epilepsy, and smell Parkinson's Disease before a person has symptoms.

"However, electronic noses are now being developed and so far, it's looking like they might work really well, so I'm not sure if scientists are going to become more or less interested in animal noses. But when you have animals with trainability and smelling capability as excellent as that of rats, we really should be looking at the possibilities."

Garret had never thought of such things, even though his detective training had included a workshop in scent recognition. In Elsie's presence, he felt as though he was awakening to a whole new sensory domain. "Why do you think humans can't smell as well as other animals, Elsie?"

"There are several theories about that. Some say our sense of smell develops only to meet needs. A person stuck in the desert might learn to smell water. Some say our brains shrunk our olfactory lobes to make room for our other senses. Some think our olfactory lobes shrunk to protect us from a world of stink. Scientists are just starting to study human super smellers, some of whom have a funky genetic mutation."

"So, what do you think of my idea, Elsie?"

"It's intriguing. I'll talk to my mother about it. I do think she might be willing to let me look at our rats' smelling ability. We are still researching the potential of our own breed or rats."

"Does anyone besides your mother get to decide on the direction of the research?"

"My parents used to have a network of scientist friends who they liked to discuss things with, but that seems to have ended when my parents divorced. My mother has a close friend who's a physician who she talks to about research ideas."

"Are there any other relatives involved in your family's business?"

"There are hardly any relatives. My dad was an orphaned only child, and my mom had an older brother who died young and a sister who joined a religious cult and disappeared."

"Does your brother Toby help with the lab decisions?"

"Toby wants no part of the lab. He hates the whole idea of animal research."

"So how come Toby has been estranged from your father but not from your mother who's trying to bring another animal researcher into the lab?"

"Let me be honest, Garrett. Toby rejected our father out of jealousy because Dad turned out to be his rival for the attention of his research assistant, Charly, the same Charly who our father left our mother to marry.

"I think that Toby's animal rights obsession is more of a cover-up for his conflict over his feelings towards our father. They had a loving relationship until Charly started to play on Toby's teen-aged vulnerabilities. Charly used Toby to make Dad jealous and get him to divorce Mom. She uses her beauty like its bait on a fishhook.

"I'd guess that if Charly hadn't been in the picture for the last seven years, Toby and my father would be the best of friends, and they would have become research partners and we'd still be a family. But who knows? Maybe that's just wishful thinking on my part."

"I'm so sorry, Elsie. It seems like you're also a victim of this awful attack on your father. Do you have any other relatives you can fall back on other than your brother? Is your brother going back to school?"

"I have Maya, our family's adopted person. She's my second mother and I'm super lucky to have her. She's my best friend in the world.

"I'm not sure what Toby is going to do. He's very conflicted. I think he wants to at least finish this semester and maybe then he'll help out in the lab if Charly and our father aren't there anymore. Perhaps that's also my wishful thinking. Toby has always been a second father to me, and I miss him."

"Do you still have grandparents, Elsie?"

"My father was raised by his grandparents who are long gone. My father doesn't have any other living relatives that I know of.

My mother's mother Sara is in an Alzheimer's unit. She hasn't known who we are for years. My mom still goes to see her once in a while, but she doesn't know who my mom is either.

"My grandfather Jay, my mom's father is in an assisted living facility and my mom and I visit him at least once a week, or at least we did before my dad wound up in the hospital; not so often for these last few weeks. Before the divorce, my dad used to visit Grandpa Jay too. They also had a good relationship before Charly blew everything up.

"Grandpa Jay still understands most things but he's too forgetful to live alone. He can't remember to turn off the stove or pay his bills. We opted for assisted living for him after he turned on the water in the bathtub, forgot about it and went to bed, flooding his entire house. Then he got lost driving his car on a few occasions and he burned and cut himself trying to cook.

"He's in a good place now. He gets prepared meals, and he has a companion there with whom he shares his love of rock and roll. My Grandpa Jay used to play a mean guitar. His friend Simon was a drummer."

"No aunts or uncles? No cousins, Elsie?"

"My grandfather Jay has a sister who should be in a nursing home, but she refuses to go. The trust pays for her to have home care. She's been widowed for ten years, and she never had children. She used to come to our house for the holidays, but she doesn't travel anymore.

"My mother's mother Sara had an older brother who had kids, a little older than my mother, but Uncle Phil wound up divorced. His wife and kids resettled somewhere, and my mother doesn't even know where any of these people are nowadays.

"You know what, Garrett? I think you can probably cross everyone in my family off of your suspect list. And thanks for dinner."

51

OCTOBER 20 - MIDDAY

Feeling guilty for not having visited his grandfather for more than a year, Toby agreed to take Elsie for a visit before heading back to school. They found Jay in the recreation room of his luxurious assisted living facility, playing Jenga. He still had one steady hand that could pull the blocks out of the tower with ease.

Jay was always delighted by Jenna's and Elsie's visits, and he was thrilled to see his grandson. Together, they grabbed some goodies from the snack bar and walked back to Jay's apartment. His balcony provided a magnificent view of a pond and a treed hillside, and it was warm enough to sit outside and enjoy the brilliance of fall foliage.

"How's your mother? How come she didn't come?" Jay asked as soon as they settled.

"She's attending to a fire alarm at the retail plaza, Grandpa, but she's doing better with the MALS. She's hardly had any pain for the last few days, and she's eating better." Elsie said. "The nerve block seems to have calmed things down and she's starting to hope that she can recover without surgery."

"I certainly hope so. The woman has suffered enough. And how's your father doing?"

"Mom and I visited him early this morning," Toby said. "Today's the fifth day since they started the transcranial magnetic stimulation and the nurses are very encouraged. As of yesterday, he's been able to swallow pureed foods from a spoon. If they can get more calories into him, he won't need the feeding tube. I'm pretty sure he knew I was there this morning. I don't know how I know that. It's just a feeling."

Elsie added, "he's also making more purposeful head and mouth movements, like trying to turn towards the person who's feeding him or speaking to him, but he still needs bolsters alongside of his head when he's upright.

"His primary nurse thinks he's also starting to be able to execute 'one blink for yes and two for no.' He's also trying to move his left fingers when the therapist rubs his hand with the faux fur. I just wish Mom and the hospital would let me bring one of our rats in for him to pet, but the idea gets shot down every time I bring it up.

"He's also spending more time awake, but here's the bad news, Grandpa. He's not going to be on Mom's insurance after next week, so he won't be able to stay in the hospital and get treated. We don't know what's going to happen to him. It's up to Charly and she seems to have wiped her hands clean of the husband that she stole. Now, there's a hospital social worker looking into chronic care facilities that Dad could be transferred to."

"Yeesh! I guess that's progress except it sounds like he's on his way to a horrific existence. Poor bastard, but he's a two-timing fool that August Rincade. He had it so easy, so perfect, and he gave it all away for that Charly. Serves him right for two-timing my Jenna, but he shouldn't have ended up like this. No one should wind up like it sounds like your father is going to wind up. I feel sorry for the poor rat bastard. I used to love August, but I can never forgive him for what he's done to my family.

"But it won't surprise me if Jenna forgives him and decides to help him. My daughter's heart is too tender. She could hate that man and still be unable to let him suffer. I'd stop her from helping him if I could. He doesn't deserve our help. He's ruined the family and the foundation, but your mother has always been a sacrificial lamb who has to rescue others, generous to a fault my Jenna. Her mom Sara was like that too."

"Mom says she's not going to help him, but I guess she still has a week to change her mind. We sure don't want to see Dad in some flea bag nursing home. If he can continue to receive good care, maybe he can still recover."

"From what you're telling me, it doesn't sound too hopeful, Elsie. So, what is your mother going to do about the lab?"

"Mom interviewed a good guy a few days ago. I think she might make him an offer. We liked him too."

"And what are you going to do about the lab, Toby?"

"I've been thinking about it a lot, Grandpa. Elsie and I both believe that Dad's work on hormonal treatment is going to give way to genetic treatment, and that's probably going to be engineered by artificial intelligence. Some scientists have just altered the genes of fruit flies to turn them into cocaine addicts, so now there's hope that genetic manipulation could also cure cocaine addiction.

"There are new directions to go in, but Mom isn't ready to open that door just yet. She knows it's coming but right now, she's too preoccupied with Dad's unfinished project."

"She'll get there, she has to," Jay offered. "Your mother always figures things out. I'm a thousand percent relieved that August won't be her perpetual project anymore. I could just see him twisting her arm to do one more trial, one more tweak of the data and your mother would give in, and she'd never be free of the leech and that bitch. And what's going to happen to Charly the homewrecker?"

"Mom fired her." Elsie said with a look of satisfaction. "I was there. Mom had the IT guy lock her out of the computer. She came into Mom's office to complain about it and when she was done, Mom said, 'you're locked out of the computer, Charly, because you're fired. You have ten minutes to clean out your locker and turn in your keycard. Your and August's final paychecks will be in the mail. Your health insurance is covered until the end of the month, eleven days from now. You have the option to purchase your own insurance through my plan. I never want to see you on these premises again.'"

"I wish I had photographed the look on Charly's face. I'd have to call it horror. Her expression probably put a small stitch in the big hole in Mom's heart. So, I guess that creep is now out looking for a new job. She certainly hasn't been visiting Dad. By the way, Grandpa, did you happen to catch Charly's ice hockey exhibition when they were show-ing it on the news a few days ago?"

"No, I guess I missed that. I haven't been watching too much news lately. Like thoughts of Charly and your father, the news is too depress-ing. What about any news regarding Grandma Sara?"

"Sorry to say, same old, same old. Mom checks in with the nurses regularly and nothing changes. Sadly, Grandpa, Grandma has no lucid moments anymore. She doesn't recognize anyone, even the nurses who take care of her every day. She calls everyone Shelby or Baby."

"Well, that's never good news. How about any breaks in the police case?"

"Maybe. Yesterday, the lead detective impounded Dad's car and they got some fingerprints off of the interior door handles and the con-sole which could be from Elsie and me, since we brought the car from the hotel back to Dad's townhouse. Then Charly had it cleaned by a detailer, so, we also have to hope it's not the detailer's fingerprints.

"However, the detailer didn't do a very good job. Under a black light, some tiny dots of urine fluoresced, correlating perfectly with where Dad would put the rat cages in the back whenever we trans-ported them. We had recently picked up some Sprague-Dawley rats for a comparative study of hormones.

"The police also found some long hairs on the driver's seat uphol-stery that probably aren't mine or Charly's. They're still going over the car and waiting for some results from the police lab.

"Say, Grandpa, where's your buddy Simon? He's such a cool guy. I wanted Toby to meet him."

"Poor Simon's in the hospital again. They took him yesterday for maybe an intestinal blockage. Simon lost some of his intestine to cancer a decade ago and he's had gut troubles ever since.

"Simon moved into the apartment across the hall from me about a year ago after his wife passed. He's become a very good friend, Toby, maybe the best I've ever had. He used to be an optometrist, but he sold his business to a corporation and retired comfortably.

"Not too long before your parents' divorce, Simon had a conversation with your father about some optometry equipment he was interested in. I understand August was going to look at that equipment when he had his stroke.

"Simon has an interesting family. He has two nice kids, a son who's a successful contractor and a daughter who's an optometry technician but she's divorced from a deadbeat dad. Her son Desmond, Simon's grandson, is a real piece of work. He has angry looking tattoos, and he dresses like a tough guy. He's almost thirty years old and he's never had a job. I think he's a druggie and maybe a dealer."

"I saw him a few times," Elsie said. "It's like he works hard at making himself look scary."

"Desmond visits Simon often on the pretense of being a devoted grandson, but what he's really after is money. Simon's too soft-hearted and maybe a little soft-headed and he gets extorted by the kid all the time. It's like your father August and Charly extorting the trust. That's what Simon and I have in common, people taking advantage of the wealth of us successful old geezers.

"Right after Simon moved in, August was visiting me, and Desmond was visiting Simon at the same time. Desmond actually tried to hit August up for some cash. I had to laugh because August never carried cash. He was 'plastic man.' I remember him showing Desmond his empty billfold. That was right before the divorce.

"You probably know, Toby, but your father stopped visiting me after the divorce. I think he was too embarrassed to show his face around here after sponging off of the Laudren Foundation for all of those years.

"The next time Desmond visited, he asked about August, and I remember telling Simon and Desmond about what a deadbeat your father had become. I'm sorry, but I've lost all respect for that man, my ex-son-in-law.

"I don't know why Simon gives into that dirtball grandkid of his so easily. At least August was a professional with a purpose. Desmond is a real dreamer-schemer, wheeler-dealer slimeball. I wouldn't give that kid a dollar.

"I know August's your father, Toby and Elsie, but I don't want to give him any more handouts either. He's a double-crossing rat bastard and I hope your mother can finally get rid of him and not continue to take care of him."

Elsie heaved her shoulders, sighed and reached for her grandfather's hand. "Hang in there, Grandpa, I know your buddy Simon's a great guy and a good friend and I hope he'll be okay."

"I hope so too, Grandpa," Toby echoed, "but I'm afraid I've got to go now. I have to take Elsie back to the hospital to meet Mom and then I'm heading to the airport.

"It was great to see you, Grandpa. Keep on rocking."

52

October 20 – Evening

Kristy Findalson's first edition of Charly's interview had no takers, but she was determined to get a video out there before the hockey hotshot got put on ice. She spent hours editing and splicing and when she finally had it pared down to two and a half minutes' worth of safe-for-TV smut, three media outlets made her offers. Kristy took the deal that gave the best royalty rate. All of her instincts told her that this was a story that other networks were going to devour.

The producers were especially enthused about the interposition of the stock film clips and photos that Kristy had purchased and included in her video. They showed scantily clad women performing amazing athletic feats: tennis pros, Olympic gymnasts, divers, figure skaters, sprinters, volleyballers and a certain pro golfer who loved to tease the camera and make a mockery of golf's conservative dress code.

As video clips streamed, Kristy voiced over, "the golfer you see right now claims that the less she wears, the better she hits the ball. Another golf celebrity has started a topless golf league. After all, it's been shown that bras restrict chest muscle expansion and breathing. Bra straps restrict rotation of the scapula and increase rotary motion in the shoulder joints.

"The constraints of clothing on physical performance are appreciated in most every sport from football to cycling, so what's up with this archaic, irrational dress code for golfers? And what ever happened to knickers? Why can't male golf pros show some leg when they're hiking those hilly fairways? And why don't they go topless or wear muscle shirts so we can see their biceps and delts when they're driving the ball four hundred yards?"

Kristy's banter with Charly about female athletes having to be sex objects to get media attention was interspersed with images of renowned athletes in skimpy outfits. Kristy threw in excerpts of the tapes of Charly's ice hockey performance as they discussed Charly's theory that nobody watches women's ice hockey because these highly proficient athletes don't show any skin.

The camera then focused on Kristy. "Here I am, folks, little old athletics analyst Kristy Findalson, reporting to you while all covered up. I'm not even wearing anything form-fitting. Scarves are my fashion friends; they conceal all sorts of flaws. Fabulous foundation conceals my imperfect skin. Humans have applied war paint, facial decor and coverups forever.

"But even though I'm wearing makeup, you can still see my face, unlike women whose cultures demand that their faces be covered. You can see my actual hair, unlike people whose heads have to be hidden." Images of women in burkas and head covers then flashed across the screen, alternating with the images of the nearly naked athletes. Then, there were clips of skilled, graceful athletes in more modest apparel.

"With the mobility of today's fabrics and the advanced engineering of garment construction, today's athletes can find all kinds of clothing to optimize their performance and appearance. The long-legged look of male gymnasts' pants gives their top-heavy bodies more appealing profiles. The fringed sleeves of a spinning skater can make the movement more captivating. The long compression shorts worn by sprinters can boost thigh muscle power.

"It took a while, but even basketballers learned to stop wearing droopy shorts that restricted the motion of their knees. Will judo participants ever ditch their heavy dogis? Tradition is the 'reason' for doing something when there's no rational reason to still do it.

"Fellow females, let me tell you something: sex is in the mind of the beholder and that applies to almost the entire human population, especially sports spectators. Most people appreciate those of you who are liberated enough to show off your well-honed bodies. And some people appreciate athletes who don't display their bodies. Athletes, you have all kinds of options. Please dress accordingly.

"Ice hockey players have to sensibly cover up to stay safe in their sport," Kristy said, as profiles of Charly's pretty face and figure and her ice hockey performance were shown again, along with a clip of the World Cup winning U.S. women's ice hockey team.

"And Charly Swift-Rincade has proven that athletes don't have to be sex objects to be appreciated. Hey sportscasters, show some love for the exciting women's sport of ice hockey. Our U.S. team is the best in the world. And thank you, Charly Swift-Rincade.

"This is Kristy Findalson with another celebrity athlete profile, signing off."

~ ~ ~ ~ ~

The major networks loved the Findalson tape after it was shown by lower tier media outlets on the evening news. More than two dozen premier broadcasters picked it up for the late-night news. In the waning baseball season of October, most any other sports news was somewhat refreshing, but Kristy had managed to hit a universally sensitive nerve.

~ ~ ~ ~ ~

Charly was outraged when she saw the tape. It had nothing to do with her husband being a victim of a crime or her being in a desperate situation. Kristy Findalson was the scum on the bottom of the journalist barrel, and Charly wanted to kill herself for having consented to this garbage.

Then, Charly remembered that she had maybe blown the whole interview by getting drunk. She hit the rewind button and watched the tape again and then she watched it a third time. Then, she checked into her memory file and realized that Kristy Findalson had only used film from before Charly had made a drunken fool of herself. She should be grateful that Kristy hadn't exploited her further. It could have been a whole lot worse, but the journalist had apparently been respectful and it was her own fault that her entire effort was a failure.

Then, the story got some attention from some athletic clothing and sports equipment sponsors, and Charly suddenly found herself looking at some endorsement offers to promote hockey sticks, helmets, and compression leggings. But the offers would barely cover her rent, not her addictions to clothing, facials and Brazilian blowouts.

Charly should have been sending Kristy Findalson a thank you bouquet for embellishing her celebrity status. Instead, she was drinking a gin and tonic and feeling sorry for herself.

53

OCTOBER 22 – AFTERNOON

Charly had called several divorce lawyers and left messages. She'd sent email explanations of her situation, but no one had responded. Finally, she came across a law firm that promised to provide an online consult within three hours of receiving completed online forms. Charly filled them out quickly and spent the rest of the time making herself camera worthy.

Charly had seen website pictures of the divorce lawyers associated with The Eagle Beagle Law Firm and she hoped it was the guy. The man looked older and more experienced. The woman actually looked too young, but she was attractive and probably a draw for the men who were seeking divorce.

Charly decked herself out in a silky orange shell under the white jacket she had worn for the Findalson interview. A giraffe patterned scarf concealed her rat tattoo. Dazzling hoop earrings dangled amidst the red tendrils that cascaded down her long neck.

~ ~ ~ ~ ~

The lawyer assigned to review online inquiries that day wasn't actually a divorce lawyer. Adam Vader was a former fireman who went to law school and now specialized in insurance fraud fires. It never ceased to amaze him how many failed businesses mysteriously burned down in the middle of the night when no one was there. He had as many cases as he could handle.

However, one day out of every month, each of the dozens of lawyers and paralegals who worked for The Eagle Beagle Law Firm, were required to do tele-law consults and reel in more customers.

Normally, Adam Vader would have responded to Charly's inquiry by telling her that an expert from the firm's family law division would get back to her within the next two business days. There were several lawyers and paralegals who knew how to handle her issue, getting rid of an impaired spouse. In this state, divorcing an incapacitated person was difficult. Adam knew that much; he could learn the rest.

Adam Vader just happened to know who Charly Swift-Rincade was. An avid consumer of sports news, he had seen Charly's skating performance as well as her recent interview. He could not resist the opportunity to engage with her. Maybe he could become her legal representative in other matters if not the divorce issues that she had checked off in her online form.

Maybe Adam could even date this Charly Swift-Rincade. Wouldn't that be a kick in his ex-wife's teeth? Sending alimony checks to his ex every month had made Adam feel like he was regularly experiencing tooth extractions.

Adam did a quick review of divorce laws pertaining to incompetence. Then, he memorized some data pertaining to women's ice hockey. Then, he undertook a quick shave and he combed his hair. He flipped his desktop computer around to feature a backdrop of his diplomas.

This ice queen was what most men could only dream of. It didn't bother him in the least that she was trying to divorce her disabled husband. He hoped it could be an opportunity. Adam was fantasizing that maybe Charly could even become his escort for a quick trip he had to make this coming week.

Adam's current girlfriend had bowed out. The fire technology conferences that Adam liked to attend were always in big cities where she felt like a fish out of water. Her absent sense of adventure was chilling their relationship. Adam was looking forward to spending a few days away in Seattle. He'd never been there. He had even bought a ticket to see a pro hockey game between the Seattle Kraken and the Calgary Flames at the futuristic Climate Pledge Arena.

~ ~ ~ ~ ~

The face on Charly's computer screen didn't look like the picture of either of the divorce lawyers whose photos she had seen on The Eagle Beagle Law Firm webpage. Adam Vader was younger and much better looking.

Adam tried to appear entirely professional, but Charly's instincts told her that she could reel him in if she wanted to. She could see it in his eyes. He didn't live that far away, and he could be a welcome diversion.

Charly also really needed a lawyer. She had already learned that divorcing an almost comatose spouse was a costly and prolonged process. After filing for the divorce, she'd have to wait for an overburdened court to assign a legal representative to August, and even that could take months. There was no easy way out.

~ ~ ~ ~ ~

Adam Vader wound up driving for almost five hours to get to the West Willow Hotel where Charly agreed to meet him. Charly showed up a half-hour late. She wanted to make him anticipate. When she did arrive in a slinky zebra striped turtleneck, orange spandex leggings and genuine snakeskin stilettos, she drew the eyes of everyone in the dining room. Adam felt as hungry for her as he was for dinner. She was just the diversion he needed.

The date went exceptionally well. After dinner they walked around the hotel's gardens and then they had drinks at the bar. Adam wound up spending the night with Charly in the premier suite of the West Willow Hotel. He drove her home the next morning so she could deposit her car and pack up. They'd leave for Seattle that afternoon.

If this Adam dude didn't work out, Charly still had some old ice rink friends in Seattle that she could probably crash with while she waited for the legal help she needed. But so far, Adam seemed like an acceptable option. He was an opportunist who had instantly gone gaga for her. She'd keep him around until he set her free from August. Then she'd decide what to do.

<h1 style="text-align:center">54</h1>

OCTOBER 24 – AFTERNOON

Elsie and Jenna both did double takes when they walked into August's hospital room. He was holding his head up without the bolsters and the left side of his face seemed to be trying to smile. His raised his left index finger and his thumb twitched.

"He's been trying to move his mouth and his fingers since this morning, after he had his transcranial treatment," Neil said with a broad smile. "And I have some really major news for you that I just found out about. Have a seat. This is big."

August emitted a raspy noise, and they all turned in his direction. He seemingly wanted to participate. They moved their chairs closer to him. "I'm so glad you want to hear about this too, August, Old Buddy. I am going to miss you, but you are quite the special guy with a special option.

"After I reported this morning's changes to Doctor Siegle's physician assistant, I told her that August was going to be discharged from our hospital at the end of the week and that he was going to be in a facility that would not have the staffing to continue the treatment.

"An hour later, Doctor Siegle called our doctor and told her he was interested in August's response to the transcranial magnetic stimulation and that he could provide August placement in his research facility. His project is funded by a private investment firm and August's costs would be covered. The hitch is that family support is a requirement of the treatment protocol.

"Emotional support by a loved one is considered such a critical element in coma recovery that Doctor Siegle provides a pull-out bed in August's room and expects the attending loved one to sleep and be there for most of the day and night. There's a private bathroom as well as a communal kitchen and lounge for the family members of the patients. It sounds like an extraordinary opportunity."

"I'll go," Elsie said without hesitation.

"No, you will not," Jenna said just as quickly. "Your job is in our lab, Elsie. Charly doesn't have a job; she's the one who needs to be at her husband's side. And how am I supposed to run our lab without you as well as without your father and Charly? Elsie, please!"

Elsie's eyebrows jumped skyward. "And you think Charly is going to go and sit there and be with Dad? You see how much she chooses to be with him here, even when he's right in our back yard, even when she doesn't have anything else to do, except maybe primp for the cameras. Dad needs someone who actually cares about him."

Elsie turned back to Neil. "How far is it from here to Doctor Siegle's facility?"

"Google says about four hundred fifty miles by road. There are both paid and volunteer ambulance squads that will do transport relays for long distances, but ten hours on the road wouldn't be ideal. There's a chance they will transport him by helicopter which would be about ninety minutes."

"But if it's that far away, how can we visit? You've said it yourself, Neil. Dad responds to Toby and me. He needs for one of us to be with him. I have to go, Mom. Tara can fill in for me with the training for a few weeks, and you need to hire Adrien Kysilia to run the lab. Tara's competent and reliable and she'd appreciate more hours. Adrien seems like a good guy. I'd like to work with him, but I have to go with Dad."

"Elsie, please. I need you to orient Adrien if he accepts my offer. And Elsie, your father needs his wife to be with him, not his daughter. Remember? Your father left you and me to be with her. And what the hell else does Charly have to do right now? I need you here, Elsie. You are my rock and my sunshine."

Jenna turned back to Neil. "Does Charly know about this offer to provide care for August?"

"Both Doctor Wittel and I have tried to reach her, but since she appeared in that news clip the other night about women athletes in skimpy clothes, Charly's voice mailbox has been full. She hasn't responded to texts, and she also hasn't visited for three days, while August has definitely made progress. He's lapping up the milkshakes and puddings and he's more consistently able to maintain eye contact.

"I'm glad you're both here now. Doctor Wittel has to give Doctor Siegle an answer today. There are other brain-injured patients that can fill that empty bed. This is really a rare opportunity, and the offer may be off the table very soon."

August made another noise. When they all turned towards him, August locked eyes with Jenna and then he blinked once. Then he looked at Elsie and blinked once, and then he looked back at Jenna.

Jenna looked down and spun around. Tears spilled down August's cheeks. Neil found himself holding his breath.

Elsie turned her microphone up. "Mom, you have to let me do this or I can't work in the lab anymore. If I have to go live on social security somewhere by myself, I'll go do that. You have to let me go to be with Dad unless you can corral Charly into doing it.

"Let me go at least for now, at least to see if Dad has a chance. You can't let him go to a warehouse nursing home when there's an opportunity like this. I couldn't live with that, and I don't think you could either. Please, Mom."

Jenna remained turned away and silent.

"Mom, you have spent major chunks of your, Toby's and my inheritance helping strangers on so many occasions. How can you turn your back on my father? Mom, please."

Jenna turned back to Elsie with tears streaming down her cheeks. She stared at August with his droopy right mouth and saw his tears. He again made an indistinguishable noise. She looked at her daughter whose face was also wet with tears.

Jenna picked up her phone and called her lawyer. "Stan, please start proceedings to wrest power of attorney for August Rincade away from

Charly Swift-Rincade and get it reassigned to Elsie Rincade as soon as possible. It's an emergency."

Jenna turned back to Neil. "What does Elsie have to sign for her father to be transferred to Doctor Siegle's care?"

"But what if Charly says no?" Elsie asked.

"The police can't even find Charly," a voice said from across the room. Doctor Iris Wittel was walking towards them with a tablet and a clipboard full of papers. "I asked Detective C.C. McAllister to see if she could track Charly down and the police just confirmed that Charly has disappeared. Her car is at her townhouse but there's been no one home for the past two days."

"The hospital attorney is shaking in his shoes over this, but I say the greater liability for our hospital would be to not authorize this transfer. We believe August is stable enough to make the trip. We also believe that with intense input, he has a chance to recover, and we did not want to send him to the county chronic care facility.

"I say we let Elsie sign for Doctor Siegle to take over and Jenna, you cosign to help protect Elsie. Neil and I will sign as witnesses. Should Charly have an issue with our sending August for this extraordinary rehab opportunity, she can take us all to court, but I think we'll win. August deserves a chance at recovery, not a life sentence of custodial care."

"So, what are all of those papers you've got there?" Jenna asked.

"I downloaded most of it from Doctor Siegle's website. Some permits for our hospital are also included. It is a lot of paperwork. I've gone through it briefly. Here's what you need to understand.

"Doctor Siegle's patients may be randomized to undergo various investigational therapies in addition to transcranial magnetic stimulation. Depending on the patient's individual circumstances, they may also be treated with hyperbaric oxygen, hormones, stem cell infusions, exosome infusions, ultraviolet blood irradiation, photo-biomodulation of the brain through intranasal light catheters, transcranial ultrasound stimulation, acupuncture, pharmacologic agents, psychedelic therapy with psilocybin, and other novel treatments.

"Your signatures will affirm that you understand the risks and that you will not hold anyone who has created or administered these treatments accountable for any adverse outcomes. Each of the papers you are going to sign lists dozens of potential adverse outcomes from each of these potential treatments, but the risk level is very low.

"You will also be confirming that you will be responsible for transferring August to another care facility if and when Doctor Siegle decides that he is not responding to treatment, and that could be as soon as in two weeks. Max Siegle's facility is not a permanent solution for those that continue to need custodial care.

"As of the past year, about a third of Siegle's patients have recovered enough to be able to go home. Most have wound up in chronic care facilities. A couple of patients who first came under his care about fourteen months ago are still receiving care in his facility because they are making slow progress. The hope is that a few years of rehab will cost less than many years of total dependency.

"Regrettably, you are not going to have time to read and think about what you are going to be signing for. Just reading all of it could take days. I have to send these documents back in about an hour and a half or that empty bed in Doctor Siegle's facility is going to be offered to another stroke patient.

"I'm afraid your only real choice in this matter is whether or not you consent to turning August into a lab rat."

55

October 24 – Afternoon

C.C. McAllister and Garrett Towser had struck out in their attempts to track down Jenna Laudren's sister. Her name didn't come up in any data banks, anywhere. Just as Jenna had said, her sister seemed to have completely vanished.

There was also no evidence that Shelby had ever tried to contest her father's transfer of wealth to Jenna. For years, Jenna expected her sister to show up and start a legal battle for a share of the trust, but that hadn't happened in more than two decades. Jenna suspected that Shelby might even be buried in some unmarked graveyard. She was certainly lost to the family.

Although they had given up on finding Shelby, C.C. was still clinging to her theory that it was a family member who went after August. Who else could have known that he wanted to go see some lab equipment in the college science department? Everyone in August's lab as well as in Celia Fromme's lab had been interviewed and no viable suspects had materialized.

Garrett had been assigned to check out representatives of the company that manufactured the optical coherence tomography, as well as the personnel in the college animal lab. None of that proved helpful.

The college lab director did know who August was because he was one of several adjunct professors who occasionally lectured for a course called "Introduction to Research."

August had also visited the college's animal lab on occasion over the years, but the lab director didn't know of his interest in the OCT equipment. Most recently, he had brought her some Laudren rats for her deafness research, but that was months before she acquired the OCT equipment which was only a few weeks ago. Her team was still learning how to interpret what this technology enabled them to see. She couldn't imagine that anyone in her lab would have been ready to demonstrate it to someone else.

Charly's disappearance had moved her to the top of the suspect list, but C.C. still hadn't been able to cross off Toby, Elsie or Jenna. Charly seemed the least likely to have a motive while her marriage to August had embittered all of the others. C.C. then decided that Toby was also less suspect because he wouldn't have had reason to know about August's interest in new equipment. His disinterest in the lab was very apparent.

Whoever had used an OCT equipment demonstration as a lure was keenly aware of August's enthusiasm for this technology. Elsie admittedly knew exactly how this bait had been dangled, Jenna seemingly knew of its expense and Charly knew how the OCT would impact their research. Who else could have known?

The fingerprints taken from August's car also hadn't helped. The prints were from all of these suspects plus Toby's friend Brigham, and some other people who couldn't be identified. The long hair's DNA had been documented, but its owner remained unknown. The only thing that could be concluded from the search of the car was that the detailer had done a lousy job.

Had Charly not disappeared without notifying the police as instructed, C.C. would have arranged for the car to be returned to her so she could sell it. But now it was evident that Charly didn't even need a car. She had fled from the investigation with someone's help, and they didn't even know where to start looking for her. Still, she didn't seem like the most likely suspect.

Ultimately, it occurred to Garrett that maybe Grandpa Jay would have known about August's interest in OTC. Elsie had mentioned that she and Jenna visited him regularly and for all practical purposes, he seemed to be the only person outside of the immediate family, the housekeeper, and the lab that these people had regular contact with. Checking out Jay Laudren in his assisted living facility became Garrett's next assignment.

Garrett went to call Elsie to find out where Jay Laudren was residing when he saw she had left him a voice mail while he had been on the phone with C.C. It said that she and her father were being transferred to another facility by helicopter in about an hour, and she didn't know how long she'd be gone. It could be a long time. Tara, the other primary trainer in the lab, had been informed that Garrett might come by to learn more about training.

Garrett was surprised at how Elsie's sudden, unexpected departure and nebulous return date had upset him. He was also worried about Freyja. Elsie and that baby rat seemed to have such a strong bond. Would the other trainer be able to compensate for Freyja losing her friend?

Garrett felt compelled to check in on Elsie's unit at his earliest opportunity, even though he had mentally put his police rat training project on hold. He couldn't help feeling a sense of relief when he stopped by the lab and Tara informed him that Elsie had taken Freyja with her.

56

October 24 - Evening

Elsie let her mother know that the helicopter had touched down. The landing pad was just a five-minute ambulance ride from the hospital, an old two-story building. While August was getting checked in, Elsie called Jenna again to tell her what she had learned about the place from a staff member who had taken her around the facility.

The building had previously been a sixty-bed hospital that served a rural community. After the 2020 pandemic had put it into deep debt, the hospital was bought by a national health care corporation.

The corporate officers quickly decided that this old hospital was too run down to renovate. It also wasn't financially profitable, so they terminated all of the staff and shut it down. The locals would just have to drive a few hours to the city if they needed medical care or jobs. The corporation would invest in an ambulance service.

The building was set to be demolished when a group of venture capitalists involved in neuroscience investments made an offer to buy the property. If the ingenious and daring Maximillian Siegle could demonstrate that their patented system was as successful a remedy for stroke patients as these investors hoped, they'd be able to sell the equipment to every health care facility in the world.

Doctor Siegle's patients occupied the upper floor of the building. On the first floor, another physician was using transcranial magnetic stim and other experimental modalities on patients who had suffered traumatic brain injuries, but whose systems had not been contaminated with stroke-inducing drugs.

More than half of these patients were pediatric. Two had shaken baby syndrome. Five of the children including two teenagers were wards of the state. All had been diagnosed as being minimally conscious, but in need of custodial care at taxpayer expense for the rest of their lives.

The pediatric neurologist who was conducting this research was not publishing results for fear of being attacked for experimenting on children. The first child she had tried the treatment on was her nine-month-old nephew. When JoJo was six months old, he was dropped on his head by a babysitter, and he didn't get medical attention until his parents came home from dinner two hours after the accident. The sitter thought that JoJo was just sleeping. He had had a massive brain bleed.

For three months, JoJo seemed to be in a minimally conscious state, interrupted only by seizures. When Doctor Siegle used artificial intelligence to figure out how to adapt the magnetic settings and the timing for an infant's skull, JoJo started to show improvement.

Then a plea from the pediatrician who knew about JoJo's case resulted in another successful treatment of another brain injured child. Now, some more young children were being given a chance, and it wasn't costing taxpayers a dime. But fear of hateful protesters kept these experiments a closely guarded secret.

Each of Doctor Siegle's patients was in a private room that also accommodated the supportive family member. Nothing was plush, but everything was comfortable. In addition to Elsie's pull-out bed, August's room had a recliner and a bed that faced a window with a view of treetops and songbirds. There was also a TV, a locker for Elsie's stuff, and a desk with a chair, computer hookup and phone charger.

"I'll call again as soon as we get settled," Elsie promised. Then she hung up before Jenna could say a word.

~ ~ ~ ~ ~

Elsie stepped out into the hallway just as a woman emerged from a room on the other side. The woman paused for a minute as she stared at Elsie. Then she said hello and introduced herself as Davita, support person for her son Andy, who had a major stroke at age thirty-two.

Elsie learned that Andy had been accepted for Doctor Siegle's project because his local doctor had eagerly pursued Siegle when Andy's initial progress was dismal. Andy had been a healthy man with a successful computer business. His family was still in shock from finding out that his stroke had been caused by cocaine. Now, after a few weeks of Doctor Siegle's protocol, Andy could sit up and shake his head yes and no. That was a whole lot better than his first few weeks in which he had been essentially vegetative.

Davita was Andy's support person because Andy's wife Tina had three young children at home, ages two, five and seven. The family also had a dog, a cat and a gigantic mortgage, and now Tina had no income, just a huge pile of medical bills that she had no way to pay. Tina's parents were trying to help, and her friend had started a GoFundMe drive that was at least keeping food on the table. Davita had no idea how they'd get by if and when Doctor Siegle terminated Andy's treatment.

Davita herself was a widow who could barely survive on social security. She had recently loss her eighteen-year career as a respiratory therapist along with her retirement benefits when the corporation had shut this hospital down. Had she not become part of Andy's treatment protocol, she would have sold her home and moved to the city where she could hope to find new employment.

Elsie could empathize. It was one more cocaine catastrophe that impacted innocent lives. While Davita went to get herself a complimentary beverage from the communal fridge, Elsie went to check out the rest of the unit. In the family lounge, she encountered two men working on a gigantic jigsaw puzzle. Neither of these guys seemed very adept at jigsaws but they were very congenial.

Elsie learned that one of the men was the husband of a twenty-nine-year-old woman whose stroke was caused by her birth control pills along with cigarettes. The younger man was the eighteen-year-old brother of a twenty-two-year-old patient whose stroke had been caused by a fentanyl overdose.

Elsie learned that the contraceptive victim was doing very well after two months on Doctor Siegle's protocol, and her husband was optimistic that she'd be able to come home in another few weeks. There was no doubt that the treatment was helping.

The fentanyl victim had been in the facility for eleven days and he'd not made observable progress. His brother, who had given up his college acceptance to be the support person, feared that his big brother was destined to spend the rest of his life in a nursing home.

"Yeah, two weeks is the cut-off, they tell me. I keep telling my poor brother that he's got to wake up. He only has three more days to show he's salvageable, but he can't awaken, the poor fool. His brain damage is too severe."

~ ~ ~ ~ ~

When August was finally wheeled into his room, his nurse Sally introduced herself. She explained that August had just been imaged and cultured from head to toe and lots of test results were pending. A nutritionist would be selecting August's diet based on the bacteria in his intestines.

An acupuncturist would be doing a neural treatment every fourth day, alternating with every other day neural massage. Physical, occupational, speech and music therapists would be visiting daily. Supportive family members would also be instructed in how to assist with therapies and participate to the extent that they could.

Elsie could order meals from the cafeteria, and they'd be delivered to the unit. There was also an exercise room and a laundry room. When Sally asked if she had any questions, Elsie opted to address the big one. "What's the policy on therapy pets?"

"Funny you should ask," Sally said. "There's a cat in the room next door and that patient has made real progress since we let the cat in. It's an old, deaf, white cat named Willy Wonka. He purrs into his person's ear and our stroke patient can now stroke Willy.

"We don't really have a policy about therapy animals, we go on a case-by-case basis. The family of the patient at the end of the hall visits their person with a chihuahua named Stella. She doesn't bark at anyone, and she definitely knows that it's her job to cuddle with her person."

Elsie took a deep breath. She had given Freyja a sedative before the trip, and it would be wearing off in the next hour. She had no idea what the rat would do if she could smell the cat in the next room. Zonked out in a halter hammock under Elsie's oversized sweatshirt,

Freyja hadn't yet stirred. Maybe showing her to Sally while the little rat was peacefully sleeping was the best way to introduce her to August's new nurse.

"I'm so glad to know pets are okay because I brought one along for my father." Elsie took the sleeping rat out from under her shirt. "This little girl is from my father's research lab. She's barely ten weeks old. Her name is Freyja. She's sedated right now, but when you see her awake, you'll understand.

"My father was very excited about this rat pup's exceptional intelligence, and he had become attached to her just before he had his stroke. I'll send her back to the lab if it's a problem, but she's very low maintenance. She sleeps in a hammock in her cage, she comes when she's called, and she does her business in a litter box."

Elsie put Freyja under August's left hand, and he immediately moved his fingers. He opened his eyes and looked around. He looked at Elsie and blinked once. Then he looked at the rat under his hand and he blinked again and then he closed his eyes. There was almost a smile on the left side of his face. He moved his fingers some more. The rat continued to sleep.

Sally said she'd run it by Doctor Siegle on morning rounds, but she doubted it would be a problem. She was already intrigued by the little black and white speckled rat. It was adorable if you could get past the tail. Sally was also impressed by her patient's response to the rodent. August's limp hand was trying to make purposeful movements.

Elsie called Jenna and told her that things were going well, and Freyja would almost certainly become part of the treatment plan. She wouldn't have to send the little rat back unless the smell of the cat next door caused a problem.

But Elsie was optimistic. She had watched a dozen or so YouTube videos in which pet rats and cats had become best friends. She wondered if Willy Wonka next door could now be smelling Freyja.

57

October 27 – All Day

D.E.A. agent Spencer Parrow notified detective C.C. McAllister that his lab had just processed more cocaine specimens from the college in her precinct. These samples had the same chemical signature as in the case of August Rincade.

The victim had been found passed out on a bench in the central campus plaza. She was ambulanced to the E.R. for a massive heart attack. She tested positive for cannabis, cocaine, amphetamines, and benzos. She stabilized after three days in intensive care.

The heart attack sufferer was a young woman who was found to have four packets of this cocaine concealed inside the padding of her bra, in addition to the big dose found in her system. The specimens were from the same strain that was causing heart attacks, strokes, disability and death on college campuses around the country. Spencer Parrow desperately wanted to stop the distribution of this poison.

Identified initially as Jane Doe, the victim's facial photo didn't match anyone in the college's files, though her image had been captured on several campus security cameras during recent weeks.

Nobody admitted to knowing who she was when a group of bystanders greeted the ambulance squad that came to rescue her. The paramedics suspected she was homeless and taking refuge on the campus. She had no identity.

The hospital staff wondered if she was an escaped human trafficking victim. No one had inquired after her. She spoke broken English when she regained consciousness, and she was generally uncooperative. She would only give her name as Aylin O. The address she had given didn't actually exist, but she insisted that's where she lived. Her fingerprints weren't on file. She didn't match the description of any missing persons. A cheek swab had been sent for DNA identification.

Aylin was furious to learn that her heart had been seriously damaged, and she was suffering from heart failure. She would need to be on medication and supplemental oxygen until the injured cardiac muscle showed some signs of recovery, if it did. Her sky-high cardiac enzymes stopped climbing after the first twelve hours, so there was a chance of recovery. Aylin scowled when she was told she was lucky to be alive, though she didn't seem to comprehend how disabled she might now be.

C.C. McAllister got permission to interview Aylin in the cardiac care unit. The woman was petite and pretty, even with an oxygen cannula in her nose. C.C. immediately got the impression that Aylin was very skilled at playing the role of an ignorant immigrant, while she was probably very astute. She spoke with an indistinguishable accent.

C.C. also sensed that Aylin was fearful. Would her loved ones pay a price if she ratted out her supplier? Aylin was actually terrified that she might be found in the hospital by the people who held her three-year-old son in custody while she was supposed to be making deliveries. The buyers must have been raging because their orders had never arrived, and the police must have found the cocaine that was stashed in her bra. She hoped they hadn't also found the phone she had thrown in a garbage can when she realized she was about to pass out.

Aylin only knew that she should never trust anyone. This old policewoman could be the person who was there to hold a pillow over her face. She could not believe that law enforcement would rescue her if she betrayed the others. It had to be a trap. Her son's life was at stake. She had to play it cool, and she had to get out of the hospital as fast as possible.

Aylin decided to deal with this policeperson by scapegoating one of her customers who owed her money. Desmond Yarborg had failed to pay her when she had performed a service for him a few weeks ago, because the target had a bad outcome. She had done her job maybe too well, but Desmond had copped out of the deal. She should have known better than to trust him, he was a total turd.

Aylin knew Desmond's license plate number and she offered it up as a diversion. C.C. texted the number to Garrett Towser and tasked him with tracking down the driver, while Aylin hoped that would be the end of this police inquiry.

Ayla didn't know that Detective C.C. McAllister had taken precautions against her doing another disappearing act. If Aylin was the distributor of this lethal drug, she was a killer who needed to be contained. A police guard was posted outside the door of the cardiac care unit, and C.C. alerted Spencer Parrow that he needed to send his best shaker-downer for this case. C.C. also had some of Aylin's hair whisked off to the police lab for an emergency analysis.

~ ~ ~ ~ ~

From the address associated with the license plate number, Garrett was able to tail the driver from his residence to a downtown club where he was found in what was probably the last billiards hall in the region. The place was apparently a refuge for the few people who didn't like computer games or didn't like to drink alone.

Desmond Yarborg was higher than Mount McKinley at two in the afternoon and he reeked of beer. When Garrett Towser showed him his badge and told him he was a suspect for dealing bad cocaine to a woman named Aylin who was in the hospital, the other pool players exited the place at the pace of racehorses.

Desmond was still cogent enough to express outrage. He admitted to using coke once in a while just for fun, but he swore he wasn't a dealer. He said Aylin was the dealer and that she was the only one he bought coke from because she always had the best stuff. He wanted to know why she was in the hospital. Was it bad?

Desmond had quickly deduced that because of a medical crisis, Aylin had been busted, and she had pointed the police at him because he had recently stiffed her on a deal. But Desmond hadn't paid her because she had messed the whole thing up with bad coke, so he wasn't going to get paid either.

Desmond Yarborg's Grandpa Simon had been very bothered about his good friend Jay Laudren having a rotten ex-son-in-law. The bastard was taking advantage of Jay's whole family and the family trust that Jay had spent his lifetime building. This dude was a cheater and a parasite, and the family hadn't been able to get rid of him. This August Rincade guy was going to drain Jay Laudren's entire estate dry and ruin his family's philanthropic foundation.

"I know how to take this guy down," Desmond had told his grandfather. Desmond was thinking maybe Jay Laudren would also reward him for fixing the problem of August Rincade. Desmond had seen Jenna and Elsie during some of his visits to his grandfather while Simon was hanging out with Jay. About a month ago, when Jay's family had come to visit, Desmond had noticed that Jay's daughter Jenna looked sick, and that the granddaughter Elsie sure had her problems. Desmond figured he could do them all a big favor and make his grandfather feel like their savior. Fatherless Desmond liked to fancy himself as his grandfather's hero.

Desmond's dealer Aylin was known to do just about anything for money, but Desmond wasn't a pervert. He only exploited Aylin's access to drugs. When she said she could get the date rape drug, Rohypnol, Desmond promised her that it would be a great deal for her to help him pull off a little scheme he had come up with to appease his Grandpa Simon.

Desmond had provided Aylin with a script about some lab equipment that his grandfather knew that August was interested in. Jenna had once asked Simon about this expensive optical coherence tomography because she knew Simon had been an optician.

Once Aylin lured August into the college science building with a phone call about the phony OCT demo, she engaged him at the coffee bar and put the Rohypnol in his coffee. When it looked like he was starting to fade, she quickly escorted him to the family rest room adjacent to the coffee bar. Once he went down, she blew the coke up his nose. Then, she was supposed to get him to the hospital while playing the role of an escort.

In the meantime, Desmond was supposed to move August's car to the West Willow Hotel. They'd make Rincade out to be a cheating, thieving coke head. Then Jay Laudren's daughter Jenna would have the ammunition to kick the two-timing dude out of her lab. Desmond was impressed with the cleverness of his plans.

It was never in Desmond's plans for August to have a stroke, and when he did, Aylin panicked and ran out of the science building instead of staying with August and going with him to the E.R. Then she and Desmond took his car to the hospital so they could deliver August's I.D. Desmond stunk of beer, so Aylin insisted on doing the driving.

After August's hospitalization, Aylin had disguised herself as a hospital housekeeper emptying garbage cans just to find out what had happened to him. Then, Desmond turned around and said he wasn't going to pay her for turning Rincade into a vegetable. Now, it appeared that Aylin was going to try to frame Desmond because she had become a victim of her own bad drugs. He never should have trusted her. She had screwed up his brilliant plan to appease his grandfather and help out the family of his grandfather's friend.

Grandpa Simon was not appeased. He was now complaining that August Rincade had become an even bigger burden on Jay Laudren's family and an embarrassment to their philanthropic foundation. Desmond wasn't going to take credit for any of that.

Desmond was regretting everything until it suddenly occurred to him that August Rincade probably wasn't the issue. The police probably only knew that Aylin dealt cocaine, not about her connection to Rincade. Surely, Aylin wasn't so stupid that she would tell them. This just had to be about bad cocaine putting her in the hospital.

Desmond wasn't dealing cocaine, and if bad cocaine caused Aylin to suffer a heart attack, she deserved it. Desmond knew of two other users who could identify Aylin as a coke dealer if it came to that, so he figured he was in the clear. Aylin was the one who was going down and

he'd just cooperate with this Officer Garrett Towser. If Aylin was dealing bad cocaine, she needed to be put out of commission.

What Desmond didn't know, was that the DNA of some long hairs
Detective C.C. McAllister had taken from the pillow of the hospital
bed of Aylin O, had just been reported to be a perfect match with
the alien hairs that had been extracted from the upholstery of August
Rincade's car.

While Desmond was trying to explain to Garrett Towser that he
had no other connections with this Aylin person other than having
bought coke from her on occasion, C.C. McAllister was arresting Aylin
O for the attempted murder of August Rincade, on top of the cocaine
dealing charges.

Aylin would soon be telling the police how Desmond's Grandpa
Simon and his friend Jay Laudren had put Desmond up to taking out
August Rincade, and how Desmond never even paid her for being his
accomplice.

58

October 31

Toby drove six hours to Doctor Siegle's facility to give Elsie a break. He and his girlfriend Liz stayed in a nearby bed and breakfast. While Toby hung out with their father, Liz drove Elsie to the nearby town so she could run some errands.

Elsie needed more supplies for Freyja and for a project she was undertaking. She was devising an olfactory stimulation experiment for both her father and Freyja. It went well beyond coffee, mint, antiseptics and the fox urine that Elsie had ordered from a lab supply company.

Toby could not believe the difference in his father after seven days in this treatment program. August could sit up in his recliner and he had clearly tried to express happiness with his twisted mouth when Toby first walked into the room.

August was also making attempts to speak, moving his mouth and emitting some vocalizations. He could nod his head appropriately and there was little doubt that he was following conversations. He'd gained a pound or two and with a haircut, he looked a lot less like a total stranger, though he still didn't look like the father that Toby wished he had been closer to.

Toby was encouraged to see August limply using his left hand to cradle and stroke Freyja. When he relaxed his hand, the little rat ran up his arm and licked his neck, ear and scalp. Then, she ran down his right arm and tried to burrow into the right hand which still wasn't moving. She licked and pushed at his fingers with her nose and then licked his hand some more. Then she ran back up his arm, across his chest and down his left arm and settled into his cupped hand.

Sally, August's primary nurse, gave Freyja a treat and August bobbed his head as if to say thank you.

"Did Elsie teach Freyja to do that?" Toby asked Sally.

"Not at all. When Freyja first woke up after their trip here, Elsie was worried that the smell of the cat in the next room was going to scare her. Just before Freyja first opened her eyes, her little nose had started to violently twitch.

"Then, when it seemed that Freyja had become fully awake, she leaped onto August's chest, and she ran up and down his head and body sniffing him. After sniffing him all over, she curled herself around his head and started licking his scalp. Now, she's working on getting him to use his hands. It's maybe just a fantasy on my part, but I could swear this little rat knows what's going on with your father and she wants to make him better.

"Elsie is also wandering if rats can sniff out brain lesions. Rats are known to lick their wounds which has been shown to promote healing. Little Doctor Freyja has been licking August's scalp right over the area of his head where he had his brain bleed. She doesn't lick other parts of his head, but she licks that area a couple of times a day. The skin wounds from his brain surgery are still healing, so we don't know if she's responding to the wounded skin, skull or brain, but she definitely focuses her attention on that particular spot.

"Of course, we realized that baby Freyja had been attached to August before his stroke, so we didn't know if she would be inclined to do her rat therapy like this for a stranger. However, Elsie and Freyja have now been spending some time with Andy, the patient in the room across the hall, and Freyja's behavior suggests that she also knows that Andy is suffering. She even seems to know what part of Andy's brain was impacted by a cocaine-induced stroke.

"Doctor Siegle wants to introduce Freyja to some of the other patients, but Elsie worries about how that might impact this little healer. Can feeling everyone else's pain become too painful for an empath? Elsie also doesn't want to reduce the time that Freyja spends with August. When given the option of her nest or August, she consistently chooses to sleep in August's hand or on his head.

"Elsie is wondering if Freyja's behavior is unique to her, her family or her breed, or if any domesticated rat might be able to assist a brain injured patient. We do have other patients' family members asking for a therapy rat like Freyja, and Doctor Siegle and two of his investors have become very interested in Freyja's impact on August. I suspect if Freyja starts to have a positive effect on Andy, everyone in this facility is going to want a rat.

"Now, Doctor Siegle and your sister and mother are in the process of designing an experiment. Your mother is going to send us some young rats that already have their basic training and who have demonstrated high levels of compassion. She'll also send us some just weaned rats who haven't yet been trained but they are accustomed to being handled. She'll also send along the equipment that Elsie needs to teach our people how to do the training. Our only problem with this plan is that we have too many people here who are interested in doing this. Elsie thinks Freyja might be able to help select the best candidates.

"Doctor Siegle is enthralled with the idea that rats could aid brain injured patients. Rats are so much easier to manage than other pets. He's also wondering if the compassionate nature of rats can make them natural healers.

"What has Doctor Siegle especially intrigued is that Freyja keeps licking the same spots on his patients' heads that he's been treating with magnetic stim. We wonder if Freyja can hear or smell something in those areas? Can she hear altered blood flow? Can she smell the chemistry of the tissue growth factors that induce healing? Could she be sensing the magnetism? Is there some electrical signal that she can pick up on? Do her whiskers detect some vibration emitted by traumatized tissues?

"I've learned from Elsie that rats are able to see ultraviolet light rays that humans can't, so we wonder if Freyja can she see an aura in the injured area. It's now understood that some humans can see light waves that most humans can't. People with a rare condition called synesthesia have some cross wiring in their brains' sensory pathways. Certain frequency sounds might cause them to see certain colors. Certain odors might cause them to hear certain sounds. Some people with synesthesia experience specific tastes when they see certain colors.

"Perhaps, Freyja has some sensory apparatus that we don't even know about? It's been demonstrated in more than one study that rats can be so empathetic that they can feel their partner's pain.

"Everyone here is very excited about this, Toby. Doctor Siegle has allowed animals in here all along because a fair amount of data shows that relationships with pets can improve the outcomes for victims of stroke and brain injury, but he had never previously considered rats.

"Now, having learned about how naturally compassionate rats are, and having also witnessed Freyja's behavior and your father's accelerating progress, our lead physician is ecstatic about the possibilities. There's suddenly some indescribable sensation penetrating the minds and hearts of all of the nurses and family members who are caring for someone here. If I had to give it a name, I'd call it the optimism of discovery."

As the time passed, Toby was continually amazed at how his father was starting to communicate with his head, his eyes and a few facial muscles on the left side, He was swallowing semi-solid foods. He seemed happy to hear that Jenna was doing much better with her MALS problem. She was no longer considering going for surgery. Maybe all she needed was a periodic nerve block. Maybe her body was healing itself.

August's half smile went wide when Toby explained that he was planning to take a leave of absence from his veterinary school curriculum at the end of the semester and work with Elsie in the lab, and then he planned to reconsider what he wanted to do. Elsie, Jenna, and Adrien Kysilia all had some great ideas for their next project and Toby was starting to share their enthusiasm.

August did drift off to sleep after Toby started telling him about how Adrien Kysilia was going to start working in the lab. Toby redirected his conversation to Nurse Sally.

"So, what happened with the cat in the room next door? When Elsie first got here, she was texting me that I'd have to come get Freyja if she was too afraid of the cat."

"It's been no problem at all, thankfully. Elsie even took Freyja next door to meet Willy Wonka and after they sniffed each other, Freyja seemed pretty relaxed. Willy is ninety something years old in cat years and Freyja apparently doesn't perceive that he's a threat. We were also greatly relieved to see that Willy didn't look at Freyja like she was lunch. This might sound sappy, but I was there, and it was almost like this sweet, old cat and this loving, little rat mutually recognized and appreciated each other as therapy animals. I don't know how else to describe it.

"In the meantime, Toby, your father is improving every day, maybe even hour by hour. Yesterday, he scored perfectly on a yes and no cognitive test. If he can recover motor function, he could conceivably become self-sufficient.

"We have hope, more than hope. We are optimistic."

EPILOGUE

So, the old lab rat said to a young one: "I've got my scientist so well trained, she gives me a treat every time I do something senseless."

ACKNOWLEDGEMENTS

I am most indebted to Lorrie Lambert, PhD, author of *The Lab Rat Chronicles: A Neuroscientist Reveals Life Lessons from the Planet's Most Successful Mammals,* an informative, thought provoking and entertaining read.

Thanks are also extended to editors Nancy Costo and Amy Schapiro and to publisher Katie Mullaly of Surrogate Press.

ABOUT THE AUTHOR

Dr. Beverly Hurwitz, originally from Brooklyn, New York, has spent her professional life as a physician, educator, and author.

In her youth she won awards for scholastic journalism and served as copy editor for her college newspaper. Before attending medical school, she spent a decade as a health and physical education teacher in rural public schools.

As a medical fellow, Beverly specialized in the care of children with neurologic disability. After three decades of clinical practice, she spent eight years as a medical case analyst/writer for administrative law judges in federal and state court systems. In recent years, she has been writing novels and hiking books.